THE
SONGS
OF MY
FAMILY

JILLIAN ARENA

Diana,
It was a pleasure
to meet you! I'm so
glad that you enjoyed
the story.
♥, Jillian ☺

THE

SONGS

OF MY

FAMILY

A NOVEL

atmosphere press

Published by Atmosphere Press

Cover design by Matthew Fielder

atmospherepress.com

This book is dedicated to my husband, Josh. Thank you for constantly reminding me that nothing is out of reach. You are the catalyst behind every dream I've fulfilled.

Also, to my children, Jacob and Jocelyn. You fill my heart in ways I never knew it could be filled prior to motherhood. You inspire me to keep creating and to never stop working to be the very best version of myself.

I love you all.

PROLOGUE

Myra pushed open the door to the police station with a feigned air of confidence she had been practicing all morning. She hadn't seen the children since the day of the accident, the day that had changed both her life and theirs forever. She shifted uncomfortably at the memory and pinched her face tightly to hold back any emotion that might spill out onto her features.

"May I help you?" the woman behind the front desk asked, not bothering to look up from the stack of paperwork in front of her. Myra tucked a blond curl nervously behind her ear and noticed that her hands were trembling ever so slightly.

"I'm Myra Jenkins," she answered, almost in a whisper. "I'm here to see the Garcia children." The woman behind the desk stopped shuffling the paperwork and shot Myra a look filled with some mix of disdain, judgment, and pity. It was a look Myra had become rather accustomed to in the recent past.

"Yes, Ms. Jenkins. Officer Martin has been waiting for you. I'll let him know you've arrived."

Myra glanced at her watch. It didn't really matter what

time it was. She had nowhere else to be. She had lost her job. Her social calendar wasn't exactly full of extracurricular activities, and her kids were in school for another four hours, but somehow it gave her comfort just to stare down at the familiar face of her Cartier. It had been a Christmas gift from Greg two years ago. It seemed like decades ago now, a whole different life, a life in which the word Cartier actually had some relevance to her happiness. It might as well be a Swatch these days, for all she cared. As she turned over the memory of that Christmas morning in her head, the woman's face reappeared at the plate-glass window.

"He'll see you now, Ms. Jenkins. You can head through that door over there. Let me buzz you in." She pointed to a heavy metal door to her left.

"Thank you," mumbled Myra. She could see Officer Martin coming out of the hallway as she stepped toward the door. The buzzer sounded and she turned the handle, feeling her heart pounding in her chest.

He was there to greet her as the door swung open, a wide smile plastered on his face, wildly inappropriate for the situation at hand. Myra found herself wondering if perhaps Officer Martin wasn't as uncomfortable as she was.

"Well, hello there, Ms. Jenkins. Come this way. I'll bring you back to the kids if you're ready."

The statement was ridiculous really. Of course, she wasn't ready. She'd never be ready, but it had to be done. It was only right, after all.

She followed slowly behind Officer Martin as he led her down the hallway to a closed door. They stopped, and he glanced at her briefly and gave her a nod of encouragement before placing his hand on the knob. She nodded back, breathing deeply and calmly to shake the dizziness that had set upon her. The handle turned, and before she knew it, she was stepping into the room, claustrophobia setting in instantly as she laid eyes on their faces.

There were three of them, two girls and a boy. All had the same creamy, mocha skin, coffee bean eyes, and shiny black hair that she had seen in the pictures of their parents. The oldest, a girl, especially resembled her mother, although her eyes had a steeliness about them that Myra did not remember seeing in the mother's picture. She instantly felt responsible for that, and a wave of regret washed over her, another feeling she hadn't quite adjusted to yet.

The youngest, the boy, had just turned five if she remembered correctly; the girls were nine and sixteen. The boy sat in the chair, his dangling legs swinging back and forth, eyes directed downward to the fidgeting hands on his lap.

The youngest girl smiled meekly at Myra, and the older girl pinched her gently. Myra couldn't tell if she was meant to see it or not, but the smile quickly disappeared from the younger girl's face.

The oldest girl stared straight ahead, apparently fixated on some minute detail on the bare wall ahead of her. She didn't blink and sat stone still. Behind them stood a tall, lanky, middle-aged man whom she remembered from the court proceedings. She had seen him sitting with the prosecutor and presumably he represented the children's interest in the case. The tension in the room was palpable, as was the silence.

Officer Martin glanced nervously from Myra to the children and back again before breaking the lull.

"Kids, I'm sure you remember Miss Jenkins." Another interesting choice of words, Myra noted to herself. It would be pretty hard for them to forget her ever, let alone less than a year after what she had done. "And Miss Jenkins, I'm sure you remember Mr. Randall, their caseworker. I'll just leave you five to it, then." He moved eagerly toward the exit, pausing briefly as if he might say something else, before changing his mind and leaving the tension of the room behind him with the click of the shutting door.

None of the children moved, and neither did Myra. She re-alized her throat had become as dry as sandpaper, and she smacked her lips together nervously a few times, trying to think of anything to say. The oldest girl cleared her throat and Myra thought that maybe she would begin the conversation, but no words ever came. Finally, Myra spoke.

"You look a lot like your parents." The two youngest children glanced sadly at one another and the oldest shot Myra a look that could freeze the Atlantic. Myra reached her hand absently to her hair and began tucking invisible strands behind her ear. "They were very beautiful people," she said.

"What do you know about them?" snapped the oldest daughter, still eyeing her. "You didn't know anything about my parents, and you probably never would have tried to get to know anything about them if you hadn't killed them." The girl's voice rose an octave, and angry tears welled up in her eyes. "Why are we even here, sitting in a room with you? Nothing you can say to us is going to bring them back. This is just stupid!" Myra, unsure of how to respond to the outburst, felt her mouth drop open and the color drain from her face. She looked to Mr. Randall for support, but he was bent over his cellphone, clearly uninterested. She stood there looking like a fish, her mouth opening and closing without sound, before the girl continued.

"Well, get on with it," she spat. "I can think of about fifty million things I'd rather be doing than sitting in this room staring at the lady who killed my mom and dad. I'm sure you have plenty of important things to do with your day as well, being a big-shot lawyer's wife and all. What the hell could you possibly want with us anyway? Why are we here?" The girl's eyes were wild, her arms flailing around her in exasperation. Myra felt her face flush and hot tears sting the backs of her eyes. This seemed to please the girl, and an unmistakable smirk of satisfaction spread across her face.

"I, I came to ... I have something to give you," Myra stammered. Her hands plunged into her purse, scrambling to find the manila envelope she had tucked inside earlier that morning. She could feel all the children watching her as she fumbled. Suddenly all the zippers and snaps on her pocketbook that had given it so much character on the shelf at Bloomingdale's seemed an unnecessary pain in the ass. She finally felt the package, pulling it from the purse with a sigh. She looked back to the children, then down again, turning the package over and undoing the clasp. "It might not seem like a lot right now, but I'm hoping it will help you in the future." She pulled three stapled stacks of paper from the envelope and shuffled them in her hands as she scanned their faces. They sat there waiting, the two youngest looking confused, the oldest, arms crossed, looking angrier than ever and clearly ready to spew her next round of insults at any moment.

Myra proceeded cautiously. She made a motion to hand the papers to the boy, the closest to her, to hand down the line, but thought better of it. She stepped toward the oldest and handed her the stack. The girl grabbed it and set it on her lap without even bothering to glance at it.

"What are these?" she asked, still staring at Myra.

"It's paperwork for your accounts. I set them up for each of you, for when you're older, ready to go to college. I just thought ... " The girl cut her off.

"Excuse me, Ms. Jenkins. That's awfully kind of you, but I just have one question." Although her sarcasm wasn't all that subtle, Myra couldn't help but hope that perhaps the girl was softening.

"Of course. What is it?"

"Well, I was just wondering if you know our names," she asked calmly.

"Excuse me?" Myra asked.

"Our names, Ms. Jenkins. I was wondering if you know what they are." Myra shifted uncomfortably from one foot to the other.

"Well, of course I do!" she began. The hand shot back up to the invisible strands as she ran down her mental Rolodex, only to find that, indeed, she had no recollection of any of the children's names. She tried out a few Spanish-sounding names in her head, but none of them seemed right. The color, again, returned to her face, and the tension re-gripped her body. The oldest girl's face had settled into a satisfied sneer as she watched Myra's discomfort.

"Yes, that's what I thought. You know what I think of your paperwork, Ms. Jenkins?" Myra just watched as the girl ripped the pages in half, one by one, and discarded them on the floor in front of her feet as she spoke. "We are not a charity case, Ms. Jenkins. In fact, before you killed our parents, we were living rather comfortably. So please, don't insult us with your stupid gifts and expect it to make everything all right just so you can sleep at night. I have to watch over my sister and brother now, and I will not teach them to take handouts from people like you, people who think they can buy their way out of anything. In fact, I'll make sure they turn out nothing like you. Are we done yet?" she asked impatiently, turning her attention back to Mr. Randall, who still seemed completely unaware of what was happening around him.

Myra stared at the girl, astounded that she was only sixteen and yet capable of cutting her down so efficiently with only a few brief sentences. Clearly, the conversation was over. She glanced down again at the stack of torn paper on the floor before quietly turning and walking to the door. She could feel three sets of eyes boring into her back.

"For what it's worth, you have no idea how sorry I am. If you ever need anything, I will do whatever I can to try to make it right," she said, not bothering to look back. She stepped through the door and began walking down the hallway, head down. She crossed the main room and felt all eyes on her. The booming voice of Officer Martin rang out behind her just as she reached the door.

"How did it go?" His cheery inquiry trailed off as he registered the look on her face. Myra walked out the door, through the lobby, out of the heavy front door, and down the steps, eyes fixed on the black Land Rover Sport at the end of the parking lot.

THE SONG OF DISINTEGRATION

CHAPTER 1

Myra sank into the cool leather seats of the Land Rover, thankful to be safe and protected in her own space where nobody could see her. She sat there for a moment, stunned into silence, wondering what she had expected in the first place. Why had she come here? Why had she done this? The girl knew; Myra hadn't gotten one over on her. She had called Myra out completely. Of course, there was no way for the girl to really know the true motives of her visit, but hadn't it been more of a suggestion from Greg than her own heartfelt idea? An "attempt to save face," he had so lovingly called it. But the girl had seen right through her. Even Myra hadn't realized how feeble it had been, how irrelevant to the suffering all of those children were now going through. They didn't want her money; they wanted their parents back, and obviously Myra couldn't give them that. How insulting it must have been for her to try to replace their lost family with a stack of paperwork. She couldn't blame the girl for her hurtful words. And to think, Myra hadn't even known their names. After all that she had done to them, she didn't even have the decency to re-member what their parents had named them. She had just looked at the paperwork that morning and hadn't even real-ized that she had forgotten their names. She slammed her hands onto the steering wheel, letting the tears finally come.

"Idiot!" She screamed into the silence of the car. She slammed her fists once more for extra measure, desperate to take her anger and embarrassment out on something. Her mind flashed back to the conversation with Greg.

"Well, of course, you'll get off, Myra. I'm the best lawyer in this damn city." He brushed a hand through his salt-and-pepper hair, pacing the kitchen floor. "You do realize you've ruined us, though, right?" Myra's spine had straightened at the words. He didn't even glance at her as he said them, too lost in his own selfish thoughts. All they were going through and he could think only of how the neighbors were going to perceive *him*?! "Do you realize how hard I've worked to get us where we are, Myra? The cars, the house, the private schools for the kids – do you think it's all free? I've bent over backward to make a name for myself, and you've gone and trashed it with one foolish act!"

Myra couldn't stand it anymore. She picked up the glass of water from the counter in front of her and threw it in his face. He finally looked at her, astonished, angry? She couldn't tell. She didn't care.

"How dare you?" she thundered. "Is that what you think this is all about? I made a mistake, Greg, a mistake I will pay for the rest of my life! Are you trying to tell me you've never made a mistake?"

"*You* are not the only one who will be paying for it, Myra!" he interrupted, wiping the water from his face with a dish towel. "Me, the girls, you've ruined it for us all. I'm *your* hus-band, they are *your* daughters, that's all people see now. No matter that I've won 98 percent of the cases I've taken on in the past decade; no matter that Ella is on the high honor roll or that Samantha could kick a soccer ball from here to the next county! Nobody sees those things anymore, Myra!"

"Have you forgotten, Greg, whom I was driving home that night?" Myra's tone had taken on that of a cornered animal. She was fierce, ready to pounce, her words cutting into the room like blades. She stared at him, silently daring him to respond. Instead, he turned curtly on his heel and stomped out of the room, leaving her still holding the empty glass. She didn't move until the sound of his footsteps tapping on the tile disappeared. She set the glass down and clenched her fists, trying to regain her composure and calm her breathing.

"Bastard," she muttered. She could feel their marriage slipping away even then, in the beginning of the whole nightmare, but it was early enough that she still held on to the faith that he would change his mind, see it her way, and support her, not just as her lawyer but as her husband. They had been together for fifteen years, since well before his success. They had married out of love, not necessity. Surely, they would rekindle that flame and get through this together. She was lost in these thoughts when she sensed somebody else in the room. She looked back up from the counter to see Greg leaning against the door frame. He looked tired, older somehow, but the fact that he was there at all gave her hope. Maybe he was coming in to apologize after all. She felt herself soften a bit.

"Listen," he said, his best business tone in effect, "as your lawyer, I think we need to sit down and strategize. Fighting is not going to help us win this case. We can talk personal stuff later when this is all over." She felt her features harden all over again.

"Are you fucking kidding me?" she said quietly. "You're not worried about me, about us, our family, not at all. All you give a shit about is winning this damn case and keeping your little 'streak' going. That is how you refer to it, right? Your winning streak? How many cases are you at now, Greg, anyway? If I remember, the number was getting pretty high. You were really impressing all of your bigwig buddies at the firm. You're kind of a hotshot these days, aren't you?" She felt hatred burning in her chest. Her Tiffany's necklace felt like a choke chain. She suddenly felt the need to be free of it all, and, before she knew what she was doing, she was ripping the bauble from her neck. Little diamonds went skittering across the marble countertop and onto the floor. Both of them just stood watching them catch the light and settle in various corners of the kitchen. Myra took a few deep breaths, clutching the remnants of the necklace tightly in her hand. None of it meant anything. It was all bullshit.

"Myra, you need to calm down. Have a cup of tea, a glass of wine, whatever, just relax a little if you can." His tone was sympathetic, almost condescending, as though she had truly gone and lost it. He had no idea what she was going through. "It's not about my streak, it's about you. All I'm saying is that we need to come up with some pretty aggressive tactics if we want to get this over with quickly. I was thinking maybe we could offer the kids some money or something. Not through the court, something personal. Maybe we could set up some personal accounts in their names. College funds maybe? If nothing else, it would be a great attempt to save face and certainly might sway the general public's opinion of you as a 'rich, careless housewife.' I believe that was the latest headline. If we can win over the public, we can win the case." Myra couldn't help but question whether or not it still had more to do with saving *his* face than hers, but she was too tired to argue. She dutifully poured herself a glass of wine and, laying the pendant and remaining chain near the sink, headed toward the couch.

Now, sitting outside the police station, she couldn't believe how foolish she had been to listen to him. In hindsight, it didn't really matter that she had gotten off with the most minimal of sentences. The prison she was living in was worse than any she could imagine. Her telephone had stopped ringing. Friends no longer cared to be associated with her. Her children were teased and ridiculed at school about their "Murderer Mommy." The giant bear hugs they used to greet her with upon their return from school had been replaced with meek smiles as they walked through the front door and headed straight to their rooms. Dinners were quiet, without conversation. Greg had left her, the stain on the family name too great for him to bear. He had quietly slipped from the radar, moved a few counties over, and begun his own practice. Another chance at success. The only upside to this was that he was ordered to pay alimony and child support that more than covered her expenses.

She had lost her part-time job as a teacher's aide at the preschool downtown. The principal had calmly explained to her they had been receiving complaints from the parents of the children in the class. No parents wanted their children being taught by a woman involved in a scandal. She could do little other than resign, her dignity still intact. Her days had become a string of lonely moments tied together by an equally lonely string of nights spent watching bad sitcoms until the early morning hours. She felt as though she had become a zombie.

She put the car in drive and started home. She was filled with dread at the prospect of the giant house and of trying to fill hours in it before the kids got home. There was only so much laundry to wash and so many times a person could vacuum in one day. Her house had never been so clean. She couldn't stand it. She missed tripping over the kids' stuff scattered throughout the rooms, missed Greg's shoes kicked off carelessly by the door, his jacket thrown over the back of the couch. She missed caps left off of toothpaste and dirty clothes next to the hamper instead of inside it. It was as though nobody dared to make a mess and risk disturbing the quiet that had settled over the house. It was the saddest thing she had ever experienced in her life. Sadder than the day they had to put their golden retriever to sleep, sadder than the day Greg walked out of the door, sadder even than the day her grandmother had passed away. This quiet infiltrated every nook and cranny of their lives, creating huge voids and vast expanses of distance between them all. It had completely taken over.

Myra pulled into the long driveway, reaching for the garage clicker thoughtlessly. She glanced at the mailbox as she passed, realizing that she hadn't gotten the mail in a few days. That would give her something to do later and kill at least a little time sorting through the envelopes. She pulled into the garage and let the door close noisily behind her, allowing her engine to idle just a little longer than she should have once the door was closed tightly. The keys jingled joyfully as she walked into the kitchen. The noise made her cringe. She turned on the kettle and busied herself readying a cup of tea. The warmth felt good against her skin when she picked up the steaming mug. Nothing seemed to warm her these days. She slumped down at the kitchen table cradling the mug, replaying the past year over and over, the steady tick of the clock the only noise to offset the terrible string of memories.

CHAPTER 2

The front door flew open at three thirty, and Myra jumped in her chair, sending little drops of cold tea shooting across the tabletop and onto her hands. She realized she must have been sitting here for hours, staring vacantly out of the back slider door, failing to even notice the beauty of the lake right before her eyes. How had the entire afternoon escaped her? She found that she was actually less shocked than she should be. This seemed to be happening more and more often lately. She jumped up and grabbed a paper towel just as Sammy sauntered into the kitchen, earbuds in, pressing buttons on her pink iPhone.

"Hey, Sammy!" Myra chirped, trying to sound upbeat. "How was school?" Sammy brushed a long strand of blond hair from her face and glanced at her mother, shrugging.

"All right." She reached into the fridge and grabbed an apple. Before Myra had a chance to ask any more questions, she saw Sammy turn the music up and walk from the room, backpack slung lazily over one shoulder. Myra sighed sadly and went in search of Ella. She found her sprawled across the beige loveseat in the living room, feet propped up on one end, *A Tale of Two Cities* opened in her hands.

"Hey, Ella, how was school?" Ella laid the book down on her chest, open to the page she had been reading. She gave Myra a look full of pity. A part of Myra hated this look, although another part was grateful for her effort. At least Ella tried to pretend that Myra hadn't wrecked everything for them. It took everything she had, Myra knew, but day after day she dutifully answered her string of questions before retreating into her own little world.

"It was good. I got an A on my chemistry exam," she offered. Myra wasn't surprised. Ella had always been an amazing student and had kicked off her freshman year at Thomas Junior-Senior High with the same enthusiasm as she had in all of her previous years of schooling, despite the turmoil that had descended upon them.

"That's great, honey!" she said in her best mom tone. Ella smiled and drummed her book methodically. Myra could tell she was waiting to see if there were any more questions. When she didn't ask any, Ella picked up the book and resumed where she had left off, leaving Myra standing there wringing her hands nervously. With at least two more hours until she had to start getting dinner ready, she plopped down in the armchair and flicked on the television. Ella lowered the book and peered at her over the top.

"Really, Mom? I'm kind of trying to read."

"Oh, yeah, right. Sorry," Myra said, clicking the TV back off and rising slowly from the couch. "I'll just be up in my room then." She walked from the room slowly, pausing at the base of the stairs to watch Ella. Her dark hair, a trait inherited from her father, flowed over the pillow, giving her the likeness of a sleeping princess. She chewed her thumbnail, clearly gripped by some pivotal moment in her story. Myra smiled to herself. Ella would be okay. She was tough as nails and had handled all of this with such grace. She couldn't believe what a beautiful, strong young woman she was becoming.

It was Sammy that she worried about. Sammy, just on the cusp of becoming a teen, going through that awkward stage of trying to find out who she really was, tossed so haphazardly into a world of adult problems before she was ready. Not that any of them had been ready, but Sammy was a sensitive soul and Myra knew that the past year had taken the greatest toll on her. She had retreated into herself completely. The iPhone and earbuds had become almost permanent accessories, removed only during school and soccer practice. The only time she seemed herself at all these days was on the field. She had been an exceptional soccer player since she started at age five. Myra would stand on the sidelines and marvel at her even then, her petite frame darting around the larger girls, her foot always in contact with the ball as she moved up and down the grass. She had a sureness about her on the soccer field that couldn't be rattled. There, she knew her place, knew exactly what was expected of her, and exactly how to make sure she lived up to those expectations. When she was playing, her mind could focus solely on the ball, and all the other problems in her world disappeared completely. These were the times Myra felt the happiest too. It was as though nothing had changed except the fact that Greg wasn't standing there next to her and Ella, helping them cheer Sammy on. She had hoped that starting the seventh grade and being in the same junior-senior high school as her sister might help to ease some of the tension, but Sammy was different these days. As if on cue, Sammy shoved past her, stirring Myra from her daydream.

"Whoa, watch where you're going!" she said jokingly. Sammy only glared at her and continued to the kitchen, the apple core perched between her thumb and forefinger, heavy bass emanating from her earbuds.

***

Myra awoke a few weeks later with the realization that Christmas was only three and a half weeks away. She sat up against her pillows and stretched, wondering how this had escaped her attention. Without a job or a social calendar, she realized she had basically lost track of days, weeks, and months. It had all just lost a bit of importance. Why had neither of the girls said anything about it? In previous years they had been all too eager to supply her with long lists full of Christmas wishes, even going so far as to name the exact stores where certain items could be found as they got older. She threw the covers back with a bit of enthusiasm. Christmas shopping might just help to raise her spirits. The thought of spending the day shopping for her girls filled her with an energy and excitement she hadn't experienced in almost a year. She threw on a robe and headed downstairs to make the girls breakfast.

Twenty minutes later the girls stumbled in. Sammy's hair was piled atop her head in a messy bun, and her face was still red with sleep. Ella's hair hung down her back, wet from a shower, and she was fully dressed and ready for school, makeup carefully applied.

"Good morning, girls!" Myra cheerfully acknowledged them. The eager tone raised both girls' eyebrows.

"What's gotten into you?" asked Sammy critically, but Myra's optimism was unscathed.

"Well, I woke up this morning and realized that Christmas is right around the corner!" she said, placing a bowl of cereal in front of each of them. She stood back, waiting for the glow of excitement and realization on their faces. They exchanged a quick glance and started in on their breakfasts. "Well, that's cool, right? In all the excitement lately, it just completely slipped our minds!"

"You call this excitement?" Sammy countered, gesturing around the quiet house with her spoon. She laughed to herself. "I'm pretty sure excitement is not what caused *you* to forget that Christmas was coming up." Ella nudged her with her elbow.

"Stop being a brat, Sammy. At least Mom's trying to make an effort. You just walk around with your stupid headphones in all the time." Sammy glared at Ella and Myra fought to maintain her composure.

"Calm down, girls. It doesn't matter why I forgot, only that I did. But that being said, there's still plenty of time. I'll go get a Christmas tree today while you're in school and get some shopping started. We can decorate tonight. I'll get everything down from the attic and we can put on some Christmas carols and make cocoa! It will be—"

"Bullshit, Mom. It will be complete bullshit, and you know it." Sammy threw her spoon defiantly onto the counter and jumped up from her stool.

"Excuse me! Sammy, you watch your mouth and sit back down right this second. It's not bull anything, it's Christmas."

"And it's ruined, Mom. It's fucking ruined just like everything else and it's never going to be the same, so stop trying to act like you're some perfect mother, and just get it through your head. We don't want Christmas presents, Mom. We just want our lives back to normal." She turned on her heel and stormed from the room, leaving the kitchen in ominous silence. Her words hung there, clouding the space with tension. Myra fidgeted with the front of her bathrobe, avoiding eye contact with Ella who sat stirring her cereal in quick little circles, making a milk cyclone in the bowl.

"Well," Myra finally said to break the silence, "you'd better hurry up and eat. The bus will be here any minute." Ella pushed her bowl across the counter.

"Thanks, but I'm not really hungry. Mom?"

23

"Yes, Ella," she sighed.

"I think a tree would be a great idea. I'll help you decorate tonight, okay?" Myra's shoulders slumped with defeat, but she offered Ella a feeble smile.

"Thanks, honey, that would mean a lot." Ella slipped from the stool and out of the kitchen. Myra leaned against the sink, rinsing out both of the cereal bowls for an unnecessarily long time, listening to the girls' bickering coming from the top of the stairs. She had to make this right, but it seemed impossible. How did Sammy hate her so much? How could she fix it? Certainly not with Christmas presents, not this time. This type of hatred cut right through to her bones, unlike the bursts of temporary anger caused by a week's worth of grounding or losing television privileges. This was a primal anger coming from Sammy, so pure and unabated that Myra feared it might eat her alive if she didn't find a way to help her work through it.

CHAPTER 3

The mall parking lot was jampacked, a glaring indication on a Tuesday that she was not the only one who had just realized that Christmas was only a few weeks away. The Land Rover crept up and down six different lanes in front of the food court before Myra found a spot to park. She pressed the car lock button on her keychain, surveying the stretch between where she stood and the entrance to the mall with a little sigh. She tightened her leather jacket around her, slipped her ungloved hands into the pockets, and turned her face down against the chill air nipping at it. She counted the clicks of her heels on the pavement to divert her attention from the cold, and by step eighty-seven, she opened the door and found herself surrounded by garish, glitzy decorations, overplayed Christmas carols, and the pushing, trampling crowd of the mall during holiday season. For a brief moment, she wondered if it was indeed worth it, before pressing onward through the mob.

She passed the center of the mall, where employees had painstakingly re-created Santa's cottage in the North Pole. A long line of pre-kindergarten children stood waiting with their parents, guided through a winding maze of velvet ropes and overly cheerful staff dressed like elves. Amid the countless who were crying, screaming, and pulling on their mother's coats, she spotted several who were smiling and laughing, the magic of the holiday dancing in their eyes as they eagerly anticipated divulging their greatest wishes to Mr. Claus himself. She couldn't help but remember Ella and Sammy with that same look. It seemed like ages ago now. She walked slowly, relishing in their delight, before dipping into what was once Sammy's favorite clothing store.

Myra perused the racks with mild interest. Nothing she saw seemed to make her think of Sammy. She passed soft, pink silk blouses and too-tight black minis, cream-colored cardigans with pearl buttons, and a table messily strewn with an assortment of handbags. It was all too girly, too cute. Sammy had no interest in things like that these days, although she used to love to play dress-up, rummaging through Ella's pretty dresses and sparkly shoes until Ella would come in and kick her out of her room. It seemed that these days Sammy liked to keep herself under the radar, although Myra couldn't help but think that the girly part of her was still hiding there somewhere, waiting to re-emerge.

She was almost through the entire store before she saw it, the perfect gift. A pair of silver hair combs stared up at her from a rack next to the checkout counter. They were simple, relatively plain even, the only adornment a single pearl set in the center of each comb. Myra smiled at the tasteful mixture of elegant and unassuming —perfect for a girly girl who didn't want anybody to know she was one. Without hesitation, she plucked them from the rack and placed them gently on the counter. The checkout girl smiled at her.

"Will that be all today?"

"Yes," replied Myra, "and I would love it if you could please gift-wrap them for me." The girl scanned the bar code and then pointed to the gift-wrap table located just behind her.

"Sure thing, just bring it around the back of the register, and Julie will take care of that for you." Julie nodded agreement over her shoulder and turned back to the gift she was currently working on.

Myra was waiting patiently for her gift to be wrapped when she saw her walk in. The long dark hair, the flawless olive skin, the way she carried herself, dark almond eyes fixed straight ahead of her. Myra was certain it was her before she even got close enough to get a good look. Her face flushed, and suddenly she was roasting in her jacket. She glanced nervously at the gift-wrap desk, noting that there was still one other person's item in front of hers. She ducked carefully behind the earring rack next to her, determined not to be seen but also able to keep an eye on the girl should she get too close. Another girl walked in behind her, far less beautiful and with the hardened features of a difficult young life.

"I'll be over there, Emilia," the second girl said, pointing toward a rack of fleece jackets. Emilia nodded, her eyes still forward. Now Myra was certain it was her, as the girl's name came rushing at her in a wave of remembrance. Emilia—how had she forgotten it? And the siblings—it was all coming to her now. Carina and Marco, she thought. She shifted her weight from one foot to the other in aggravation. Where had this information been hiding when she'd needed it most, weeks before, as the young girl berated her in front of her siblings? Emilia moved with grace through the store, stopping at racks to feel a fabric or at tables piled with trinkets, turning some over in her hands before replacing them. Myra peered through the earring rack, more and more eager with each passing second to receive her package and leave the store. The gift-wrapping girl had just picked up the gift ahead of hers and was slowly unrolling the shiny red paper onto the table. Myra found herself wondering why Emilia wasn't in school. When she looked back up, she didn't see her anywhere. Her heart leaped. Where did she go? Myra absolutely did not want to be spotted. She scanned the store anxiously but didn't see her anywhere. It was only when the earring rack began to spin that Myra realized it. The girl was directly in front of her, on the opposite side of the rack, checking out the jewelry. She thought of pushing the rack back, but thought that might bring added attention. Either way, it was too late by the time she thought to react. As the rack reached its halfway point, Myra's eye caught Emilia's, staring directly into hers. The girl's grip hardened on the plastic case, and she stumbled backward a step before regaining her composure. She straightened her back, never taking her eyes from Myra. The same steeliness that Myra had remembered from the day at the station settled over her face, and a slight smirk crept across her mouth. Myra just stood there, frozen, feet glued to the laminate floor. Emilia plucked a pair of sparkly dangle earrings from the rack and held them up, turning them over in her hands but never looking away from Myra. Her smirk became a grin, and she watched Myra's face carefully as she slipped the earrings into her coat pocket, silently daring Myra to say a word. Myra paled, tried to look away. Just as she thought she was going to get sick right there in the middle of the store, the ringing voice of Julie called out to her that her package was ready. Myra spun so quickly that she almost lost her balance and yanked the package from Julie's outstretched arm. She dashed to the store exit with an unnecessary swiftness and didn't stop until she was safely outside of the mall and back at her car.

CHAPTER 4

She drove home in silence, a mixture of shock and disbelief clouding her thoughts. What had Emilia been trying to prove? Why hadn't Myra said anything? What power did this girl have over her? She took a deep breath and rolled down the window a crack to let some fresh air into the confined space. She didn't know whether she should be angry or sorry. This girl had another thing coming if she really thought that she could torture Myra, although hadn't Myra tortured her? Her mind battled with itself, one part convincing her that she deserved the girl's coldness, the other countering that everything that had happened had merely been an accident, despite any other speculation put forth by the media. Her eyes welled with tears when she thought of the children spending their second Christmas without parents. The events of that evening replayed in her head, the same tattered reel that had been on a loop for almost a year.

***

She could still feel the weight of the keys in her pocket as they stood at the front door, exchanging hugs and air kisses with their hosts. Marianne's charm bracelets tinkled on her wrists as she grabbed Myra's hands in hers.

"Thank you both so much for coming! We've had a marvelous time. Are you sure you have to leave so soon?" Myra nodded in the direction of Greg, a smirk dancing on her lips as they watched him sway ever so slightly as he tried to get his jacket on.

"Yes, unfortunately, I think it's time to get somebody home and in bed." Marianne giggled quietly, aware of swaying herself as she patted Myra's hand.

"Good luck with that. We'll see you soon?" Myra nodded and opened the front door, grabbing Greg by the hand as she went. He stumbled out behind her and closed the door, leaving the din of the holiday party on the other side.

"Great party, huh?" He mumbled. Myra smiled at him, happy to see him at ease. He had been so stressed out lately, taking on more cases than was necessary, spending more and more hours at the office. He deserved a night out, and she was glad to see that he had taken advantage of it and allowed himself to let loose. The keys jingled as she pulled them from her pocket and beeped the car unlocked. They hurried into the car and she started it, blasting the heat in an effort to warm the frigid interior. Myra put the car in drive and started the ten-minute drive home.

Greg leaned his head against the seat and closed his eyes.

"I may have had a bit too much to drink," he said, clutching at his belly. "I think I'm definitely going to regret this tomorrow!" Myra chuckled.

"Well, it's Sunday, so there's nothing forcing you to leave the couch. Even hot-shot lawyers need a day off once in a while, right?" The car hit a small patch of ice as they neared the center of town and they slid a bit before Myra righted the wheel. "Whoa." Her grip tightened on the wheel and Greg sat up straight.

"What are you doing, honey? Be careful."

"I'm being careful! I just hit some black ice. I couldn't see it." Ahead of them gleamed the giant Christmas tree that the city had decorated each year. Its soft glow bathed the downtown street, reflecting off the snow and giving it the feel of a storybook town. Myra was struck by how quiet everything was. The stores closed down for the evening, the residents and store owners tucked behind closed doors in an effort to lock out the cold. She didn't remember the last time she'd seen this street so quiet, although she couldn't really remember the last time she'd been out past midnight, either. Greg jumped in his seat suddenly.

"Oh, shit. I think I'm going to be sick Myra." Myra looked at him, yanked from her daydream.

"Sick?"

"Yes, pull over." Before she could look for a place to do just that, Greg had grabbed the wheel, jerking it toward him. The car changed course suddenly, and Myra was unable to stop it fast enough.

"Greg!" She heard herself scream, grasping for the wheel and slamming both feet down onto the brake. The car shot up over the snow and onto the sidewalk, the brakes rendered useless on the icy pavement. Myra was gripped with fear as the car went into a tailspin. It must have been only seconds, but it felt like an eternity. She saw them just as they saw her, their eyes meeting hers for the briefest of moments as they stepped out from an alleyway tucked between two of the shops. Before anybody had time to react, the car was upon them, throwing their bodies out into the road as if they were paper dolls. The car slowed from the impact and continued to glide smoothly down the road about thirty yards before bumping ever so softly into the brick side of a clothing store. Myra sat still for a

31

moment, mute, stuck in the juncture between what was and what is, that instant before shock sets in when everything that has just happened is glaringly clear. The sharp smell of liquor and vomit snapped her out of it. She reached for Greg and shook him, trying to make sure that he was okay. He mumbled something incomprehensible and stared dumbly at her. She saw no signs that he had hit his head, but, just in case, she laid it gently back against the seat so that he could rest until the paramedics came. Suddenly, her mind was as sharp as a tack. She did a quick assessment of her own body, wiggling her toes and fingers, checking herself for blood, only to find that she was fine. The contents of her purse lay strewn across their laps and on the floor, and she searched through until she found her phone. She dialed the numbers quickly, running through the details of the accident in a manner so efficient it was as if she had watched the entire thing from an outside perspective. Once she had been assured that the police and ambulance were on their way, she clicked the phone shut and unhooked her seat belt.

The brisk air bit her face as she left the car. At first, she saw nothing and thought that perhaps she had imagined the young couple. Her heart raged in her chest as she made her way back toward the spot where Greg's SUV had jumped the curb. When her eyes fell upon the two shadows lying in the snow, she realized she had lost her voice. She screamed so hard she was sure she would wake the world, but no noise came out of her throat. Myra ran to them, desperate to see their chests rising and falling. They had landed about two feet apart, the woman's empty glove still in the man's hand. There was no blood, no screaming, nothing. Both had their eyes closed. For all the world, they might have been sleeping, choosing this icy street as their bed. Myra grabbed at their wrists in turn, searching for a pulse. Nothing. She shook them both, still trying to scream. Nothing. The seconds ticked by, but time stood still. Her breath wouldn't come. The warm radiance of the Christmas tree faded, and the twinkling stars disappeared behind a cloud of black.

When the paramedics arrived, they might have thought that three people had been hit. Myra awoke to an officer shining a light into her eyes and a flurry of commotion surrounding her. Lights flashed from every direction, and sirens broke through the silence of the street. Lights flicked on in apartments above the storefronts, and the world came alive, despite all the death of the evening. The bodies were covered with white sheets as Myra was poked and prodded by paramedics. It seemed as though everywhere she turned her head, there was another officer, asking her questions she couldn't possibly answer until she found her voice. She just sat there, mute and grief-stricken, trembling in the icy night. She watched as the officers dragged Greg from the car, his jacket soiled with vomit and still stumbling from his overindulgence. They checked him for injuries, preferring not to question him, realizing it would probably be useless.

The following twenty-four hours whizzed past like a jet plane. Myra's voice finally returned, although it was unrecognizable to her own ears. Her tone had taken on the gritty hoarseness of a woman in agony, overcome with grief. She numbly went through her account of the evening's events with one officer after another, signing statements with an automated flick of her wrist. For some reason she never mentioned Greg grabbing at the wheel, only that she had hit some ice. At some point in the evening, the news channels caught wind of the tragedy, and she saw her face flashing across the television screens on the other side of the pane glass in the waiting area. When the police had pulled Greg from the vehicle, they had been overwhelmed by the thick stench of alcohol, a tidbit that the media had grabbed onto and run with. Never mind that Myra had consumed only one glass of red wine throughout the evening; the speculation that she might have been drunk driving was already racing through the town like a wildfire, and a wildfire in a small town has no trouble finding kindling.

Upon arriving at the station, Myra had been administered a Breathalyzer test, which she passed, but that fact seemed to fall on deaf ears all around. She felt her first flicker of resentment toward Greg. He had sobered up since the accident, but Myra hadn't yet had a chance to talk to him alone.

It was close to ten the following evening when Myra and Greg finally stumbled through their front door, exhausted and drained. Greg's mother sat stick-straight on the couch, her eyes fixed on the evening news, hand covering her worried mouth. She flipped the television off when she heard them come in, standing too abruptly. She looked at her son with pity before turning an angry glare toward Myra.

"The children are sleeping. I've made sure that they didn't see the news today, and I've kept them inside so that they didn't hear anything from the neighbors. You have a lot of explaining to do." Myra noticed she wasn't talking to them as a couple, but was instead staring straight at her. Although she didn't know it at the time, this was how it was going to be from here on out.

"Linda, I'm exhausted. You don't even know what happened. Greg doesn't even know what happened. It wasn't my fault—" Linda held her hand up in the air, motioning for Myra to stop speaking.

"This is for you two to figure out. I don't want to hear a word. I just hope you realize what you've done." With that, she picked up her coat and walked out of the front door, slamming it behind her. Myra was too tired to think straight. She didn't bother to explain to Greg that he had caused all of this, didn't bother to scream at him or slap at him as she might have wanted to. Instead, she headed up the staircase, peering into the girls' rooms as she passed, thinking only of how she was going to tell them in the morning. She climbed into bed and fell into a dreamless sleep.

CHAPTER 5

Myra had managed to pull herself together after her incident at the mall. She had picked out a beautiful tree from a lot near town and had it strapped to the roof of the Land Rover. The struggle to get it into the house had proved to be the best medicine for her weary mood; her adrenaline was coursing as she pulled it bodily through the garage door and into the living room. When finally it stood erect in its red base, she stepped back to admire her handy work. This was the first time she had ever had to do this alone, she realized with a pang of sorrow. But there was also something else that stirred in her; she thought it might be pride and the first glimmer of recognition that life would go on.

When the girls got home from school, even Sammy smiled at the scent of pine filling her nostrils.

"Great pick, Mom!" said Ella. "It's totally perfect." She kissed her mother on the cheek before taking the stairs up to her room, two at a time.

"Good job, Mom. How did you get it in the house?" Sammy

asked, her curiosity for once greater than her anger.

"I just ... did it. I dragged it and then I just put it in the stand." She couldn't help but hear the surprise in her own voice. She had never been the type of woman to take out the garbage or mow the lawn. Those had always been Greg's tasks. Putting up the Christmas tree was on the same scale as was stringing the house with lights. In the past year, she had learned to do the first two tasks, almost thankful for the attention they took away from the mundane life she was leading. Christmas would be no different. She felt invigorated at the prospect of creating something beautiful within the bones of the oversized house. "Maybe you will help me decorate it tonight?" she asked quietly. Sammy shrugged.

"Sure. After my homework, okay?" She patted her mother on the shoulder and headed up the stairs. Myra held onto the moment, afraid to let go of Sammy's kind gesture, never knowing if or when the next might come.

After dinner, the quiet house was transformed. Christmas carols echoed off the vaulted ceilings as box upon box of ornaments were torn opened and strewn across the living room. The girls rummaged through them searching for their favorites as Myra strung the tree with lights, stepping back every few seconds to make sure they were evenly spaced as she had seen Greg do so many times. Her heart was bursting. For the first time in a year, she felt like a family again. She was half-expecting Greg to come bounding into the room, serenading them all with his loudest version of Elvis's "White Christmas." His absence was the only reminder that "normal" had taken on an entirely new meaning. For a brief moment, she thought maybe she should call him and invite him over to help, but the idea fizzled as fast as it had come. Greg had made it quite clear that there was no longer room for Myra in his life. He had spoken to her only once since the day the divorce was final, and that was simply to let her know that he didn't want to pursue a friendship with her, feeling it would benefit the girls more if it were a clean break. Although Myra couldn't have disagreed more, she didn't argue. There was rarely a point in arguing with a defense attorney; she had learned that lesson early on in their marriage. Following that conversation, drop-offs and pickups had consisted of the same quiet that had swallowed up the other aspects of their lives. For some reason, however, as she stood watching the girls carefully place colored balls and homemade ornaments on the branches of the towering Douglas fir, she felt a stir in that little space in her heart that had been reserved for Greg for so long. The CD began to skip, jerking Myra from her thoughts. She drifted over to the player and slapped it gently, setting the tune back on its regular course.

After the girls had gone to bed, Myra poured herself a glass of wine and plopped onto the couch, staring at the Christmas tree fully decorated and lighting up the room. It dawned on her for the first time that they had not had a tree the year prior. Her eyes settled on a photograph set up on the mantel of the stone fireplace. She and Greg and the girls, rosy-cheeked and smiling, winter hats pulled down over their ears. She remembered the trip to Vale fondly. It had been the first time that both of the girls had known how to ski well enough that they could tackle all of the harder trails that she and Greg loved, together. This picture epitomized what she had thought that their marriage was made of. She had always pictured them as "together forever," the one relationship among those of all of her friends and colleagues that would stand the test of time. Greg had been her best friend since high school, and that friendship had blossomed into a love that she had never known was possible to feel. Once they had the girls, Myra had felt complete. She loved every second of being a wife and mother. As Greg's practice had grown, there had been moments of tension between them, but Myra felt that was just part of the process of growing as a couple. His success had allowed her to stay home with the girls through their youngest years, and for that, she was grateful beyond words. It wasn't until after the accident happened that Myra was finally able to see just how much he had changed at the core. He was no longer the Greg who took her to Friday night football games in high school, or later to fancy Friday night dinners while his mom watched the kids. He was Greg, powerful defense attorney, winning victories left and right, caught up in the glory.

But it wasn't just him. After the accident, she had been able to see the changes in herself as well. She realized that maybe football games and even fancy dinners had lost their value to her as well. She was far more concerned with shiny baubles, fancy cars, and her oversized house than she ever thought she would be. But Christmas had passed the prior year without expensive gifts or holiday cheer, and, just like that, she was brought back down to earth. She hadn't missed the opening of presents or showing off her new jewelry to her friends as much as she had expected to, but her sadness at watching the children do without a normal Christmas was enough to put her over the edge.

They had tried to keep Christmas as normal as possible for the sake of the girls. Granted, there had been no tree, nor the gigantic pile of presents to which they were accustomed, but the effort was there. Myra awoke early to prepare the same fancy breakfast she had made ever since the year she and Greg had married. They made mock "mimosas" from orange juice and sparkling water and toasted each other. They plastered on fake smiles and wrapped their arms around each other as they watched the girls open the few gifts wrapped for them. But as soon as the girls had gone to bed, the façade faded away, and they found themselves in the midst of yet another argument.

"I can't believe you didn't even get a tree," Greg exclaimed, gesturing to the bare spot next to the fireplace where the tree normally went. Myra was walking out of the room but turned on her heel at the comment.

"Greg, it's been a little complicated around here. I've kind of had some stuff on my mind. Not to mention, it's not something I generally do by myself. I never heard you make mention of going to get one either." She realized her posture had become defensive.

"I can't think of everything, Myra. I've been busy trying to keep my wife out of jail for the holidays." Myra eyed the glass of Scotch set on the coffee table in front of him, trying to cast her mind back to remember how many he might have had.

"I'm not doing this, Greg. You've been drinking, and you're getting nasty. It's not fair, and I'm not going to listen to it." She placed her hands on her hips and stared at him, hoping he might acknowledge that he was getting out of line.

"God forbid I tell the truth, right? Better if we all just tiptoe around and pretend like none of this is happening just so we can spare your feelings, right? That sounds like a much better idea, dear." Myra could feel herself shaking. Up until this point, she had taken on the burden of this entire drama unfolding before them. She had never mentioned, to Greg or to the police, his own involvement in it. Her eyes narrowed, and, when she spoke, it was in a voice she had never heard herself use.

"Do you really want to talk truth, Greg? Because I have some truth for you! Would you like to know what caused the car accident that night? You did, you insolent bastard. You pulled on the fucking steering wheel because you were going to get sick. I lost control of the car because of YOU, and you were too damn drunk to even realize it." Myra could feel the tears streaming down her face, rage building inside of her. "For three weeks I have covered your ass, and truthfully, Greg, I don't even know why. Maybe I am afraid to see us both in trouble! Maybe I'm afraid you're the only attorney around who might be able to get me out of trouble, and I'm scared, if you're in trouble too, you won't be able to represent me. Maybe I don't want our children to see me throw their father under the bus. I have no idea, but what I do know is that I am NOT the one who should be explaining myself. I am NOT the one who should be on the defensive. I wasn't drinking. I didn't jerk the steering wheel. I didn't kill those people, Greg. YOU did, and I've been sparing you the guilt of that knowledge since the day it happened."

She stopped as abruptly as she had begun, her resolve fading, her shoulders sinking, no longer having to carry the weight of the truth. Greg stared back at her, confusion and anger contorting his face. The air was thick with tension, with only Myra's sobs cutting through the silence. It felt like ages that they both just stood there, acclimating themselves to their new circumstances. It was Greg who finally spoke, one simple sentence disintegrating whatever was left of the relationship they had known.

"You're fucking crazy, Myra." He got up and stormed out of the house, leaving Myra standing there listening as the garage door rumbled open and his BMW screeched down the icy driveway.

Greg filed for divorce a few weeks later. Myra had been relatively shocked, despite the predictability of his actions. They had barely spoken since Christmas night, and it was never brought up again. To this day Myra wondered whether or not Greg knew she was telling him the truth that night. He never asked, and she never offered, preferring to avoid any additional conflict for the sake of Sammy and Ella. They were already going through so much. Still, at this moment, she couldn't understand why or how she had let the whole world believe that she had caused the deaths of that poor, innocent couple, but there was no going back now. She had been dealt her hand, and she had folded under pressure and let Greg emerge victorious. Even if the truth were told now, nobody would believe her. She sighed heavily and rose from the couch, flipping off the Christmas lights before heading up to bed.

CHAPTER 6

The house was a lot taller than Myra had ever realized. She had found the giant yellow ladder still tucked behind the shed in the backyard, exactly where Greg had left it. She once again impressed herself with her own strength, dragging the ladder across the yard, opening it and positioning it at the left front corner of the roofline. Now, standing at the top of the ladder with a string of white lights dangling precariously from her free hand, she had the same feeling in her stomach that she generally associated with riding the ski lifts in Vale. She resolved not to look down and instead focused intently on holding the string of lights in place while avoiding putting a staple through the wire. The first shot of the staple gun startled her, and she wobbled a bit before regaining her composure. She couldn't help but let out a little laugh at her own surprise. She must have looked like an idiot up here. She found herself silently begging God not to let her fall off of the ladder. She could only imagine the headlines. "Murderess Housewife Turns on Herself, Jumps from Roof and Hangs Herself with Christmas

Lights." She giggled again, amused at the thought. She pressed in one staple, then another, as her mind created one zany headline after another. Before she could believe it, she was standing safely back on the ground, admiring the mildly crooked string of lights spanning the entire roofline of her home. She was utterly impressed with herself! It hadn't been nearly as hard as she thought it would be. Before she could think it through, she was in the car headed to the twenty-four-hour Walmart just outside of town.

***

"You're doing a lot of decorating, I see," said the clerk behind the counter. He eyed her curiously as she pulled Christmas paraphernalia from her cart, piling it so high in front of the register that she could barely see the top of his head on the other side.

"Oh, yes," Myra responded. "I've decided to do it all myself this year." She pointed to a giant Santa and reindeer displayed in the windows. "I'd like one of those sets as well. Do you keep them in stock?"

The clerk nodded his head.

"Yes, do you need some help loading all of this into your car? It's an awful lot. Quite the undertaking, if you ask me. You're really going to do it all by yourself?" Myra scanned the pile, littered with boxes of colored and white lights, oversized ornaments to hang from the fascia, tinsel, a blow-up penguin in a Santa hat and mittens, giant beaded candy canes, lengths of artificial spruce garlands, and a set of handmade wreaths to adorn the double doors at the front of the house.

"Yes, I suppose it is, isn't it? Hmm. Well, I will definitely need some help loading it up. And, you, what time do you get off of work?" The young man looked at her strangely, not quite understanding the question.

"Me, ma'am? Well, I'm off in just about fifteen minutes or so. Why do you ask?" Myra smiled politely.

"That's just perfect. How would you like to make an extra five hundred dollars today?" The boy smiled crookedly at her, clearly assuming she was joking around.

"Well, that would be pretty nice, but my pay's not all that great."

"Oh, I meant from me. Are you capable enough to come and help me decorate my house? I need to have it all done today for when my girls get home from school. It's a surprise for them." She smiled back at him.

"Yeah, I could help you out. Five hundred bucks, for real?" He looked at her in disbelief.

"Listen, money's about the only thing I have these days. If I can use it to help brighten up Christmas for my girls, then so be it. Luckily, I get to help brighten up yours, too, in the process. I'm in the black Land Rover right out there," she said, pointing out of the front window to her car in the parking lot. "If you can send somebody out to help me load up, I should be ready by the time you're done and you can follow me home, okay?" The young man nodded just as Myra handed him her credit card.

***

By the time the girls' bus pulled up at the end of the road, Myra and Scott (as she later learned he was named) had somehow managed to get every single decoration unloaded from the car and placed meticulously throughout the yard. The leafless branches of the giant oak tree at the base of the driveway now boasted tightly wound strands of colored lights. The drive itself was lined with glittering, waist-high candy canes in red, green, blue, and white. The giant blow-up penguin waved gently back and forth in the late afternoon breeze, and Santa and his reindeer surveyed the entire scene with contented grins from atop the midsection of the roof. The giant tin ornaments hung lazily from the fascia of the house, others dangled from the branches of various trees scattered throughout the yard. Myra and Scott stood side by side, admiring their progress. Myra's heart was ready to explode with joy. She couldn't believe she had pulled it off.

The same surprise registered in the faces of her daughters as they ascended the lengthy drive. The sun had just begun to dip down below the house, allowing the tiniest shimmer of the lights to show. Although the full effect wouldn't be felt until dark, it was instantly obvious that Myra had pulled off something pretty incredible. Even Greg had never exerted this much effort on Christmas decorations. The quiet house was singing, and the noise was music to all of their ears.

CHAPTER 7

It seemed as though the holidays passed in a blink of an eye. Trash cans full of used wrapping paper lined the side of the house, waiting for the next pickup. The refrigerator swelled with leftover turkey, stuffing, mashed potatoes, corn pudding, green bean casserole, pearled onions, cranberry sauce, and gravy. Myra had made enough to feed a small army, despite the fact that it was only her and the girls celebrating this year. The New Year loomed ahead of her and she couldn't help but feel hope that it would bring some positive changes and feelings of normalcy. The previous Christmas had brought with it so much turmoil and chaos that she had been sure it could never go back to the way it used to be. Although it had certainly been different without the presence of Greg and his parents, it had been happy and stress-free in the way Myra had remembered from years before.

Sammy and Ella traipsed into the kitchen midmorning, happy to be able to sleep in on their school break. Greg would be there around noon to pick them up and take them back to his house for their second Christmas celebration.

"Good morning, ladies!" Myra said, "Are you excited to go to your dad's today?" Ella nodded and Sammy shrugged.

"It will be nice to see Grandma. We haven't seen her in forever, it feels like!" Ella said, sighing dramatically.

"What's for breakfast?" Sammy chimed in.

"Well, 'breakfast' was served three hours ago when I got up. I'm not sure what you girls are eating!" Myra teased. Sammy smiled, and Myra happily noticed the clips she had bought holding back Sammy's hair. "Our brunch menu is significantly shorter. It consists of oatmeal or frozen waffles, so you pick." Myra was already reaching for the freezer door, knowing full well which the girls would choose. "Are you all packed to go?"

Not surprisingly, Ella's head nodded at the same time that Sammy's shook back and forth. "Well, miss, you'd better hurry up and get to it after you eat. You know Dad doesn't like to wait around." It saddened Myra to know that her children would have to leave their beautiful home this year to spend half of their vacation cramped into their father's two-bedroom apartment, but she maintained that it was important for the girls not to feel involved in her own tension with Greg.

The car horn honked in the driveway less than an hour later. Greg was annoyingly early, as usual. The girls hustled up the stairs and Myra couldn't help but laugh, watching Sammy haphazardly throw the contents of half of her dresser drawers into her duffle bag as Ella leisurely strolled from her room with two neatly packed totes. They were so different. The horn honked twice more and Myra headed back down and opened the door, signaling to him that the girls would be just a minute. He nodded his head in acknowledgment and turned his gaze back forward. She laughed a bit, wondering how long it might be, if ever, until he would yet again speak to her. Ella and Sammy pushed past her, shaking her from her thoughts, planting simultaneous kisses on either cheek.

"Bye, Mom, see you in a few days!" Ella offered. Before Myra knew it, the doors of the BMW were slamming and the car was rolling down the steep drive. She still stood in the doorway until they were out of sight, wondering what she would do throughout the next few days. She wandered back into the house, plopping onto the couch to watch a few minutes of television. She sat flipping through the channels aimlessly, preoccupied. Maybe she should take the decorations down. It would certainly be a lengthy project without the help of Scott, and it would keep her busy while she was alone. A knock on the door jerked her from her thoughts. Perhaps one of the girls had forgotten something. She leaped up, wondering briefly if she had perhaps locked the door, but the knob turned freely when she grabbed it. The briefest moment of hesitation set upon her as the door swung open, and, when she saw whom she was face to face with, she instantly knew what her gut had been trying to tell her.

Standing on her doorstep was Emilia, her long black hair shining in the sun. Her almond eyes were red-rimmed, as though she had been crying. Myra grasped at her chest without realizing she was doing it. How had the girl known where she lived, and why was she here? Myra pushed the door open a little farther and looked beyond her, searching for the other children or anybody else who might be with her. She felt exposed, taken off guard, and a little bit afraid of this girl. Was she here for revenge, having just spent the holidays without her parents?

"Well, hello, Emilia. What are you doing here?" She stammered, still clutching at her heart. The girl's steely eyes penetrated to Myra's core. She didn't blink or look away, just stared at Myra with such apathy that it would have unnerved a grown man. "How did you get here?" she asked, still searching the street below the house for the sign of anybody else who might be accompanying the girl.

"I walked," she stated, not bothering to explain herself any further. Myra's heart was pounding, and her palms had begun to sweat.

"Why? What do you want from me?" She realized she sounded frantic and tried to internally talk herself down to a calmer frame of mind, but, try as she might, the thoughts were racing through her head. What was Emilia doing on her front step? Was she here to hurt her? Somehow it didn't feel like it, but Myra's feelings had deceived her before. The girl shuffled her feet uncomfortably on the doormat, showing her first signs of what seemed like humility. Her eyes lowered a bit before again meeting Myra's.

"I need your help." She looked away again quickly, and Myra's fear turned to confusion. She released her hand from her still-pounding heart and stared at the girl in doe-eyed bewilderment.

"I'm sorry, you need my help?" Myra stammered. "I don't understand." The girl looked embarrassed and more than a little distressed, as though she herself couldn't believe she was standing on the doorstep of the woman who had killed her parents, asking for aid of any kind. Myra racked her brain, trying to think of what this girl could possibly want from her.

"Do you have a few minutes so that we could talk?" Myra couldn't wrap her head around what was happening. Was she really going to consider letting this girl into her house? This girl who had every reason to hate her? As if she could read Myra's thoughts, Emilia continued, "I'm not going to, like, do anything to you or anything. Believe me, this is as unexpected for me as it is for you, but you told us if we ever needed anything ... " Myra hadn't blinked, felt as though she couldn't speak. The girl's discomfort was growing, and she shifted her weight and wrung her hands. "Listen, if I had anywhere else to go, I would be there. Trust me. I don't ... I just don't have anywhere else to turn."

CHAPTER **8**

Myra's resolve was fading, and she found herself slowly stepping to the side and opening the door wider so that Emilia could enter her house. Emilia nodded a curt thank-you and stepped through the door. Myra couldn't take her eyes off her. This stranger in her home who was in many ways no more of a stranger to her than she was to herself; their lives were inextricably woven together these days.

Emilia scanned the house slowly, starting with the staircase on her left, moving through the living room and dining room, and through the passage to the kitchen. She walked to the wall of pictures hung in the entryway and touched a photo of Sammy and Ella.

"They are yours?" she asked. Myra nodded solemnly, still wary. "They're pretty."

"Thank you," she offered. They both stood nervously eyeing each other before Myra decided that she would eventually have to break the silence and move them from the foyer. "Can I get you a cup of tea?" Emilia shook her head.

"No, I don't drink it. Maybe just some water, please." Myra could see it was taking every ounce of effort for the girl to be pleasant with her. She wondered what Emilia could possibly need so badly that would lead her to her doorstep. Money, she assumed, although the girl had scoffed at her first attempt to provide that. She led Emilia into the kitchen and poured them each a glass of water before ushering her into the dining room. Emilia sat stiffly in one of the chairs, folding her hands neatly in her lap as Myra took a seat across from her. They sat in uneasy silence for a moment, avoiding eye contact, both fidgeting with the fringes of the cloth placemats on the table.

"What can I do for you, Emilia?" The girl looked up.

"You remembered my name." Myra nodded.

"Yes, I'm sorry about the other time. I ... " The girl shook her head, clearly not willing to hear the apology.

"Why I'm here, Miss Jenkins. It's not easy to discuss with you. I just have to preface it with the fact that I think we can both agree you owe me one." Myra sat up a little straighter, not sure how to respond to the comment. "I need help, and I have nobody to turn to. You remember my brother and sister, I would imagine." Myra nodded.

"Carina and Marco, yes." She was eager to prove to the girl that she was not the heartless monster she had been painted to be. She did know their names and would always remember them, of course. Emilia smoothed her hands down over her jeans, taking a deep breath. She looked as though she was trying not to cry.

"Well, I assume you can understand that they are all I have left now of my family." Myra looked back down at the placemat in front of her. "I don't really know how to say this, Miss Jenkins, so I'm just going to say it. Our closest family members are in Mexico and they are poor and won't be able to take care of us all. Seeing as we were born in the United States, the state does not have the right to just deport us, so we have been

52

placed in the foster care system, naturally. None of us are babies, as you know, and it is rare to find a family who wants to adopt a grown child, especially one with two semi-grown siblings. They have found a temporary home for Marco and also for Carina, but they will be separated, and I cannot go with either of them." She stopped talking and looked up, searching Myra's face for a reaction to what she was saying.

Myra was stone still, trying to register where Emilia was headed.

The girl cleared her throat and continued. "The only way to keep us together is if we can find a family who will foster us together. Once I'm eighteen, I can go and find a job and an apartment, and then, when I'm twenty-one, I can adopt them myself. I just turned seventeen after our last meeting in September, so it wouldn't be for that long." Myra's jaw dropped as she realized what Emilia was asking.

The girl gestured to her surroundings. "You have the room, and you'd never know we were here. We'd be quiet as church mice. My brother and sister are young, but they are very well-behaved. As soon as I turn eighteen and get my own place, I can pick them up from school and keep them on the weekends. I can essentially be their mother. You would only need to be involved enough so that the state would believe that they were under your full-time care until I can legally adopt them myself." Her tone had shifted, and Myra could feel the sense of urgency in her voice. Her eyes welled with tears as she waited for any sort of response. "Please, Miss Jenkins. They're all I have left."

Myra's body felt weak and tingly, as though she might pass out. She couldn't believe what was happening. Certainly, she owed this girl and her siblings some help, but she had her own girls to think about as well. How would Sammy and Ella react to even the mere thought of this? Hadn't they been through the mill too? Didn't her daughters deserve as much respect as this girl did? Her mind was racing, flooded with emotions and confusion. She didn't know what to say as the girl stared at her, desperate for an answer. Her throat felt dry and cracked as she searched for words.

"Emilia ... I ... I don't know what to say. I'm a little taken aback. There are no aunts or uncles, nobody that you can turn to?" The girl waved her hands frantically in front of her.

"I'm trying to tell you that! No, there's nobody besides an uncle in Mexico. My father hated him. We've only ever met him once. He's not a good man, and he's poor. My brother and sister deserve better than that!" She was yelling now and tears were streaming down her face. "I knew I shouldn't have come here. Stupid and pointless. I don't know what I was thinking. I never should have asked." She stood abruptly, knocking over her water glass accidentally with her sleeve. She made a motion to clean it up, thought better of it, and ran for the front door, slamming it behind her and leaving Myra in stunned, cavernous silence. She watched the water from the glass pool on the tabletop before it branched out and made a little stream toward the edge of the table. It drummed the throw rug beneath as it fell, the noise acting as a reminder that this was real, had actually happened.

Myra's mind raced. She was yet again ashamed of the way she had reacted in front of the girl. She couldn't help but feel that she had again let her down. This feeling was topped with a double dose of confusion. How was she supposed to have reacted? How would anybody have reacted in the same situation? It was entirely unexpected, perhaps even more so than the events that had led her and Emilia to this point in the first place. She pushed her chair out and paced into the living room, leaving the water to puddle on the carpet. Her stomach twisted and lurched as she replayed the conversation in her head. Clearly, the girl must be desperate if she had come knocking on the door of the one person whom she likely hated the most in this world. The one person who had, in fact, caused all of this strife, at least to the best of Emilia's knowledge.

How she wished she had told the truth from the beginning, told the police about Greg, how he had grabbed the wheel. Perhaps things would be different then. Perhaps she would have been able to reach out and give Emilia a hug, offer her some support, and open her doors without a second guess. But she had her own girls to think about, she reminded herself. How would Sammy and Ella react to even the thought of this? It would be a constant reminder to them of the events that had turned their worlds upside down.

THE SONG OF
SEEDS

CHAPTER 9

Myra tried to busy herself for the rest of the day to keep her mind occupied. She dragged the ladder back out from the side of the house and climbed to the top of the roof. Down came the lights, the ornaments, and Santa and his reindeer. The giant, waving penguin was deflated and neatly folded. Everything was packed into plastic crates labeled "Christmas" in Myra's tidy penmanship before being dragged down the basement steps and stored until next year. All the while, she couldn't help but hear the pleading of Emilia's voice in her head.

It was late, the sun dipping down into the horizon behind the house, by the time she finished. She made herself dinner and poured a glass of wine. The tick of the wall clock exaggerated the silence in the house. She reached for her cellphone and turned on some music to help her stay distracted. Try as she might, she could not ignore the events of the day. She knew she would have to respond to Emilia at some point, knew that she would have to make decisions about what she had been asked. Was it even something she would consider? She placed her fork gently on the side of her plate and leaned back into the chair, racking her brain. If it was something she was truly thinking about, obviously she would have to talk to her girls about it. She couldn't imagine making the decision without their input. She drummed her fingers on the table, overwhelmed at the mere thought of the conversation. She reminded herself that Emilia must have been truly desperate to show up on her doorstep. Clearly, the girl was in need of help, and she did have a point. It was Myra's fault that she'd been separated from her parents. She wasn't sure she could bear the guilt of being responsible for her separation from her siblings, as well.

The full weight of what she had been asked finally hit her. If she said no, she was proving to this girl that she was indeed the heartless monster that she'd accused her of being. If she said yes, she was inviting the tension that would come with living with a girl who hated her, as well as putting her own daughters in a situation that might be too much for them to handle. There was clearly no right answer. Any way she looked at it, Myra realized that things were bound to change yet again.

***

Four days later, when Greg's BMW pulled up the driveway, Myra was as ready as she'd ever be to talk to the girls. Greg exited the car and headed to the trunk, removing the girls' bags carefully and placing them on the ground. The girls followed behind him, grabbing their respective luggage and heading up the walkway to the front door. Myra swung it open as they neared, waving quickly at Greg before grabbing their bags and ushering them inside.

"Hey, guys, how was Dad's house?" she smiled. Greg

stepped through the door behind them, laden with boxes and bags full of Christmas gifts.

"Where do you want these, Myra?" She flinched, having not heard her name from his mouth in a considerable amount of time.

"Just drop them at the bottom of the stairs, please. We'll put them away later." She returned her attention to the girls.

"Did you have fun?" Ella nodded, and Sammy shrugged in her typical fashion. Greg swept in to hug and kiss each of the girls. He nodded at Myra and wished her happy holidays quickly before heading back out to his car, closing the door behind him, and leaving the cold air outside.

Myra paced back and forth, trying to be inconspicuous with her discomfort. She watched as the girls tore through their bags, pulling one gift after another out to show off, talking over one another. Dinner simmered in the crockpot in the kitchen, Myra having made every effort to make sure that the scene was set for her to have this dreaded and unexpected conversation with her daughters. She could barely believe she was even entertaining the idea, but the days since Emilia's visit had been almost unbearable. She kept seeing the girl's face, tear-stained and filled with disappointment and anger. She must have run through the conversation fifty million times. It didn't seem to matter which angle she approached it from, Myra knew that she wasn't going to be able to pretend that it hadn't happened and move on with her life.

"Mom, what are you doing?" Sammy said, snapping her back to the present.

"Huh?" Myra realized both girls were staring at her.

"Ella asked you a question like three times and you're just standing there with a weird look on your face. What's wrong with you?" Sammy's face was scrunched up in disgust.

"Oh, I'm sorry. I was just thinking about something, that's all." She smiled gently at them both. "I wasn't trying to ignore you, Ella, just a lot on my mind."

"Well, you've had like four days to sit around and think about all the stuff on your mind, so maybe you could try paying attention to us for a few minutes."

"Sammy, don't be nasty," Ella chimed in. "It wasn't even that important." Sammy rolled her eyes and started up the stairs, dragging her bags behind her. "You okay, Mom?" Ella asked.

"Yeah, I just have some stuff I need to talk to you girls about." Sammy stopped on the staircase and looked back down, exchanging an unsure glance with her sister.

"Like what?" she asked. Myra shifted uncomfortably on her heels.

"We'll talk about it over dinner. Why don't you both go and put your things away and get settled? It's going to be okay." She wondered why she'd had to add that last part, instantly implying negative subject matter.

"Yeah, the last time you said that, pretty much the whole world blew up, Mom. I think maybe I'll just skip dinner tonight," Sammy said, starting back up the stairs. Myra let her go. She didn't have the energy to respond right now. Ella picked up her own things and followed behind.

"She has a point, Mom." Myra sighed and shook her head. This was not off to a very good start.

CHAPTER 10

The girls made their way into the kitchen a little over an hour later. Myra had spent most of the time pacing the tiles and wringing a dish towel in her hands, juggling words in her head to try to form the perfect opening sentence for the upcoming discussion. She realized with some annoyance that she was no closer to coming up with anything than she had been at the start. She smiled at the girls, piling overly generous portions of crockpot chili into their bowls. Sammy was the first to break the silence.

"So what is it you need to talk to us about?" Myra realized with some shock that it was the first time she had seen Sammy without her earbuds dangling around her neck in quite a while. She giggled nervously and placed steaming bowls in front of each of the girls, gesturing toward the dining room table. The girls again exchanged uneasy glances and calmly took their seats. Myra sat before them at the head of the table. She spooned up her chili and dumped it back into the bowl several times before making eye contact.

"Well, I had an unexpected visitor while you were away at Dad's, and I think that it's something we need to discuss."

"From who?" questioned Ella. Again, nervous laughter.

"Well, it was really quite strange, actually. It happened just after Dad picked you up. Um, Emilia came by." Both girls looked confused.

"Who's Emilia?" asked Sammy, her brow furrowed in consternation. Myra could feel her stomach churning, knowing that once this conversation was had, it could never be un-had, and fearing the further damage it might do to her girls. She cleared her throat.

"Uh, Emilia Garcia." she offered, hoping they might pick up on it. By her immediately stunned countenance, Myra could see that Ella had put it together instantly. Sammy still looked unsure, but catching Ella's expression, realized she was missing something.

"What? Who is that?" Myra could feel the blood rushing to her face. Her cheeks felt like they were on fire as Ella just stared at her in disbelief.

"What did she want?" she demanded.

"Who? Who is Emilia?" Sammy asked again.

"The girl from the accident." Ella snapped back without turning her gaze from Myra. "What did she want, Mom? Why was she here? Are you in trouble? Did something happen?" Myra shook her head vigorously.

"No, no, nothing happened. Nobody's in trouble. She just wanted me to help her with something." Sammy had slouched down into her chair, clearly feeling vulnerable at the thought of the Garcia family back in their lives. Her wide-eyed expression reminded Myra of when she was a little girl, caught doing something she knew she wasn't supposed to do. Ella, however, had straightened in her chair, her protective nature taking hold.

"What could she possibly want from you, Mom? She hates

you." Myra winced. "I didn't mean it like that, but honestly, you offered them money and they didn't want that. What else can you do for them?"

"How did you know about that?" Myra demanded. She had worked hard to keep the girls from knowing anything about their meeting, feeling it unnecessary information.

"Does it matter?" Ella countered, but Sammy was already answering the question, her voice meek.

"We heard you on the phone with Grandma one night through the vents." Ella shot her a look of unmistaken annoyance, their secret revealed.

"What else have you two been eavesdropping in on?" Myra asked, feeling flustered. She realized it was irrelevant, but was eager to take some of the attention off her visit from Emilia.

"I think we get to ask the questions right now, Mom," challenged Ella. Myra was surprised; she had expected this reaction from Sammy, but not Ella. Sammy had always been the more aggressive of the two. Ella preferred to step back and survey the situation rather than reacting to her emotions. Myra sat back in her chair, defeated.

"Okay, fair enough. Let me tell you what happened." She started in on the story, searching the girls' faces for receptivity the entire time she spoke. About halfway through, she noticed that Sammy had started to cry softly. Ella automatically reached her hand out and grabbed her sister's, and Myra was instantly grateful that they had each other through this whole ordeal. Despite their differences and all the chaos that had engulfed their lives, they had really managed to stand by each other, a feat that she and their father had not been able to achieve. She couldn't help but feel proud of them now as she, yet again, threatened to upset their world, and they sat there stoically, listening to every word without interrupting.

By the time Myra had finished speaking, the chili sat cold and hardened on the table. The girls still held hands as they glanced back and forth from each other to the tabletop. Myra was exhausted. She felt as though she had just run a marathon, and a sudden desire to crawl into bed for the next week washed over her.

"Do you have any questions or opinions you want to talk about?" she asked quietly. Sammy shook her head, but Ella nodded.

"Are you going to do it? Let them move in?" Myra shrugged.

"I honestly don't know what to do. That's why I wanted to talk to you girls about it. I've been agonizing over it since she came here, and the only conclusion that I could come to was to ask you what you thought about it. Admittedly, I could have come up with something better, I suppose, but ultimately, it's a decision that you both deserve to be as much a part of as I, if not more. I'm not trying to put pressure on either of you or force you to make decisions you are uncomfortable with, but this was the only logical way I could find to handle the situation. I weighed my options carefully: Do I tell you? Do I not tell you? At the end of it all, if I didn't at least consider her request carefully, I don't know that I could forgive myself. Not that my guilt should fall on either of you, but you do have the right to be part of the decision-making process. You are my babies, and I love you both more than life itself. I've made a lot of mistakes over the past year, and I'm trying my best to remedy them without screwing up your lives any further. I hope that you can both understand my plight and that you know I came to you with this out of a good place in my heart." Myra felt overcome, yet again questioning her decision to consider this in the first place. Was it putting too much pressure on the girls?

"I think you should do it," Ella said. Myra looked up, surprised.

"What?"

"Me too," Sammy offered, wiping a tear from her cheek. Ella squeezed her hand.

"Girls, this is a big decision. I think that you really need to think about it before you just agree. I want to make sure you are really sure about it before you give me an answer, okay? Talk about it, ask me questions. It doesn't have to be decided tonight, okay?" Both girls nodded in unison, and Myra smiled.

"I think I'm going to go to bed, okay, Mom? I'm beat." Ella stood up, pushing her chair in before walking away, and Sammy followed suit, picking up their chili bowls and depositing them in the kitchen sink.

"Me too, Mom. I'm exhausted." Just like that, the girls whisked from the room, leaving Myra alone with her thoughts. She cleaned up the kitchen slowly, reveling in the sounds of their feet shuffling down the hallway overhead and water running through the pipes in the kitchen from the upstairs bathroom where they were readying themselves for bed. She was so happy that they were home and couldn't believe how well her conversation with them had gone. Their resilience took her breath away. She could barely even believe what they were considering, and yet both of her daughters had listened carefully and embraced the opportunity to help another family without a second thought. In the midst of her fatigue, she couldn't help but feel immensely proud of them and even a bit proud of herself and Greg for raising them to be such kind and understanding individuals.

CHAPTER 11

Myra decided to let the week pass without any further mention of the Garcia children and Emilia's request. Although her daughters had readily agreed to the arrangement, Myra herself was not so sure that they had thought it through completely. Saturday morning came without so much as a word uttered about their conversation. The girls both sat hunched over bowls of cereal at the dining room table while their mother traipsed through the kitchen, humming something indiscernible.

"So, Mom," mumbled Sammy, "Ella and I are going to clean out the office today."

"For what?" Myra asked absently, adding the cream to her coffee.

"For the kids," Sammy answered. Myra stopped stirring and looked up at them, both girls now awaiting her response.

"Oh, well, I hadn't ... I didn't think ... we haven't really discussed it much. I just ... are you sure there are no questions you want to ask me? Like I said, this is a big decision, girls.

Plus, I'm not even sure it's possible. I haven't even spoken to Emilia any further. What if the state says no? I don't think it's just as easy as me saying I will take them." She realized this all as she was saying it. She hadn't even thought about that yet. What if it wasn't even possible? What if she told Emilia of their decision and it turned out to just be another disappointment? She realized she was feeling suddenly flustered.

"We already thought about that, but just in case, we thought it might be nice to get some stuff ready for them," added Ella. Myra could hardly believe how proactive the girls were being. It almost seemed as though they were excited at the prospect.

"May I ask you a question?" she asked. Her daughters nodded simultaneously. "Okay, well, if you don't mind me asking, why are you both so eager to do this? Don't get me wrong ... it's admirable that you want to ... I guess I just thought it might be a hard thing for you to fathom. I mean, what if you don't get along? It's three more people in our house, three more people to fight over the remote, the shower, who does the dishes and takes the trash out. Have you thought about any of that? I'm not trying to discourage you, but I want to make sure that you've really weighed this out." Sammy smiled and Ella answered.

"Yes, Mom, we've already talked about that stuff. We have two TVs and an extra bathroom. Not to mention, the more kids, the fewer chores we have to split up." Sammy giggled. "We'll get along, Mom. We both really want to help them. I can't imagine what it would be like to lose both of my parents. It might be hard at first, but nothing's been easy lately. This can't be much harder than anything else we've been doing." Myra sighed. She certainly had a point there.

"Okay. If you're sure, then I will go ahead and see what I can do about contacting Emilia. But, girls, I need you to listen. This is very important. Once we tell her this and begin the process, there's no turning back. We can't make an offer like this and then change our minds. If either of you has *any* reservations about this, promise me that you will let me know before the weekend is over. I won't be able to contact Family Services until Monday anyway. This is big, girls, and I want you to know that no matter what your final decision is come Monday, I am extremely proud of both of you. It seems a bit premature to go cleaning out rooms, but I suppose they could use a good once-over anyway. I don't even remember the last time I've gone through the guest room or the office." The girls nodded in agreement and exchanged a smile.

By noon, work had begun on clearing out the office. The French doors that had remained closed since Greg's departure were flung open. Boxes filled with ancient tax documents, bank statements, and old photos littered the foyer as they were pulled one by one from the room. Two trash bags full of Greg's old clothes rested against the front door. His mahogany desk was pushed bodily by both girls until it crossed the threshold as well. The ceiling fan and windowsills were dusted, and cobwebs were sucked from the corners and crevices. The floor was vacuumed and mopped, the curtains pushed aside and the windows opened to eliminate the musty odor that had permeated the neglected room. Baseboards were scrubbed and the closet was emptied, until, finally, all three of them were standing back to survey the product of their hard work. The room, now purged of its clutter, was a lot larger than Myra had remembered. Still, to fit three children in here seemed a bit ambitious.

"Will they all be comfortable in here?" She wondered aloud. She had to remind herself that the prospect of the Garcia children living with them was still just a minute possibility.

"Well, we have the fourth bedroom upstairs, Mom," Ella offered. "Do we really need a guest bedroom? I mean, we don't have a lot of visitors these days, and I'm sure Sammy and I can

share a room when Grandma comes to town." Myra considered it. Of course, they could use that room. Why hadn't she
thought of that?

"Absolutely. I think it's a great idea."

"Awesome!" answered Ella. "Let's get started on it." Myra
knew they were getting way ahead of themselves. After all, she
still didn't even know whether or not this was going to be possible. Just because Emilia had come to her with the idea did
not necessarily mean that it had been properly researched as
a possibility.

"Let's just slow down a little bit, okay? I think we've done
enough for today. We still have to get all of these boxes out to
the garage," she said, surveying the disarray. "The spare bedroom is pretty much set up already anyway, so if this all pans
out, I think we can just make a few minor changes to make it
comfortable. I just don't want us to get too far ahead of our-
selves, okay?"

"Yeah, I think she's right," said Sammy. "Besides, I'm exhausted!"

"Oh, no, you don't!" responded Ella. "You are totally helping us clean this up!" Sammy stuck out her tongue and Ella
laughed.

After the girls had gone to bed, Myra leaned in the doorway of the office. It smelled fresh and clean, the marble tiles
gleaming in the light of the moon that shone through the win-
dowpanes. She couldn't believe it had been a year since she
had been in this room. She remembered the last time she had
closed the doors.

***

Greg moved out officially on a Wednesday afternoon, a fact
that had driven Myra crazy ever since. She couldn't believe
that his disdain for her had grown so much that he couldn't

even make it through the rest of the week and move out on the weekend like a normal person. No consideration was given to the girls or the fact that they had to go to school the next day, with no time to adjust to or grieve over the fact that their father had moved out. Apparently, Myra was so unbearable that he just *had* to get away as soon as possible.

"Really, Greg? You couldn't perhaps wait until the weekend?" she'd asked him.

"What's the point, Myra? Is anything going to change so drastically between now and then to make me change my mind?" His words stung, but she didn't show it.

"I meant for the girls' sake, that's all. They're going to come home from school and all of your stuff is going to be gone. You don't think that might be a little hard on them?"

"It's not like they didn't know it was coming. We've been upfront with them since we made our decision, Myra. I'm not going to keep feeling guilty about this." Myra rolled her eyes.

"Of course you're not, Greg. For the record, this was not 'our' decision, it was yours. Let's try and keep that straight, okay?"

"Oh, here we go!" he countered. "I forgot that none of this is *your* fault ... I'm the big bad guy, as usual. It was only my decision. So, what, Myra? Are you trying to tell me that you're still in love with me? That we should have tried harder?" Myra considered this, scrutinizing him from head to toe, searching for any likeness to the man she had married. That Greg had been easygoing, funny, kind, and upbeat, the kind of man that everybody found easy to be around. There had been no pretense about him at all, no showiness or want of approval from others. He had been perfectly content being himself. This Greg was different. This Greg was cocky, arrogant, snobby, and blameless.

"I suppose you're right," she conceded. He threw his hands up and shrugged.

"I rest my case." Myra shook her head. If only it were as easy as that. Unfortunately, this wasn't a courtroom, and human emotion wasn't that easy to discount. Regardless of their fading feelings for each other, the girls shouldn't have to keep paying the price. She realized the conversation was getting them nowhere. Greg must have come to the same conclusion because he flung the final two bags of his things over his shoulders and headed out the front door to his car. She followed him out, watching as he forcefully crammed them into the overstuffed BMW. With some effort, he finally got the passenger door to close and stood back to catch his breath and wipe the sweat from his brow. He looked over at Myra, arms crossed, standing on the walkway watching him.

"Well, I guess this is it," he mumbled, walking toward her. "I guess I'll be by soon to pick up anything that might have gotten left behind once I'm settled in my new place." The air between them was thick, and Myra's breathing felt constricted. She nodded acknowledgment. With nothing left to say, he turned abruptly, got into the car, and backed down the driveway. She stood there for a few minutes trying to right her breathing. She walked back into the house, closing the door slowly and softly behind her. The quiet seemed to swallow her up. She evaluated the battle scene before her: lamps and two end tables removed from the living room, an empty suitcase ajar on the bottom step of the staircase, the coat closet rummaged through, several jackets dangling haphazardly from their hangers. CDs had been strewn across the mantelpiece as he carelessly sifted through them to take his share. In the kitchen, cabinets were left open, portions of their contents removed to be taken to Greg's new place. The office, however, was the worst of it. Drawers had been emptied, papers scattered across the desktop as he separated "his" from "hers." Multicolored folders from the filing cabinet lay open, their contents partially spilling onto the throw rug beneath. An ancient Rolodex sat on the windowsill, all the important business contacts long since transferred to digital files, another glaring reminder of the simpler life they had once lived. Boxes littered the floor, half-stuffed with plaques, awards, recognitions, and framed copies of Greg's college diploma and specialty certificates. Myra felt sick and angry, hurt and confused. As much as she knew Greg had changed, she couldn't help but feel, looking at this, that she was as much to blame as he was. She had, after all, allowed him to hole himself up in here for hours on end, admiring the walls adorned with his own framed successes, talking on the phone to his high-end clientele and powerful friends and colleagues. She had let him skip countless family dinners as he succumbed to the pressures of becoming one of the most highly acclaimed lawyers in the state. She had accompanied him to his fancy parties, spent his money on private schools for the kids and pretty cocktail dresses for herself, and fawned over him each time he presented her with a new diamond tennis bracelet or a getaway to some island paradise. It sometimes felt as if the only real difference between them was that he had no remorse over whom he had become.

She walked up the stairs, stepping carefully over the suitcase. Entering her bedroom, she was hit full force with the reality of the situation. The overhead light in the walk-in closet had been left on, highlighting the empty racks where Greg's clothing had been. His dresser drawers were open and mostly empty. The night table on his side of the bed was gone, as were his pillows and the slippers that he always left on the floor at the foot of the bed. His side of the his-and-her vanity was barren. The medicine cabinet had been completely emptied and the countertop, normally a point of contention between them, was unnervingly clean. Countless times throughout their marriage they had argued, half in jest, about Greg's side of the bathroom counter and discussed his reluctance to use the many drawers and cabinets available to him for storing his things. Where he had once kept his countless bottles of deodorant, cologne, hair gels, pomades, and shaving accessories, an immaculate marble surface stared back at her. His shampoo, specially formulated for graying hair, was the only thing of his that remained in the shower. She promptly picked it up and squeezed the contents into the toilet bowl, followed by a satisfactory flush. She walked back into the bedroom and sat on the bed with the empty bottle in her hand, the only noise the subtle tick-tock of the alarm clock on her nightstand. So this was what it felt like to watch your marriage disintegrate. This was divorce. Excellent.

It took only a short while for her to compose herself. The girls would be home from school shortly and she would be damned if she would let them see her like this, wallowing in self-pity, caressing an empty shampoo bottle as if it were her long-lost lover. Before she realized what she was doing, Myra was on her feet racing throughout the house, a giant black trash bag trailing behind her. She started in the garage and moved through the kitchen, living room, downstairs bathroom, and various closets, pulling anything and everything that was left of Greg's and depositing it into the bag. She moved up the stairs, through the guest bedroom, the hall closets, their bedroom, bathroom, and closet. She went through her own drawers, removing cards, love letters, photos, and memorabilia she had collected over the course of their courtship and marriage, and deposited that too. If he insisted on leaving on a Wednesday, then Myra insisted on making it a clean break. Whenever Greg did decide he was ready to get the rest of his things, they would be ready and waiting for him.

By the time she was finished, the house was immaculate, and she was dragging two full bags down the steps. She threw them into Greg's office and slammed the French doors behind her, thankful for the curtains that separated its contents from her view. Looking at the various rooms now, nobody would have ever guessed that just hours earlier, Greg had been an inhabitant of the house. All traces of him had been wiped clean except for the picture from Vale on the mantelpiece.

CHAPTER 12

The girls were unusually perky for a Monday morning, especially a Monday on which they were returning to school after an extended break. Sammy came to breakfast without her earbuds in, and she and Ella were engrossed in conversation right up until they walked out the door to meet the school bus. Myra couldn't remember the last time she had seen the two of them so animated. She could tell that they were legitimately excited over the prospect of being able to help the Garcia children, although she herself was still filled with trepidation at the thought.

Myra left the house at nine fifteen. She had made sure to take the time to look perfect, carefully choosing a mid-length black Armani skirt and a cream-colored silk Chanel blouse with pearl buttons. She finished the outfit off with a smart pair of Manolo Blahnik pumps, a fond memory of her last pre-accident shopping spree dancing in her mind. She blew her hair dry, meticulously placing each strand in the correct place before spraying it and decorating her ears with the pearl studs

Greg had given her on their first anniversary. A touch of blush, some mascara, and a dash of red lipstick, and the look was complete. She walked into the bedroom and twirled around in front of the full-length mirror to make sure she hadn't missed anything before she descended the staircase.

The Wisconsin cold whipped up her skirt as she walked toward her car. She was careful to avoid the little patches of ice that had formed on the walkway and found herself wondering why she hadn't parked in the garage the night before. The cold car started without delay, and icy air shot from the vents, chilling her to the bone. By the time she had reached the highway, the air had finally begun to warm and her mind began to wander. She still couldn't believe that she was doing this. How would the Garcia children react? She realized that the girl might have changed her mind by this point. What if they had already been placed and separated? What if Myra was too late? She couldn't bear the thought. She stepped a little harder on the gas. The clock on the dash read 9:43 as she pulled into the local County Family Group, which she had learned through some digging was handling the Garcia case. Myra drummed the steering wheel and took a deep breath.

"Okay, Myra, here we go," she mumbled to herself. She gave herself a quick last glance in her rearview before stepping back out into the frigid air and skittering to the door.

The air in the building was stale and old, and the peeling yellowish paint gave the feeling that it had seen too much. The whole place had an aura of bleakness and sorrow about it, as did the girl who halfheartedly greeted her at the front desk. Though fairly young, she had the appearance of a girl defeated. Myra could picture her years earlier, eager and fresh, ready to save the world as she landed her first real job after four hard years of college to earn her bachelor's degree. The disappointment of real life was now written all over her face.

"Can I help you?" she asked with a practiced raise of her eyebrow.

"Um, yes, actually. I would like to speak to someone about possibly fostering a child, three children actually. I, um —" The woman cut her off before she could finish.

"Take a seat over there and fill out this paperwork. Someone will be with you shortly. Name?" she asked curtly, pointing with a clipboard stacked with papers in the direction of a collection of dingy, tattered chairs.

"Oh, uh ... okay. Myra Jenkins," Myra stuttered, taking the clipboard and searching the desktop for a pen. The woman handed one to her with a glimmer of what might have been recognition, and Myra made her way toward the chairs. The unnerving glow from the fluorescent lights above her head reflected off the paperwork, giving her an instant headache. A muted television was mounted in the corner and featured two women (or was that a man dressed like a woman?) leaning forward in their chairs wagging fingers in each other's faces while a talk show host watched in amused silence. She glanced back down at the paperwork, scanning the rows and rows of questions in front of her. There had to be at least thirty pages, and she realized she'd better get to work. The top page was all of the basics; name, address, DOB, etc. The second asked about her family, marital status, number of children, pets, size of home, etc. At the third page, she stopped.

Have you ever been convicted of a felony? Y N
If yes, please explain on the following lines:

Now, of course, Myra hadn't been convicted, but the realization that she was going to have to disclose her relationship with and/or interest in the Garcia children specifically, as opposed to any other children they might want her to foster, hit her with full force. For some strange reason, she hadn't really thought this far ahead. It was probably largely because she didn't truly believe that the girls would be so eager to fulfill the role of foster sisters so readily. Either way, she was here now, and there was no turning back. She'd promised Sammy and Ella that she would have information, any information, for them when they got home from school. Reluctantly, she circled the N and moved down the page to the subsequent questions.

The following page was one question with several blank lines following.

Why do you want to become a foster parent?

She sat with her pen perched above the first line, chewing at her lip anxiously. How to answer this one? She chuckled a little to herself. She could write, "I'm writhing with guilt over what I've done to these three poor children, and this is the only way to make what I've done right," but she was pretty sure that wouldn't go over very well. How about "This girl came to my doorstep and coerced me to take her and her siblings in so they wouldn't be separated, and I certainly do owe them one"? No, not so much. She breathed out a quick puff of air, and the girl behind the counter shot her a look. She started to write, scratched it out, started to write, scratched it out again.

She thought that it might be better, for now, to leave this page blank. She continued through the paperwork seamlessly, jumping when she heard her name called from a doorway off to the right of the seating area.

"Oh, sorry, you startled me. Yes, just one moment," she said, gathering her things together and hurrying toward the door.

"Come with me, please." the woman said, smiling dully. Myra followed dutifully as the woman led her through a winding maze of hallways and into a cramped, windowless office bathed in the same electric glow as the waiting area. The woman ushered her in and pointed to a chair, closing the door behind her and taking her own seat on the opposite side of the desk. She held out her hand without meeting Myra's eyes, and Myra handed over her clipboard. The woman scanned the first page without looking up, and Myra scanned the room. Despite the ugly paint, cheap furniture, and lack of natural light, it was quaint. The walls were adorned with inspirational posters — not the tacky cat hanging from the tree kind, but picturesque scenes with uplifting quotes. Behind the woman's desk was a shelf scattered with family pictures, birthday cards, and cheerful knickknacks. A child's painting hung on the wall above it. Myra liked her already for making the best of a mediocre situation. As the woman studied her paperwork, Myra studied her face. She had dark, silky hair pulled back into a too-tight bun. Her face was full and round, and her eyes were a crystalline blue that almost didn't look real. She had a small nose and full lips. Myra thought she might be beautiful if she would put in a little effort.

"Well, Ms. Jenkins," she started, "my name is Amanda Cooper. What brings you here today?" It was the first time in quite a while that someone hadn't said her name without flinching, and it gave her a ray of hope.

"Well, I'm interested in becoming a foster parent."

"Yes, I see that. I notice that you left a fairly significant page blank on your application here. Maybe you can tell me why this thought interests you." Amanda was all business, but she had an air of sincerity about her, a genuine interest in Myra's reasoning, a living spark within her that still fueled her passion for her job and for doing the right thing for the children in her charge.

"Well, I left it blank because that's where it gets a little complicated. I don't really know where to begin ... "

"Generally, the beginning is a good place," Amanda said, a friendly smile dancing on her lips. "It's okay, Miss Jenkins, you can relax. This isn't a test. Just try to be as honest as possible with me and I'll do the same with you. I feel like it's better to start off on that foot. It makes the whole process easier." She leaned back in her chair and crossed her legs. "So let me have it: What makes you want to become a foster parent?" Myra could feel herself relaxing in the girl's presence.

"Well, like I said, it's a little complicated. No, a lot complicated." Nervous laughter. "Well, I'm not interested in fostering just anybody. I'm actually interested in a particular child. Children, actually." Amanda perked up and raised an eyebrow.

"Go on," she encouraged.

"I, I was in an accident last year. I, um ... I ... "

"I know who you are, Ms. Jenkins. No need to go through the details again." Myra scanned the woman's face and was amazed to see no signs of judgment. Amanda didn't even flinch; her smile was still very genuinely intact as she nodded for Myra to continue.

"Oh, um, okay," she said, tucking the invisible strands of nervousness behind her ear. "Well, you know then what the outcome of that accident was, I suppose." Amanda nodded again. "Well, I want to help the children. I want to foster the Garcia children specifically, all three of them." Myra could feel her face flushing with the heat of embarrassment. She must have looked like an idiot to this woman. This woman who devoted her life to helping children and had heard so many stories, now sat across from Myra Jenkins, alleged murderer, and watched her squirm in her chair as she tried to right her own wrongs. Amanda cocked her head.

"I mean no offense, Ms. Jenkins, but what makes you think that they would want any help from you?"

Myra shrugged. It was a good point.

"Actually, *they* make me think that. The oldest daughter, Emilia, she came to me. She came to my house and asked me to help her. We ... we talked a little." Amanda sat up stick-straight.

"What? *She* came to *you?* Seriously? When did this happen?" Myra's hands fidgeted in her lap neurotically as the flush continued to creep, now reaching her ears, making them burn red hot.

"Well, a few weeks ago, actually. She needed help to keep her and her siblings together." She continued on to divulge the whole story as Amanda listened attentively, nodding her head periodically and scribbling notes here and there. By the time Myra was finished talking, she felt as though she could curl up in the chair and fall asleep. She was exhausted.

"Well," Amanda started, "I can honestly say that this is the strangest thing I have ever heard in all my years working with foster children." She chuckled a little bit. "Well, then, Myra—do you mind if I call you that? Good. If you're sure this is something that you want to do, let's see what we can do to make that happen." Myra felt a rush of excitement and nervousness. She hadn't known whether or not it would even be possible, especially given the strange circumstances surrounding the situation.

"You mean ... this *can* happen? I can foster them?"

"Whoa, whoa, slow down. I said, 'let's see.' You still have to go through an application process and training, same as everybody else. If it's determined that you are an eligible foster parent at the end of the application process, and if what you're saying is true that the kids want to stay with you, then it seems to me that there wouldn't be much keeping it from happening. The first thing is, we will need for you to finish up all this paperwork," she said, gesturing toward the unfinished stack. "Once that is complete, we'll run a series of background checks, including financial, criminal, and driving records, conduct a home study, and work on getting your training complete so you can become licensed to foster. Several different social workers will meet with you and your children, but I will be heading the whole operation, and if you have any questions throughout the process, you can call me directly. One of these meetings will take place in your home. The home study is pretty rigorous. I always tell potential fosters to let their family know that it can seem rather invasive if you're not prepared. Try to understand through the course of the process that everything we are doing is to ensure the safety and best interest of the children we are placing. Basically, the home study is a piece of paper required by the state that neatly sums up your life in a few pages. It will determine what your parenting style is and what your home life is like, and help to decide what ages and types of children you would best be able to foster. Once everything is completed, you will have to take a PRIDE training course, which will help to introduce you to the world of foster care and provide you with some realistic expectations of what your life will be like with your new addition, or additions in your case. PRIDE stands for Parent Resources for Information, Development, and Education." She smiled. "Once you've completed the course, you'll receive your certification and we'll go from there." Amanda clasped her hands in front of her and placed them on the desk. "Any questions?"

"Where to begin?" thought Myra, twirling a flyaway strand of hair around her pointer finger. "Well, yes, I suppose I have quite a few questions, but the one that seems the most important is how long this whole process is going to take."

"Well, now, that's up to you, Myra. This is one of the few government agencies that have the potential to move pretty fast, but it's really dependent on your ability to get things completed: the paperwork, the home study, your interviews, the PRIDE course. You are in charge of scheduling these things. Sadly, there are a lot of kids in the system and not enough suitable fosters to house them. For that reason, we jump at the opportunity to get any of these kids into a better living situation. In short, if you move fast, we'll do our best to move fast with you." Myra nodded.

"Okay, I can do that," she said, feeling extremely over-whelmed, but doing her best not to let it show. "I can do that, for sure." Amanda stood up and extended her hand.

"In that case, it's been a pleasure speaking with you today, Myra, and I look forward to seeing you back here soon with a giant stack of completed paperwork." Myra shook her hand rather more vigorously than she intended and picked up the stack from the desk.

"I'll be back as soon as possible." Amanda led her back out to the drab waiting area, where Myra smiled carefully at the girl behind the reception desk before leaving the malodorous building behind her.

Myra drove home swelling with some emotion she couldn't quite pinpoint. She let herself feel it for a while before trying to label it. It felt good, victorious almost. She hadn't felt like that in such a long time that the emotion felt foreign in her body, so foreign she hoped her body wouldn't attack it and try to eject it. She needed it. Despite her fear of wandering into this situation, her heart was filled with happiness that she hadn't let that fear win. Doing this *was* the right thing to do, and Myra *would* be able to help the Garcia children. She knew it. She felt inspired by the genuine kindness of her children and grateful for their ability to sway her to making the right decision. Of course, this would be a difficult transition for all of them if and when it came to fruition, but there was no doubt in her mind that they, as a family unit, would be able to come out on the other side stronger than ever.

She let out such a big breath that it dawned on her that she had been holding it tightly in for the duration of her time in the building. She felt as though she could giggle. She, Myra Jenkins, would no longer be the dejected housewife murderer that everybody in the town assumed her to be. She was going to prove to all of them that they were wrong. She was going to prove it to *herself.* She was a good woman, with a good character and a good heart, and the ability to help others. Most importantly, she was going to prove this to the Garcia children. She had made a mistake, the biggest of her entire life, and she was going to make it right, no matter what it took.

CHAPTER 13

Sammy and Ella came racing up the driveway, hats pulled down over their ears and hair trailing behind them. They pushed through the doorway and zipped into the kitchen without bothering to remove their wet snow boots. They were all voices and excitement as they pounced on Myra for information.

"Well, what happened?" Sammy questioned. "Do we get to have them come live here?"

"Yeah, do we? When do they move in?" Ella added eagerly.

"I told my friends at school we were getting new sisters and a brother." grinned Sammy,

"Sammy, you shouldn't have done that yet." Ella snapped.

"Shut up, Ella. You told Jessica! I heard you at the bus stop."

"Did not—"

"Guys!!!" Myra boomed. "Relax, would you? How am I supposed to tell you anything when you're squabbling back and forth?" She laughed. Sammy nudged Ella with her elbow before turning her attention fully to Myra.

"So, what's the word?"

"Well, first off, you both need to calm down a little bit. You don't just walk in and tell them you want to foster and suddenly you're a foster parent. There's a lot of red tape to get through."

"What kind of red tape?" asked Sammy.

"They have to, like, make sure we're not weirdos and stuff, Sammy. Duh," explained Ella.

"Essentially, yes," continued Myra. "They need to run background checks on me, and they'll want to meet you, come see where we live, you know. They want to make sure that we're suitable to take on the responsibility of extra children here. Not just me either, all of us. Their job is to look out for all children, not just those in foster care. They want to make sure that you two are ready for siblings too."

"Oh, we are!" assured Sammy.

"Totally," echoed Ella.

"I know, but I ask that no matter what these social workers ask you, you are both honest about your feelings. You are still my first priority, okay?" Both girls nodded in agreement.

"So, what happens now?" asked Sammy.

"Well, first I have to finish this novel they gave me to fill out," she said, gesturing to the papers scattered across the dining room table. "As you can see, I've been working on it, but there's still quite a bit more to do. I wouldn't be surprised if they ask for my blood type and a tissue sample somewhere in this packet. It's ridiculous. They want to know everything." She ran a hand through her hair. "It's intimidating, really. After that, they run some background checks on me, make sure I'm not a criminal or anything." The girls exchanged a dark glance.

"What about ... " Ella trailed off.

"It's fine. I wasn't convicted of a crime, Ella. The social

worker I met with today— her name is Amanda, by the way—
knew all about the case. She explained that it shouldn't affect
anything, since there was no conviction, although the fact that
there was a charge at all might hold up the process a little bit.
She didn't really get further into detail, so I don't know what
that means, but I'm going to just trust her and believe that
everything is going to work out. That's all we can do, right?
Anyway, once they've run all of their checks, there will be a
series of interviews, one of which will be done here, and if we
are found eligible, then, well, I guess we go from there." Myra
paused and watched the girls for a second, trying to determine
their mindsets. "Well, what do you think?"

"I can't wait!" said Ella, as Sammy wrapped her arms
around Myra's waist and squeezed.

"Me either, Mom. I'm really glad we're doing this."

The next few days passed in a flash, and before she knew
it, Myra was trudging back through the slushy parking lot of
Amanda Cooper's office, her completed (much to her amaze-
ment) stack of paperwork bouncing in her hands. The recep-
tionist met her with the same lack of interest as on her first
visit and gestured her back into the dingy waiting area. It
seemed like only minutes passed before Amanda's smiling face
appeared at the door.

"Good morning, Ms. Jenkins! I'm happy to see you back so
soon. Follow me." Myra rose from her chair and followed
Amanda back down the winding hallways to her quaint office
near the back of the building. They each settled into their
chairs, and Myra plopped the stack of paperwork down on the
desk with a thud.

"Well, I think I've got everything you needed here. All the
original paperwork is on top, and I've put the copies of my
license, Social Security card, and all that stuff on the bottom."
Amanda nodded her head approvingly as she picked up the
stack and thumped it against the desk a few times.

"Excellent! Well, give me just a few minutes to make sure everything is here," she said, beginning to flip through the pages and scan each one quickly, running her fingers down the lines of questions. Myra fidgeted a little, focusing on the faint buzz of the fluorescent lights overhead. The air in the room was stuffy and hot, and she loosened her scarf and removed her jacket. Finally, after what seemed an eternity, Amanda looked back up at her and smiled.

"Well, it looks like you have everything we need. I'll be in contact with you soon." She stood up and extended her hand to shake Myra's.

"That's it? There's nothing else to do?"

Amanda laughed.

"Nope, we'll take it from here. We just have to do a more extensive review of the paperwork and I will contact you within a few days. Once we've run our checks on you, we will go ahead and start scheduling your interviews, and the process will officially be underway." She smiled again, hand still extended. Myra stood and shook the outstretched palm.

"Well, in that case, I look forward to hearing from you."

The next few days seemed to stretch out forever. Every time her cellphone would ring, Myra would jump to answer it, suddenly extremely eager to hear from the placement agency, but much to her dismay, it was never Amanda's voice on the other end of the line. Finally, on a Tuesday, fifteen days after her initial visit to the office, the phone rang just after the girls had boarded the bus for school.

"Hello?" Myra answered.

"Hi, Ms. Jenkins. It's Amanda from the foster agency. How are you doing this morning?" Myra felt her back straighten.

"Oh, hello, Amanda. I'm wonderful, thank you, and yourself?"

"Just fine, thank you. Well, I'm happy to inform you that it looks as though all of your background checks came through nicely. Based on what we see so far, it appears as though you are an ideal candidate. There's only one small problem, but I don't want you to panic. We're going to need a copy of the court documentation freeing you from any criminal responsibility in your car accident. I'm sorry to bring it up. I know it was a concern to you, but, unfortunately, the state's requiring some additional paperwork on it."

"Oh, I see," answered Myra. She wasn't quite shocked, so much as annoyed. She had gone through hell and back with this whole accident and now was finally making some steps toward making it right, and it was causing problems even in this. She shoved her frustration aside. "Well, whatever you need I'd be more than happy to provide. I can drop it off this afternoon if you'd like."

"No need to do that, Ms. Jenkins. I was actually calling to schedule your first interview and you can just bring it to that. It's actually more of a character evaluation. Standard procedure, but we just need to make sure that you are mentally sound and stable enough, not only to foster, but to endure the rather rigorous process that the foster application can be. As I said, the home visit especially can feel a little bit invasive. The state wants to know everything about you." Myra couldn't help but chuckle a bit.

"Well, based on the past year and a half I've had, Amanda, I'm sure this couldn't be much more invasive." She heard Amanda let out a little puff of air on the other end of the line.

"I suppose that's true, isn't it? Well, then, how does Monday sound, about 10 a.m.? You can just come right back down here and we'll get the ball rolling." Myra agreed, but hesitated before she ended the conversation.

"Amanda, I just have one more question for you," she began, "Does Emilia ... do the children know that I've begun the application process? I just want to make sure that they are still on board."

"That's a great question, Myra, and one I meant to answer for you anyway. There's been so much going on around here that I almost forgot. Yes, I contacted their caseworker, Mr. Randall, just the other day. He approached the children with the idea and they seemed to be all for it! I opted not to tell him that Emilia had approached you, particularly since I'm still scratching my head trying to figure out how she got over to your house without it being noticed that she was gone." Myra heard Amanda stifle a giggle. "Overall, Myra, it looks like everything is falling into place."

"Thank you, Amanda. That makes me feel so much better about all of this," Myra replied. She hung up the phone, feeling what she could only describe as excitement stirring in the pit of her stomach. She couldn't wait to tell the girls.

CHAPTER 14

Monday morning breakfast was chaotic, to say the least. Sammy and Ella begged and pleaded to skip school so that they could know the outcome of the psychological assessment as soon as Myra did. Myra assured them that they weren't missing anything and insisted that they go to school. The girls finally slung their backpacks over their shoulders and reluctantly trudged down the driveway.

Myra readied herself in front of her full-length mirror with all the attention and elegance she had the first morning of her meeting with Amanda. She wanted desperately to make sure that she looked the part. This whole process had become bigger and more important to her and the girls than she ever could have anticipated. Despite her initial apprehension about this arrangement, the girls' enthusiasm had triggered her own, and the thought of being able to give back to the family that she had taken so much from seemed to fill a little bit of the empty space that the accident had left inside of her. She wondered if this made her selfish and decided that as long as those children remained together until Emilia was able to adopt her siblings herself, it didn't matter what her motivation was. She knew in her heart that she was doing the right thing.

The interior of the Land Rover buzzed with her giddy and nervous energy. She was so focused on getting through the interview that she nearly passed the entrance to the Family Group building. The car slid the tiniest bit as she hit the brakes a bit harder than necessary and turned into the lot. She put the car in park and tilted her rear view so that she was staring back at her reflection.

"All right, Myra," she encouraged herself, "you've got this. Don't let these kids down, any of them! Poised, calm, kind, and sane. Most important, sane. Don't twirl your hair or fidget or act nervous. Don't stutter and have your answers ready— and stop talking to yourself!" She giggled quietly as she tilted the mirror back to its normal place, scanning the parking lot to make sure that nobody had been watching her personal exchange with the mirror. That's just what she needed. She could see it now.

"Well, Myra, we'd love to let you foster these children, but it seems as though you were caught having a conversation with an inanimate object and that just won't do. Better luck next time."

With a deep breath, Myra swung the door open and marched intently to the front of the building. She approached the reception desk and saw the same indifferent girl sitting behind it. The girl nodded curtly and informed Myra she would let Amanda know she had arrived. Myra nodded back and took her seat under the cheerless glare of the waiting area.

She waited longer than usual this time, playing losing hands of solitaire on her cellphone until she heard her name called. Amanda's smiling face was looking out at her from the doorway, her hair coiled into the typical ballerina bun that Myra was getting accustomed to.

"Good morning, Ms. Jenkins! It's a pleasure to see you again." Myra smiled back. "Well, if you're ready, we can go ahead and get started. We're going down this way today," Amanda said, motioning to a hallway opposite the one leading toward her office. "Dr. Hayworth is waiting in our conference room to give you your evaluation. I urge you to be honest and open, and don't be nervous. He's been doing this for years and years, and he's heard it all. He's quite a nice gentleman and an amazing psychologist. If you do get nervous, keep in mind that he wants this for you and the children as much as you do. Remember that this is why we are all in this business, to help the children. Getting proper placement for our foster kids is the top priority for all of us."

"Okay," Myra answered, feeling her feet become heavier as they approached the double oak doors at the end of the hall clearly marked "Conference One." Amanda rapped briskly on the door before opening it wide and ushering Myra inside. At the head of an oblong conference table, a gentleman stood up to greet them. He smiled calmly, his thin lips spread across perfectly straight white teeth, and extended his hand.

"You must be Myra Jenkins," he greeted her warmly. "I've heard lovely things about you. I'm Dr. Hayworth." Myra nodded and smiled back. Dr. Hayworth turned his attention to Amanda. "Thank you, Amanda. I can take it from here. I'll be over to let you know when our interview is finished." Amanda flipped him a thumbs-up sign before leaving the room and closing the door behind her. "Well, Ms. Jenkins, may I call you Myra?"

"Absolutely," Myra agreed.

"Well then, Myra, let's get started, shall we? Would you like any water or coffee before we begin?" Myra shook her head. "Well, in that case, have a seat," he said, gesturing to a comfortable leather desk chair resembling his own. They both sat and the room became quiet as he shuffled through her paperwork, stopping every now and then to bookmark a page with a yellow sticky tab. She could feel her palms beginning to sweat, despite his calming presence. His gray hair was cropped close to his head, and perfectly round wire-framed glasses sat perched on the tip of his nose. His tweed suit and crooked bow tie, though they might have gone out of style some time ago, gave the impression of a well-educated if not slightly off-balance Harvard professor. She watched him carefully, noting his gentle breathing, the careful way he turned the pages of her file, and the subtle smile that seemed to remain on his lips as he read, as though he hadn't a care in the world. She decided instantly that she would really like him if the stress of the current situation weren't present. He made her feel instantly safe, welcome, and secure, and Myra could see why Amanda had described him as being great at his job. Finally, the doctor placed the papers to the side and folded his hands neatly on the table in front of him.

"Well, Myra, your paperwork looks impressive. You come from a good background, you live in a beautiful area, you're financially stable enough to foster, your own daughters are impressive in their own rights, both academically and socially, so you must be doing something right. There's only one thing that I find lacking in your documentation so far." Myra shifted uncomfortably in her seat, waiting for him to bring up the accident. She waited for him to continue. "There is a question in this packet that you didn't fully answer, and it seems to me that it might be the most important one that is asked." Myra raised her eyebrows at him. She was sure she had fully explained the circumstances concerning the accident. "Myra, can you elaborate for me on what makes you want to become a foster parent in the first place?" She couldn't help but show her surprise.

"Oh, I thought you were going ... well, never mind, yes, I ... well ... " She stopped, reminded herself silently about not fumbling over her words. She always did that when she was nervous. Poised, calm, NOT CRAZY. She took a breath. "Yes, Dr. Hayworth. I suppose I didn't answer that question in writing because it's a little hard to explain." She remembered Amanda's words: Be honest and open. "In all honesty, the thought of fostering had never crossed my mind until recently. After all, I have my own two daughters, and that has always felt sufficient." Dr. Hayworth let out a little "hmm" and shifted his hands from the table onto his lap, never taking his gaze from her. Don't fumble, open and honest. "Well, I'm sure that you read in my paperwork about an accident that happened a while back where—well, you read it, I'm sure." Dr. Hayworth nodded. She felt as though this must be what Greg's clients felt like under interrogation.

"Yes, I'm familiar with the car accident."

"Okay, well, I'm sure you're also familiar with my particular interest in the three children of the two adults that were, um … killed in that accident." He nodded again. Myra went on to describe to him the unexpected visit from Emilia and her proposition. She watched his face for a reaction as she spoke, but saw no sign of surprise or concern. He listened intently as she spoke, nodding occasionally but never interrupting. "Her visit really got me thinking," she continued. "The idea that I could help these children in any way is obviously intriguing. I'm not going to pretend that the initial appeal didn't stem from my own guilt at what has happened to them. After Emilia walked out I really had time to let it all absorb, and I realized it wasn't some selfish decision that I could make by myself. I had to think of my own daughters and what I had already put them through as well. The only way to proceed was by bringing it up to them and seeing how it was received.

"Well, you can imagine my surprise when they jumped right on board, even going so far as to clean out rooms in our house and offer to share a bedroom to create extra space."

Myra put her hand to her cheek and shook her head, thrown once again into admiration and disbelief at her children's resilience. "It hit me right there that this was absolutely the right thing to do, and, ever since that, it's actually begun to excite me a little bit, you know?" She looked over at him for some sign of understanding, but his face remained stoic. "This is an opportunity for me to help keep a family that I have already broken from breaking even more, and my gut is just screaming at me to make sure it happens. I will be great to those children, Dr. Hayworth."

Here she stopped, offering him the chance to continue the conversation in any way he saw fit. He picked up a pencil and began doodling on a pad that sat on the table in front of him, nothing in particular, some squiggles and dots, his face pensive, eyebrows furled, teeth nibbling gently at his bottom lip. He sat this way for a few moments, the only sound the shuffle of his suit as he crossed his legs in a different direction. It felt like forever before he spoke to her.

"Well, this certainly is a unique situation, Myra. I have to say that in all my years in this field, it is the first of its kind that I have seen. I understand your desire to help these children, however, my job now becomes more difficult, as it is now up to me to determine whether or not your motivation is fueled solely by guilt and your ego needing to make what's happened okay or by your genuine desire to help three children who are in need." Myra sat straighter in her chair and motioned to refute his accusations, but he waved her off before she could speak. "Please don't get me wrong, Myra. I'm not insinuating that one or the other is happening here, I'm simply explaining my process to you so that we are on the same page. Try to remember that I'm here for the best interest of the children. This being the case, I want you to elaborate for me, if you would, on your own daughters' reactions to this whole idea. Take me through your conversation with them, when you told them that Emilia stopped by and made this request." Myra cast her mind back to their dinner table discussion of Emilia's unexpected visit and recounted it to Dr. Hayworth to the best of her ability. They went back and forth like this for what seemed like hours, Myra telling stories and Dr. Hayworth asking her to expand upon certain parts. He asked her about her past all the way back to her childhood, her marriage to Greg and why it had failed, her reaction to her children being born, about the accident and the events leading up to it, how she had explained the events to her children, and their reactions. He asked her about her spending habits, how often she cooked and cleaned, her thoughts on religion, parenting, discipline, education, and even politics. By the end of the meeting, she was drained and exhausted beyond belief. Dr. Hayworth leaned back in his chair, drumming the fingers of his right hand thoughtfully against the tabletop.

"Well now, Myra, it seems to me that you are a stable, kind, caring, and genuine woman. You appear to be a good, loving mother, as well as a responsible and upstanding citizen. It seems as though you have been 100 percent open and honest with your children regarding this situation, and above and beyond that, you have allowed them to fully be a part of the decision to move forward with this process. In my personal, humble opinion, I think that you would be a great candidate for our foster program. Obviously, I am only a part of the application process and a relatively easy part at that. I assume Amanda has informed you about the home visit." Myra nodded. "Okay, good. Well, moving on from here, I'd like to have a brief meeting with your girls, just to verify that we are all on the same page." Myra smiled gently, glad that this part was over.

"Absolutely. I'm sure that they'd love to meet with you." And with that, the meeting was scheduled and Myra was walking out of the building feeling as though she could nap for the rest of the week.

CHAPTER 15

The process began moving more quickly than Myra could have imagined. The girls were interviewed, and both seemed to express the same eagerness and excitement that Myra herself had at the prospect of fostering the three children. Myra underwent several more interviews with different social workers, with Amanda heading the team, and completed her PRIDE training during the hours the girls were at school. She was asked again about her childhood, her beliefs on several different subjects, and to rehash the events of the accident, so many times she felt as though the entire Wisconsin Department of Children and Families must know her life story inside and out. Finally, it was time for the home study. The girls helped Myra clean the already clean house over and over again, all of their nerves on edge, waiting for their final judgment. Myra tried to remain light and indifferent, to reassure the girls that they were not being judged, but she couldn't help but feel the same way. There was something so strange about people observing you in your home, watching the things that made the family tick and scrawling them down to later be reviewed and graded. Yes, they were being judged. However, each time this thought crossed her mind, she replaced it with a reminder of how her home had once sung. She remembered the noise and the laughter of her life before the accident, and each time she remembered this, she realized that all the excitement of the potential fostering had given a buzz to the house once again. Her girls were laughing again, calling out her name as they rushed through the front door from school, eager to hear any news from Amanda. Her home held promise again, that life would go on and that her world could still sing. She kept these thoughts front and center on the Saturday morning that her doorbell rang and three social workers, including Amanda, stood on her doorstep stomping off the winter cold.

"Good morning!" She smiled gaily as she opened the door to let them in. They had insisted on coming on a Saturday so that, Myra assumed, they could gauge her interaction with her own children and how a typical day was spent among the three of them. She took their coats and offered them coffee or tea, which all three refused.

"Just go about your business, Myra, and pretend like we're not even here. You too, girls," Amanda said, smiling widely at Sammy and Ella perched on the bottom of the staircase. "I know it seems weird, but just try. We'll be moving around. Bob here will be checking things like fire alarms and cabinet locks and putting together a list of things that will need to be childproofed and fixed before a move-in. Annette will be observing your daily routines and I will be assisting them both. At the end of it all, we will give you a list of things you'll need to get in order, Myra. Once the fixes are made, we can schedule another walk-through. In the interim, we will be taking all the information we have gathered from all of you throughout the course of the process, as well as our observances today, and putting together a home study report that sums up everything we have learned about your family to either support or discourage the agency from moving forward and placing children in your home. That report will go before a board, which will make the final decision. And then, we will go from there. Any questions?" Amanda looked around the room, stopping on Sammy who was meekly raising her hand. "What do you want to ask, honey?"

"I was just wondering, do the kids know that we're doing this? I mean, what if they changed their mind or something?" Myra realized she hadn't shared this information with the girls.

"That's a great question, Sammy," answered Amanda. "Typically, the children would not be aware of the application your mom has put in. We tend to keep this information quiet until the application has been approved so that there are no expectations or false hope created. However, due to the sensitive nature of this particular situation, we felt it was in the best interest to have full disclosure with the Garcia children. They are fully aware that the application process is taking place, but we won't give them much more information until your family is either approved or denied. Does that make sense?" Sammy nodded. "Okay then, if there's nothing else, let's get started. Go ahead and just have a normal day at home."

The day was anything but normal. Every time Myra walked around the corner, somebody was watching her, or Bob was scribbling something down in his notebook. At one point she found an opportunity to peek over his shoulder and see a giant red X in the "no" box next to a question regarding whether or not her outlets had safety covers. She laughed a little to herself, and he quickly realized she was behind him and snatched the notebook out of her sight before continuing down the hall, which only made her laugh harder. He was a short, portly man with a glowing bowling ball of a head dusted with mousy brown hair around the edges. He wore a disapproving look and a tight, churlish grimace that suggested he probably took his job a tad too seriously and considered himself quite the expert on determining another person's worth as a parent. Myra wished she could ask him to leave, but instead she spent the day exchanging bemused glances with her daughters every time he entered the room.

The trio left just after dinner, and Myra and the girls let out a collective sigh as they plopped onto the couch.

"Holy crap, Mom, that sucked!" exploded Sammy.

"Watch your mouth, Sammy— but it did totally suck!" agreed Myra with a giggle. Ella nodded in agreement.

"I'm just glad it's over!" she chimed in. "I think I'll watch a little TV with you guys and then I'm off to bed!" The warm glow from the television filled the room, and within minutes Myra noticed that both girls had fallen asleep on either side of her. She flicked off the screen and got them both to bed.

CHAPTER 16

"Damn it, Myra. What the hell is all this about? And why haven't you told me about it? Do you know how ridiculous this sounds?" Greg was standing in the foyer, having just dropped off the girls from their weekend visit, his fists balled up at his hips and his face growing redder with each word he spat at her. "Did you plan on mentioning it to me at any point, or were you just going to wait until your three roommates had moved in and let me figure it out on my own?"

Myra silently reminded herself that she didn't really owe Greg an explanation on anything anymore, not to mention that he was the one who outright refused to speak with her, making it virtually impossible for her to divulge any information to him on her state of affairs. She was mildly amused that this was only the second time he had set foot in the house they used to share since the day he had packed his belongings. He was a lawyer, always looking for something to react to, and he had found it. In all sincerity, she knew that she should have told him about it, but she had been so busy in her own life that the thought hadn't even crossed her mind. She was careful with her response, wholly aware of the girls peering through the banister rails at the top of the stairs.

"Well, Greg, I just hadn't thought of it, if you want the truth."

"You hadn't thought of it, Myra? For fuck's sake! This isn't changing the paint color on the house or buying a new car! You're allowing three strangers to move into our home!" He exploded. Myra fought to hold her tongue and let him finish his rant. "Those three kids hate you; they probably want nothing to do with you. But here you are, Mother fucking Teresa, here to save the day, not bothering to think about how your actions might affect your *own* children. Jesus, Myra! I don't even know what to say right now. I'd love to say that I'm shocked, but I'm not. Ever since you had that car accident, you've been acting like a crazy maniac. But this takes the cake, Myra. This just takes the fucking cake!" His hands flew to his forehead, as though this effort was required to keep his brain from literally erupting out of his skull. He took a few deep breaths, and Myra watched him to make sure it was over before she responded.

"First off, Greg, watch your language in *my* home. That's the second: This is *my* home, mine and the girls, not yours. You chose to give that up and therefore have no right to influence any decisions that are made within its walls." She couldn't help but be impressed by her own calm, firm tone. "Admittedly, it was a bit negligent of me to not let you know that this was something we were considering. It truly did just slip my mind. I didn't ask the girls to keep it a secret either, since I assume that's what you're thinking. It's just been a very busy few months. The application process is fairly rigorous and time-consuming. Beyond that, I do have to wonder, if I had tried to tell you, how would that have worked? That would require the two of us having a conversation, and this little exchange here is proving that can be a daunting task for us these days. As far as the girls go, they have been a part of every step of the decision-making process, and I think they are completely ready for this." Greg's eyes flashed anger.

"Ready for *what*? They're kids. Myra! Kids can't make decisions like this. Those girls have no fucking idea what they're getting themselves into!" Suddenly Sammy and Ella were both racing down the stairs, yelling.

"We want to do this, Dad! Leave Mom alone!" screamed Sammy.

"This is why we didn't want to tell you, Dad! All you care about is yourself!" chimed Ella.

"You girls butt out; this is between your mother and me!" Greg screamed back.

"ENOUGH!" Myra boomed. All eyes turned toward her. She had never heard herself be so loud or assertive, and clearly, she was not the only one surprised by it. "That's enough!" she echoed. "Girls, calm down and do not speak to your father that way. And you ... " she said, turning back toward Greg, "you can't just waltz in here and tell me what I can and cannot do and how to live my life. In case you've forgotten, you are no longer my husband. I understand that these children are our shared responsibility, Greg, and I think we've done a wonderful job raising them. Maybe, for once, instead of putting other people down and forcefully working to prove them wrong, you could stop being a damned lawyer and take a step back. You don't have to care about what I want. Your children want this, and, as their father, for once, it would be nice if you would take the opportunity that's being thrown in front of you to realize what mature, kind, wonderful young women they are becoming. Mature and kind enough to see people suffering and to know what it takes to put their own feelings aside just long enough to see how they might help them. Maybe you could learn a few lessons from your daughters, Greg. I certainly have."

The room was silent. Greg looked sheepish. She couldn't tell if he was humbled or embarrassed, but she hoped it was a bit of both. "We are moving forward with this process, Greg. If there's anything else you have to say on the subject, please, now is the time. If not, I'd like to get on with my day." Greg's mouth hung agape. They stood there for a few moments in silence before she continued. "Well, it appears that you are finished, so, in that case, I suppose we will see you next weekend." Without another word he turned on his heel and walked out the open front door. Myra closed it behind him and stood there staring at the wood panels, trying to decide how to handle the next step with the girls. Sammy was already tugging on her arm.

"We're sorry, Mom. We shouldn't have said anything to him." Myra turned.

"You girls did nothing wrong. On the contrary, I *should* have told him—some time ago, in fact. I just seriously didn't even think about it. Don't bother feeling bad. It was bound to happen sooner or later, and at least now everything's on the table and there are no secrets, right?" Both girls nodded in unison. "Okay then, what should we do for the rest of the day?"

***

Myra leaned against the countertop, hugging her tea mug close to her chest, watching the girls. They were sharing a chair at the dining room table, hunched over the computer, fully immersed in the wonders of internet shopping. They had collectively decided that the foster kids should have some new bedspreads as a welcome gift into the home. Although the approval had not officially come through yet, Myra was allowing the girls to browse and get some ideas. It was true, the guest bedroom had not been used or updated in some time, and the current décor was on the bland side. Initially, they had wanted to redo the whole room, but Myra had suggested they leave a little wiggle room so that the children could still make it their own. The girls were definitely getting excited, and Myra was too, in spite of herself. She kept reminding herself that anything could happen. Emilia could have even changed her mind. She wouldn't know for a while yet.

CHAPTER 17

Myra buzzed around the kitchen, humming an indiscernible tune. The girls had just left for school a half hour earlier and it was too quiet. The house needed a little cleaning and there was no time like the present. She was elbow-deep in dishwater when her cellphone rang. It chirped out its happy tune three times before she was able to locate a dish towel to dry her hands.

"Hello?" She answered.

"Good morning, Myra! It's Amanda. Do you have a minute?" Myra felt her heart flutter in her rib cage.

"Oh, good morning. Yes, I'm just ... I'm not busy. How are you?" It had been weeks since she had heard Amanda's voice, and she had begun losing hope.

"I'm fine, thank you. And yourself?" Myra tried to dissect her tone. Was she calling with good news? Bad news? Her voice seemed monotone for some reason.

"I'm great, thanks. What's going on?" She could hear Amanda shuffling paperwork on the other end of the line.

"Well, I'm just going through my inbox here and it looks like I have a status update on your foster application."

"Oh, and what would that be?" She was jittery with nerves.

"Well, Myra, it looks like you're going to be adding to your brood pretty soon here. What do you think about that?" She heard herself literally squeal with joy. Her whole body relaxed.

"Seriously? Oh my God! The girls are going to be so excited. I can't ... when? When does this happen? Does Emilia know? I'm in shock." She heard Amanda chuckle.

"Calm down, Myra, you're going to hyperventilate. Yes, the kids know. The news was accepted without hesitation. In fact, they all seemed quite thrilled." Relief swept over her.

"Oh, wow, that's great. So, what happens next?"

"Well, today's Wednesday, so why don't we shoot for a move-in date of Saturday— let everybody finish out the week at school before we go uprooting them and getting them into a new school. Does that sound good?" Myra was beaming.

"That quick? That sounds great!"

"Well, okay then. I'll be in touch with you. I just have to submit the move-in date and get approval from my superiors, and I will contact you about a time."

"Perfect. Thank you so much, Amanda."

"Thank you, Myra. I'll talk with you soon." Myra was trembling when she hit the end-call button on her cell. She was so excited she could barely think straight. She picked up her car keys and headed for the garage, stopping abruptly at the door as she looked down and saw her bunny slippers staring back up at her. She laughed out loud.

"Okay, Myra, get it together." She put the keys back down and headed upstairs to get dressed.

***

"Yes, I just need to pick up my daughters a little early today, if that's okay." The spectacled secretary regarded Myra with a look of distaste.

"Do they have an appointment or something? I'll need a doctor's note."

"No, they don't. I just ... it's a special occasion and I'd like to surprise them." The secretary's stern countenance showed she was not interested in Myra's good news.

"Well, I'll have to check their attendance records. The new school statutes are very firm on the kids not missing more than ten days. Also, it's lunch break, so I'm not sure where they would be at this moment." Myra was growing impatient.

"That's fine. I think Ella may have missed a day back in November due to an illness, but otherwise, they should have perfect attendance." Clearly, Ms. Secretary was not listening, already busy clicking away on her keyboard to determine their eligibility for an early release. Myra couldn't help but think that it was rather ridiculous. The woman lifted the telephone receiver and hit a big black button on the bottom.

"Ella and Samantha Jenkins to the front office, please." The announcement echoed through the halls. She placed the receiver back down and peered back at Myra over the top of her glasses. "Hopefully, they heard that and they should be here in just a moment." Without another word, she lowered her head and went back to whatever work she had been doing. Myra stood there awkwardly, backing away from the window. She strolled over to the trophy cases, scanning the shelves packed with shiny awards.

Sammy was the first to arrive, peeling around the corner with a look of wonder on her face. She took one look at Myra's face and knew exactly what was going on.

"No way, Mom, when?"

"Just wait a second for your sister and I'll tell you both everything." Right on cue, Ella appeared, eager and curious.

Sammy threw her arms around her sister.

"It's happening!" she screeched.

"Yes!" Ella exclaimed. The girls' squealing grabbed the attention of the disgruntled secretary, who stood up, pushed her glasses up on her nose, and told them they needed to quiet down. Myra laughed, grabbed the girls around the shoulders, and together they headed back out the front door of the school.

The car ride back home was a barrage of questions. When were they moving in? Could they go shopping and get the rooms set up now that they knew it was official? Did they have to go to school or could they stay home for the rest of the week to prepare? Myra answered each question as it came. She was thrilled at the energy she was seeing in the girls, yet again amazed at their resilience.

It dawned on her that there really was a lot to do in preparation for the children's arrival and that it might be a good idea to keep the girls home to help. As their excited chatter continued, she started on a mental checklist of things she would have to get accomplished. First off, they had no mattress or furniture to put into the converted office for little Marco. Would he even want to sleep downstairs, all alone, given that he was only six? Second, they never had really gotten around to making the guest room more accommodating. Third, she realized she had no idea what kind of foods they ate. She thought it best to call Amanda as soon as she got home and get some details on what exactly the children were into.

As it turned out, Amanda had been more than prepared for Myra's phone call. "I was wondering when you might call," she giggled. "It never takes long after the initial acceptance for the new foster to contact us reeling with questions. How can I help you, Myra?"

Myra recounted her checklist to Amanda. She heard some shuffling of papers as Amanda muttered under her breath something about finding a packet. "Oh, here it is. Well, Myra, you will be glad to hear that I have exactly what you are look-ing for right here. Each of the children fills out a preference sheet when they are transferred into foster care. It's a nice way for us to help them feel a little more comfortable and in control in their new surroundings, especially since it's typically not the nicest of situations that have landed them here in the first place. They're asked a bunch of questions about their favorite foods, TV shows, pastimes, school subjects, books, you name it. It's pretty thorough. I'll scan them in now and send them over to your email, okay?"

"That would be great!" Myra exclaimed. "Thank you for everything, Amanda! I really mean it. You have been incredi-ble."

"Sure thing, Myra. No problem at all. It has been my pleas-ure, really. If you need anything else, you don't hesitate to call, okay?"

"Okay, wonderful. Thanks again. Bye." Myra swiped her finger across the screen of her phone to end the call, allowing her body to collapse against the kitchen counter. She couldn't believe this was actually happening. She could hear Sammy and Ella rummaging around in the guest room upstairs, prob-ably tearing it to pieces and making more of a mess than any-thing, but, in all honesty, she couldn't blame them. The giant house seemed to hum with anticipation and expectation. She couldn't help but wonder if its old bones had ever seen this much excitement from the Jenkins family to date. A pinging noise from her cell announced a new email, and she got right to work opening up the attachments and getting to know all the details about the three children who were about to become a part of her family.

CHAPTER 18

Friday night finally came, and the girls were lit up at the prospect of the following day. The past three days had been a whirlwind of activity, and, although excited, Myra could sense their exhaustion as they mutely hunched over their dinner plates. They had been such an incredible help: picking out bedroom furniture, comforter sets, paint colors, accessories, and even accompanying her to the grocery store and loading up one-and-a-half carts full of food and toiletries for their new housemates. Sammy stabbed her fork halfheartedly into her lasagna a few times before looking up from her plate.

"Mom, I'm beat. Is it okay if I don't eat dinner tonight?" she asked. Ella perked up at hearing this.

"Yeah, me too. I'm sorry, we know you cooked it from scratch, and it's delicious and all, but I can't even keep my eyes open." Myra smiled softly at her girls.

"Come to think of it, ladies, I'm pretty tired myself. Why don't you two go upstairs and get ready for bed? I'll take care of the cleanup and be up in a few to tuck you in." The girls slowly pushed their chairs back and ambled out of the kitchen and up the stairs. She heard the familiar sounds of the water running through the pipes and the shuffle of their feet up and down the hallway, the bang of a few drawers as they pulled out their pajamas, and she was happy. She carried the dishes across the kitchen, stacking them in the sink and turning on the water. She flipped the switch on the garbage disposal, staring on in a foggy sort of satisfaction as she dumped the contents of one bowl and then another down the hole in the sink, watching it disappear. The dishes were loaded into the washer, the counters wiped down, and the chairs pushed back in when Myra finally turned off the kitchen light and made her way to the steps leading up to her daughters' rooms.

The house seemed so quiet and peaceful, more peaceful than she had remembered it being in years. She reached Sammy's room first, the whirring of her overhead fan the only noise. It didn't take long for Myra to realize that she was already fast asleep. Myra kissed her softly on her forehead, pulling the covers up just a little tighter, even though the first signs of spring were right around the corner in Wisconsin. She remembered all the tulips she had planted last season that were just starting to think about popping up through the slowly melting layer of snow that still littered the February landscape. She thought of new beginnings and how appropriate it was that the arrival of the Garcia children coincided with all the transformations taking place in Mother Nature. She switched Sammy's light off and gently closed her bedroom door behind her.

Ella's eyes were still open, though barely, when Myra popped in through the door. "Hey, Mom. I was trying to stay awake. You almost missed me," she laughed.

"Well, I'm glad I didn't. How are you doing? Still okay with all of this stuff taking place?" Myra asked, stroking Ella's long dark hair off her forehead. Ella smiled sleepily back up at her.

"Yeah, Mom, I'm good. Sammy and I are really excited. I know it's going to be different, but I think we will all adjust to it. I have a really good feeling. Besides, it will be kind of cool to not always have to be the big sister, right? Maybe if there's two of us, Sammy will have somebody else to bug." She gave a little chuckle. "I'm just kidding. It's going to be fine, Mom." Myra smiled and gave her a squeeze on the shoulder.

"Of course it is. All right, kiddo, get some sleep," she said as she kissed her on the cheek and walked back out of the room, her mind, although heavy with lethargy, still moving a million miles a minute.

It would be okay, right? Even through all the excitement, naturally, there had been that one part of her that was terrified that she was making a poor decision. Of course, Greg had only elevated this fear, so intent was he on giving her a tongue-lashing every single time he picked up or dropped off the girls for their visits. It still amazed and half-amused her that he had barely set foot in her home for upwards of a year until he had heard the news of the potential fostering from the girls. It seemed like ever since that day, his face was constantly staring back at her from the backside of her front door, questioning her decisions on every step or threatening to fight her for custody of their own daughters. She walked down the hall to her room, plopping herself bodily onto the bed, recounting their last conversation in her head. She gave an audible chuckle into the empty space around her. Like he would ever fight her for custody. What the hell would he do with full-time custody of his daughters? He could barely take care of himself.

***

Myra was running as fast as she could. She knew she was being chased, but she couldn't see the face of the masked assailant who was closely trailing her. All she knew was that whoever it was, was FAST— far faster than she was. It would be only a short time before he, or she, caught up. She was dizzied, with no sense of direction and even less of an idea how the hell she had gotten here. She dodged through darkened alleyways, past burning dumpsters and shadows that seemed to climb the walls all around her. In her head, Greg's voice taunted her. "I told you so, Myra. I told you so. What kind of mother are you?"

"Shut up!" She screamed, pressing her hands to her ears. "Just shut up, Greg!" She was breathless by now, her heart pounding, the knowledge that she couldn't keep up her pace much longer spreading a debilitating dread throughout her entire body. Her lungs burned with the cool night air as her foot slipped on a wet patch of the black pavement. She fell to her knees, her ankle twisting at a disgusting angle. She felt herself sobbing, knowing that this was the end. She was going to die like some B-list actress in a shitty horror movie. How the fuck had it come to this?

Before she could think about it further, the unmistakable sound of sneakers smacking against the blacktop rapidly approached, until the assailant was upon her, face obscured by a dark hood and the distinct glare of a metal object glinting in hand. When the voice came, it was airy and light, as though some twisted, ethereal being had arrived to take her off to the next dimension. She felt as though she were floating, this figure above her lifting her into the vast expanse of night sky overhead.

"You killed them, Ms. Jenkins." The voice was distorted, but Myra knew exactly who it was coming from. Before she could respond, she felt cold fingers wrap around her throat. They began to squeeze tighter and tighter. Myra reached up for the hood and ripped it away from her attacker's face. Emilia's cold eyes stared down into hers as she mouthed the words over and over again. "You killed them, Ms. Jenkins. You killed them. My parents." Myra tried to scream, but no sound would come. Greg's shadowy figure appeared from seemingly nowhere, his deep-throated taunts mixing with the whispers escaping from Emilia's lips. "I told you so, Myra. This is what happens when you don't listen to me." She reached for him, but he only crossed his arms, shaking his head indifferently, a look of pity and disdain cast across his features. She continued to scream, still unable to make any noise, the grip of Emilia's hand growing tighter and tighter still. She felt the sharp point of a knife blade begin to press into her throat. Her eyes locked with Greg's for a brief moment, before closing completely as she felt her life slipping away from her.

CHAPTER 19

Myra sat up in bed, gasping for air and soaking wet from head to toe. It took her a full sixty seconds and a pat-down of her entire body to convince herself that she was safe in her own bed and not bleeding to death in an alley haunted by the ghosts of her past. She realized she was trembling, and a chill ran down the length of her spine. She threw back the covers, swinging her legs over the side of the bed and reaching for the bathrobe dropped in a sloppy pile at the foot of the bed. She wrapped it around herself, grateful for its familiar smell and texture. A glance at the clock told her it was 4:39 a.m., far too early to get up, although she knew that there would be no more opportunities for sleep on this particular night. She moved quietly past the girls' rooms, closing their doors gently as she passed, and padded down the steps, across the foyer, and into the kitchen. Her cheery yellow kettle rested atop the stove, and she thought a cup of chamomile might be just the thing to calm her nerves. She filled the kettle with tap water, replaying the nightmare over and over in her head. She set the kettle back on the stovetop and turned the dial. She tried to busy her mind by perusing through the cabinet dedicated to her vast collection of teas, reading the box labels one by one until she found what she was looking for. She plucked the box of Cozy Chamomile from the assortment of boxes, careful not to disturb the rest, stacked as they were like a game of Jenga nearing its end. She tried to find some solace in the cheerful image of a bear dressed in pajamas adorning the box's cover and eventually found herself talking out loud to the box.

"If it were only that easy, Mr. Bear. If only a cup of tea could make sense of all of this and assure me that I'm undoubtedly doing the right thing." She shook her head, placed the box on the counter, and pulled a packet from within. The water was steaming by now, and she quickly leaped across the kitchen to stop it from whistling its little tune and potentially waking the girls.

With her mug of steaming relaxation in hand, Myra moved her way into the dining room. She sat at the table, placing the mug directly in front of her, gazing down into the brew that was becoming darker with each passing minute. The clock above the table clicked by the seconds as her mind wandered.

"What am I doing?" she muttered out loud, realizing for perhaps the first time that maybe Greg had been right. Was she putting the girls in danger with this crazy idea, putting herself in danger? "Jesus, Myra. You don't even know these people." Then her mind flitted back through the many conversations she had had with Amanda over the course of her application process. Amanda had assured her that all the children were completely of sound mind and wanted—no, *needed*—this opportunity to stay together. "Okay, okay, don't let some silly dream freak you out. This is a good thing. You're just nervous, that's all. Today is going to be a huge day, and nobody knows what to expect. Shit, maybe Emilia is having nightmares tonight, too. Keep it together, Myra. You have to, for the girls. For *all* the kids."

She was suddenly too restless to sit at the table anymore. She pushed the chair back with a little too much force, grabbed the tea, and whisked herself off into the living room. She walked to the mantel and stared at the picture of Vale, the four smiling faces of what used to be her family beaming up at her. She found herself wondering—not for the first time—how she had ended up here. What would the new picture of her family look like? Could this really work? Obviously, there was no going back now. She felt compelled to make her way to what once was Greg's office, now fully converted into a bedroom. She opened the French doors one at a time, catching the scent of fresh paint and newly washed linens. She walked in, the marble floor reflecting the last of the night's moonlight through the window, and sat on the edge of the double bed that now waited inside. Originally this was going to be Marco's room, but Ella had suggested that maybe they make this Emilia's room, given that she was seventeen and Ella, being fifteen, knew what needing privacy was all about. Myra let out a little giggle, remembering Ella's conviction. And so it was decided that the two younger siblings would share the guest room upstairs.

She glanced around the room now, Greg's giant mahogany desk replaced by a simple whitewashed bedroom set and the room adorned with only a few accessories: a lamp picked out by Sammy, a clock radio, a desk calendar, and a pretty plant that Myra had found, just to bring in a little life. She admired her handiwork as she took in the shelves and the framed black-and-white Ansel Adams print she had hung herself. Maybe they were the tiniest bit crooked, but they would do. The walls were painted a pale blue-gray, a color that her computer search engine had informed her was calming and helped with concentration. She thought calming was good. Her hand ran across the comforter Ella had picked, puffy and white, with hints of the wall color peeking out through the design at the bottom and on the pillow covers. She couldn't help but think they had done quite well. It was understated and a little bit plain, but with Emilia's own touches and a little bit of color, it would be beautiful. She wondered what it was going to be like later, when this room was no longer hers, and then laughed quietly to herself as she realized it had really never been hers to begin with. She stood up, smoothing the comforter behind her, and left the room, the trail of moonlight following her out toward the foyer.

Myra walked quietly back up the stairs, one hand holding her tea, the other steadily moving up the handrail until she stopped outside of the guest bedroom just to the left of the stairs. The last time anybody had stayed there was when her mother came to help out with the girls shortly after the accident. It felt a little ironic now, as she gazed in at the two twin beds. The room had been converted quite skillfully by the three of them to have a girl's side and a boy's side. A distinct line of paint marking the center. Marco's wall space was the same blue as Emilia's, covered with pictures and decals of his favorite superheroes, his bed with a life-size depiction of Spiderman gracing the comforter, and a lamp with the same design adorning his night table. Carina's wall was painted a pale purple with a framed poster of her favorite Disney fairies and decals of flowers filling its space. Her comforter boasted the same fairies, only larger and in a different configuration. The lamp on her night table was shaped like a little fairy house. They both had their own matching dresser at the foot of the beds, and their respective halves of the walk-in closet reflected the same paint color as their sides of the room. Standing here now, she wondered how the hell they had gotten all of this done in such a short time and marveled at how well it had come out. She knew that at least the younger ones would be completely happy with their new arrangements. She sipped her tea—now mostly cold—and headed back downstairs, just as the very first of the early morning sun was beginning to climb up over the horizon through the back sliders, casting dancing, orange light across the surface of the lake.

THE SONG OF
ROOTS

CHAPTER 20

Myra, Sammy, and Ella had spent the morning tidying things that didn't need tidying, both nervous and expectant for the moment the Garcia children would arrive. Finally, the ring of the doorbell echoed through the vaulted ceilings of the house. Myra, busily scrubbing invisible dirt from the kitchen counters, heard a stampede of feet above her head as Ella and Sammy fought their way down the hall and the stairs. The three all made their way into the foyer at the same time and froze for a brief moment, staring eagerly at one another. The current of energy running through the trio was palpable. Myra reached for a hand from each of the girls and drew them into a tight huddle.

"Are you guys ready for this?" Both girls nodded their heads enthusiastically. "Okay, let's all take a deep breath together. No matter what, I need you to know how much I love you, okay?" Another nod.

"We love you too, Mom," said Ella. "Now can we open the door already?" Her brow furrowed in anticipation, and Myra reached over to smooth the tension away with her palm.

"Yep, here goes nothing!" She gave each of her daughters' palms a quick squeeze, took a deep, audible breath, and turned to face the door. Her right hand reached for the doorknob, but all she was aware of was the pounding beneath her chest, as though her heart were desperately trying to escape the prison of her rib cage. She turned the knob slowly and then stepped back as she whisked the door open, her best welcoming smile plastered onto her face. The first face she saw was, of course, Amanda's, complete with her charming grin and her characteristic bun. Amanda's natural joy bursting through gave Myra hope.

"Well, good morning, ladies! This is the day we've all been waiting for! Are you all ready?" she asked, motioning more toward Sammy and Ella than to Myra. The girls nodded their heads simultaneously, both trying desperately to peer around Amanda to catch a glimpse of their new foster siblings. A little head peeked back at them from behind Amanda's leg and showed giant brown eyes full of some mixture of trepidation and hope. Marco's tiny hand rested on the outside of Amanda's leg, and she reached down instinctively to grab hold of it. "It's okay, baby, this is Ms. Myra," she said, gesturing to her, "and these here are Sammy and Ella. This is your new home."

Myra and the girls looked through the open door as his gaze traveled back and forth from one to the other before he ducked back behind Amanda's leg. Amanda stepped off to the side, revealing the two girls. Carina stood in front of her big sister. Emilia's hands were planted firmly on her shoulders. The smaller girl looked as if she wanted to smile and run into the sanctuary of her new home, but it was obvious that her sister's grip was sending a different message to her. Her gratitude and excitement were almost palpable.

Emilia, on the other hand, stood stick-straight, eyes narrowed defensively, gazing somewhere beyond the three of them into the house. The group fell into an awkward silence, with nobody knowing quite what to do next, but before it got too uncomfortable, Amanda, used to this kind of thing, stepped in and took control.

"Why don't we get everybody inside? I've got the driver grabbing their belongings. He should be up the walk shortly if we can just leave the door open for him." She ushered the three children into the house and asked them softly to take off their shoes. She walked the five children through their introductions and then directed her attention toward Myra. "How about a tour of the house? Maybe we can show them where they will be sleeping?" Myra realized she had been staring at the Garcia children with her mouth open, still not fully able to grasp the reality of the situation taking place in front of her. She snapped back to attention with a jolt.

"Oh, of course, yes. Please, follow me." She proceeded to walk them into the living room, where Carina and Marco marveled at the wall of sliding glass doors opening to an expanse of land with Lake Monona glistening off behind it. They whispered excitedly to one another, pointing at the swing set and playhouse, left forgotten to the elements as her daughters had grown. The snow would melt soon, and it occurred to Myra for the first time that the outdoor play structures might yet again get some use. She would have to check everything for safety.

The entourage moved into the large dining area, the ticking of the wall clock filling in space as the littler children explored and Myra, her daughters, and Emilia watched in silence. The two small children continued to giggle and whisper, and Myra, noticing that this was making their older sister extremely uncomfortable, decided it was best to keep moving. They advanced to the kitchen, where Myra opened and closed cabinets and drawers to show them where they could find plates, cups, bowls, and silverware. She flung open the fridge, presenting the contents to her new housemates with the encouragement that they make themselves comfortable and help themselves to anything. They continued like this, through the pantry, out to the garage, out onto the patio, back into the house, to the guest bathroom, until they were back in the foyer. The driver from family services had been busily unloading the vehicle, and the foyer was now beginning to fill up with suitcases, blankets, pillows, stuffed animals, and the rest of the Garcia children's personal effects.

"Well," offered Myra, "if you're ready, Emilia, I can show you your room first." It was the first direct interaction between them since Emilia's arrival, and she felt as though the tension that hung in the air between them was squeezing the air from her lungs. She was reminded of her nightmare from early that morning, and suddenly felt glad that Emilia would be sleeping downstairs. She instantly felt guilty for the thought.

Emilia was clearly unmoved to learn that she had her own space.

"That's fine, Ms. Jenkins. Whatever you want."

"Please, call me Myra," she offered, and was almost certain she heard Emilia emit a little hiss from her throat in response. "It's just over here." The French doors had been closed and the curtains drawn. Myra thought this best so that Emilia would realize from the outset that she did indeed have plenty of privacy, despite the glass. She walked toward the door, reached for the handle, and thought better of it. "Why don't you open it? After all, it's your room now." Emilia remained impassive as she approached the door and slowly turned the handle. As the door swung open, revealing the naturally sunlit room and cozy decorations, Myra watched her closely. For a moment Emilia's jaw went slack and her shoulders slumped away from her ears, softening her entire appearance so that she actually looked her young age. She took a few steps into the room, her fingertips grazing the top of the night table as she looked around, taking it all in. She let her hand move to the bedspread as she pressed down firmly on the mattress. Myra wondered if the girl wasn't secretly grateful that she didn't hear any springs creaking beneath the pressure. She found herself suddenly curious to know more about what their living arrangements had been since the accident. She noticed Emilia eyeing the live plant blooming on the corner of the desk and hoped that perhaps she perceived it as a beacon of promise that life would continue. Warm tears began to form at the corners of Emilia's eyes. Myra realized the girl hadn't had a home in over a year and wondered what this might feel like for her in this moment. As though she could sense Myra's gaze upon her, Emilia quickly wiped her eyes and regained her stoic composure. It was as though she had silently reminded herself that Myra was not her friend, that she had, in fact, killed her parents, and was only filling an obligatory duty. She turned and faced Myra tensely.

"I'll grab my things," was all she said. Myra shot Amanda a concerned look over the heads of the other children, and Amanda responded with a soft smile and an almost imperceptible shake of her head, a gesture assuring Myra not to worry, that this would pass with time.

"That's a beautiful room, Myra, isn't it, Emilia?" Amanda asked. Emilia was picking up her things one by one and dropping them in a pile just inside the door. She didn't bother to respond. "Well, then," said Amanda cheerily, dropping down to a squat in front of Marco and Carina. "Are you two ready to see your room?" The younger two were clearly bursting with anticipation and couldn't hold it in any longer.

"Yes!" they exploded in unison. Everybody chuckled, and Myra glanced over and saw that even Emilia's lips parted ever so slightly in an amused half smile. She clearly adored her siblings. Before Myra could say anything, Sammy and Ella had taken over, each grabbing for a hand of one of the smaller children. Emilia's grin faded instantly as she watched the four of them giddily work their way up the staircase.

Carina and Marco whirled about the room like two little tornadoes, opening and closing drawers to discover their contents, digging through the basket of books that Myra had purchased, running in and out of the walk-in closet, and squealing with delight to each other as they rolled onto their respective beds. Carina promptly began kissing each comforter fairy on her face, her joy too large now to hide anymore. Marco was steadily rushing from one superhero picture to another, contorting his little body this way and that to imitate the way his idols were standing. Myra felt a glow washing over her body. It had been so long since her girls were this age, full of this much excitement and enthusiasm over the most minuscule things. She had forgotten how much she missed the noise, the chaos, and the imagination of little kids. Dreamily lost in the scene before her eyes, she was startled when she felt Emilia push past her into the room. She was carrying some of her brother's and sister's luggage and was clearly agitated as she surveyed the scene in the room.

"Marco, Carina," she snapped. The pair instantly stopped what they were doing and turned guiltily to face her. "That's enough. You weren't raised like wild animals. Get off those beds and come help me find a place to put your things."

"Yes, Emilia," Carina submitted.

"Sorry, *hermana*," whispered Marco, his eyes cast down now at the floor. The rest of the party hovered near the door, fidgeting, except for Amanda, who yet again knew exactly how to handle the situation.

"I've got this, for now, Emilia. Don't worry about them for a little bit. They're just excited, that's all. Why don't you go down and start to get yourself settled in your own room? Sammy and Ella can show Marco and Carina where their things go, right, girls?" They nodded in unison. "Great. It's been a long morning for everybody so far. Myra, while they all get moved in, perhaps you and I can talk for a bit in the kitchen?"

"Oh, of course," Myra responded, and with that Amanda directed her and Emilia out of the room, back down the stairs, and into the living room. Myra found herself being led to and seated on her own couch, facing Emilia, who had been pointed to a loveseat opposite. Again, she got that strange sensation in her throat, as though all the air was being sucked from her body.

"Now listen, Emilia," Amanda began gently. "I understand that this is a difficult transition, but I need you to keep in mind that it's difficult for everybody involved. Things might be a little bumpy over the next few days with your brother and sister. Remember what it was like when you went to stay in group housing at first?" Emilia nodded curtly, her face stony. "Well, there's going to be an adjustment period for them that will be similar as they start to adapt to their new routine here. Remember, Myra is in charge now. I realize that you have had to take on a lot of extra responsibility over the past year and a half, but you're safe here. Myra has done a lot of work to make sure that you stay together, and I need you to know that nothing's going to change that. Have a little confidence in the process, okay?" Emilia's nostrils flared. Her voice was cold and calm when she spoke.

"If she hadn't killed my parents, Ms. Cooper, she might not have had to do all that work to keep us together." Myra sensed her face flushing, and suddenly she felt as though she were on fire. She swallowed hard to dissolve the lump that had instantly formed in her throat, but it only seemed to come back harder. After all, the girl was right in a way, wasn't she? In that one sentence, Emilia had shattered any high hopes that Myra had had for this living arrangement. Clearly, she had been living in an alternative reality thinking that they would become some sort of a family. Emilia had made no pretense about it. She was here solely to ride out the next year and a half until she turned eighteen and could start making the types of arrangements that would eventually allow her to adopt her siblings and move on with her life. Myra held back her frustration and tears.

"Emilia!" reprimanded Amanda. "I know that you have suffered a tremendous loss, and neither I, nor Myra are trying to pretend that you haven't, but it was an accident, as you know. Ms. Jenkins extending her home to you and your siblings is an incredibly kind gesture and one that may deserve just a little bit of consideration on your part. As I said, this is a difficult transition for everybody involved, but you chose to do this. Both of you, including you, Myra, are going to have to learn to work as a team and bridge the gap that these unfortunate circumstances have created between you. This is your home now, Emilia. Let's try to make the best of everything, okay?" Her tone had softened considerably since her first outburst, one hand resting gently on top of Emilia's, the other stroking her long black hair.

"I'm sorry, Ms. Jenkins," Emilia offered halfheartedly. "I wasn't trying to offend." Her gaze lowered to her lap.

"I ... I ... of course, it's no problem" was all Myra could manage to get out, her hands fussing with a tassel on one of the throw pillows.

"Okay, then," Amanda continued. "Emilia, go and get your things sorted out. Myra, let's go into the kitchen and talk for a few. Would you mind if I asked for a cup of tea?" The squealing and excitement were still going strong at the top of the stairs as Myra and Emilia went in their separate directions through the house.

CHAPTER 21

By the time Amanda walked back out the front door, the sun was already beginning to set. Myra couldn't remember the last time she had felt this drained. The house was quiet as she clicked closed the latch on the front door, pushing out the drafty air of the cool evening. Sammy, Ella, and the little ones had been outside playing in what was left of the melting winter snow for the past hour, and Emilia had been behind closed doors since their last conversation. Occasionally, Myra had heard a shuffle or a bump, probably a box being unpacked or a drawer opening and closing, but, otherwise, the room seemed soundless. The thought of making dinner for the six of them completely overwhelmed her, and she thought that perhaps tonight they would be better off ordering a pizza. She walked toward the closed French doors, right hand poised to knock, then hesitated for several moments, too obliterated by the day's events to withstand another cutting remark from Emilia. Still, she didn't know what kind of pizza any of them ate, or if they ate it at all, really. With a little sigh, she gently rapped on the glass.

"Emilia?" No answer. She tried again, a little more force-fully. "Emilia?" Still no answer. She felt her heart skip a beat as she reached for the handle. Surely she hadn't run away? Not after everything they had gone through to make this hap-pen. She turned the knob slowly and gently nudged the door ajar, popping her head through the opening. Much to her re-lief, Emilia lay sprawled out across the double bed, mouth agape, strands of her long, dark hair spilling lazily off the pil-low and dangling down toward the marble floor. Her face looked peaceful and calm, almost as though a smile were play-ing on her lips. Across her chest was a book, open face down, her hand resting softly on its cover.

Myra pushed the door open just a bit more and walked in farther, despite the nagging sensation that she shouldn't. As she got closer, she could see tear tracks staining Emilia's cheeks and realized almost immediately that it was not just any book but a photo album that she had wrapped in her em-brace. There was a picture of a smiling couple staring up at her from the front cover, white frosting smeared across the tip of the woman's nose, her head thrown partially back in a laugh. Myra instantly recognized their faces. They were clearly dressed up, although not much of their outfits could be seen in the close-up. Emilia's arm twitched a little, just enough to reveal the title of the album below her forearm. "*Album de la Boda.*" It was their wedding album. Myra felt her breath catch, embarrassed that she was intruding on such an intimate mo-ment without Emilia's knowing. She quickly turned and hur-ried out of the room as quietly as she had come in and closed the door softly behind her.

Myra found the other four still playing outside, the still-cool air creating a blush in each of their cheeks. As she watched from the back patio, it was obvious that little Marco was punchy from exhaustion, and every now and then the

136

smile would slip from his face to be replaced by an enormous yawn.

"Okay, kids," Myra yelled, "it's time to come inside. I just ordered some pizzas and they should be here soon, so let's start to get everybody settled."

"Pizza!" Carina yelled, galloping toward the back patio and up the steps. She threw herself unexpectedly into Myra's legs, sending her backward toward the slider. "Thank you, Ms. Myra. We love pizza. Is it pepperoni?" Myra, taken aback, smiled shyly and patted the top of her head.

"I did get a pepperoni, along with some other kinds. I wasn't sure what you ate," she replied. Carina gave another light squeeze around her legs before pushing past her into the warmth of the house. She kicked off her shoes and shed her light jacket, letting them fall in a pile by the door. She started off for her room and then thought better of it, turning back to face Myra with a worried wrinkle on her brow.

"I'm sorry, Ms. Myra," she said as she reached for her belongings. "Your house is so neat. I didn't mean to make a mess. Where should I put these?" Myra reached to take them from her.

"Please, honey, just call me Myra. It's your house too now, Carina. Don't worry about it. C'mon, I'll show you where everything goes." She grabbed Carina's hand with her free one and they headed up to the front coat closet near the door. Emilia sauntered out of her room just as they were passing.

"Hermana!" Carina exclaimed, releasing Myra's hand and racing for her sister. "Where have you been? We've been having so much fun playing in the backyard." Emilia shook her off gently.

"I'm sorry, Carina. I must have fallen asleep." She shot Myra a look full of daggers. "Have they been any bother?"

"None whatsoever," Myra assured her. "They've been outside playing with Sammy and Ella for quite some time. I

137

actually just called them in to get ready for dinner. Do you like pizza?" She could hear the forced cheeriness in her voice and it aggravated her, knowing that Emilia made her nervous. Emilia shrugged in response.

"Whatever you've decided is just fine." But her eyes were trained on Carina, clearly not pleased that she was having so much fun interacting with the enemy.

Dinner that night might have felt awkward if everybody wasn't so depleted by the day. The pizza was eaten mostly in silence, with Carina and Marco rubbing their eyes and yawning in between bites. Even the older girls were visibly drained, black smudges darkening the spaces below their eyes. A few attempts were made at conversation, predominantly Ella and Sammy teasing Carina and Marco playfully. Myra was thrilled to see the interaction among the four of them, but she remained worried about Emilia and whether or not she would be able to surrender her animosity enough to adjust to the new living arrangements. All Myra could do was hope and keep trying.

Myra cleaned up the kitchen while the five kids readied themselves for bed. Emilia took care of tucking in her brother and sister who—judging by the absence of sound coming from upstairs—were fast asleep within moments. When Myra emerged from the kitchen, Sammy and Ella were lounging on the couch in their pajamas, clicking through television stations. Emilia had just reached the bottom step and stood there for a moment, looking not quite sure what her next move would be. Ella, sensing her presence behind them, turned around and peeked over the back of the couch.

"You want to watch TV with us? What's your favorite show?" She patted the couch cushion next to her, but Emilia seemed frozen at the landing of the steps for a moment before emphatically shaking her head no.

"No. I ... um, I'm tired. I think I'll just go to bed." And

without another word she slipped behind the French doors, closing them gently behind her, and drew the curtains even tighter.

"Pfft," said Sammy. "What is it with her, anyway?" Ella shot her a look.

"Seriously, Sammy? Give her a break. She's been through a lot. This isn't easy for her."

"Oh, yeah, because it's been rainbows and sunshine for us, right?" she replied, rolling her eyes. Myra hurried into the room, finger pressed to her lip as she made a shushing noise.

"Girls," she whispered, "stop it right now. I don't want her to hear this. We are all just going to have to do our best to get along. Give her some time, okay?" Ella nodded and Sammy rolled her eyes again, flipping her a thumbs-up sign.

"Okay, good," Myra said. "I'm going to bed. Don't be up too late, okay?" The girls were looking past her now, intently focused on some program they had settled on, and she received no response. She kissed each girl on the top of her head and made her way to bed.

CHAPTER 22

Myra lay awake, watching the Sunday sun starting to peek around the edges of her curtains. She'd woken suddenly, about an hour before, roused by a slightly different version of the nightmare that had haunted her now two nights in a row. Greg's words, fabricated or not, echoed through her head on repeat, slowly gnawing away at any certainty that remained that this had been a good idea. She kept going back to the look in Emilia's eyes, cold and resentful. How would she ever be able to penetrate this fortress that Emilia had built up around her? The thought alone made her want to retreat into an interminable hibernation, but clearly, that was not an option.

She found herself wondering how the six of them would possibly fill the entire Sunday that lay ahead. Was she destined to feel like a prisoner in her own home, Emilia's gaze boring into her wherever she went? Something had to give.

All of a sudden, the idea went off in her head like a flashbulb. One thing 99 percent of children could not resist was shopping, and Myra had lots of experience with that. The children had come to her with such a meager collection of items: a few outfits, a book or two each, their pillows, blankets, a toy each for Marco and Carina, along with a few personal effects and their toiletries. Although Myra had understood that the family had actually been doing quite well for themselves when they were alive—Mr. Garcia had been a successful painting contractor and his wife had been a talented dance instructor—Amanda had explained that the children had been limited in what they were allowed to bring with them when they moved into foster care. It wouldn't be fair if some children came in with more than others, and so this was their way of keeping things even across the board. Because Mr. and Mrs. Garcia had been so young and vibrant, it had never occurred to them to write a will, so anything of value had been sold. That included the family home, which had paid their funeral expenses, with the remaining money put into trusts for the children to inherit when they turned eighteen.

This had left the three children with only a few possessions and whatever had been provided to them through their foster home. Greg's child support as well as Myra's very cushy savings more than covered the family expenses, and now with the additional income given to her by the state for fostering the children, she was even more aware that there were ample funds to go around. There was really nothing stopping her from taking all five of the children out for a little treat. Maybe this would help to soften Emilia. Yes, she would make it a fun day for everybody. A little smile played on her lips as she imagined them all spending this time together. Was she being slightly unrealistic as far as Emilia went? Perhaps, but it was a nice little fantasy, and she thought she may let herself stay there for a few more minutes before she got out of bed.

***

Myra stood in the kitchen, leaning over the countertop, watching the kids eating at the dining room table. She liked seeing the table this full, the one empty chair reserved for her. Everybody, including Emilia, seemed to be feeling more vivacious after a good night's sleep. She even smiled a few times as she helped Marco get his scrambled eggs onto his fork, only to see him spill them again inches from his open mouth. Myra decided now was as good a time as any. She approached the table and plopped herself down in the empty seat with her coffee mug.

"Well, it's Sunday, and yesterday was pretty long and arduous. What do you guys say we have a little fun today?" The younger two clapped their hands. Carina almost knocked her glass of juice over, and Sammy and Ella both raised their eyebrows while smirking. Emilia remained composed.

"What do you have in mind, Mom?" Sammy asked.

"Well, here's what I was thinking. Emilia, Carina, and Marco," she said, turning to face them, "I know that things have been difficult for you lately. I thought that, now that you each have a space to call your own again, we could go out and each of you could get some things to make it feel more like home."

"Like what?" asked Carina excitedly.

"Well," she shifted uncomfortably in her seat, well aware of their older sister's icy glare and set jaw, "whatever it is that you need. I was thinking we could get some clothes, maybe some toys you like to play with, puzzles, games, that sort of thing." Marco and Carina looked at each other, eyes wide as saucers, clearly enticed, but Emilia was, yet again, unmoved.

"That's a generous offer, Ms. Jenkins, but again, I just want to remind you that we are not a charity case," Emilia said. Myra watched the smiles melt from the younger siblings' faces. It was disheartening to see them go from excitement to disappointment so quickly, and Myra was determined not to back down this time. She had to start standing her ground now, a reminder Amanda had given her the day before.

"Well, lucky for you, I can assure you that it is not a case of charity. The state gives me money each month allotted for these types of expenses, Emilia. Eventually, we will have to go and get these items, anyway. I just thought it might be a fun way to get to know each other, to make a day of it. We'll hit the mall and anywhere else you might like to stop, and then we can grab lunch before we head home. You may actually enjoy yourself, you know." She plastered an Oscar-winner smile on her face and turned back to Carina and Marco. "Sound good to you guys?" They both nodded their heads, a bit more timidly, as they looked from their sister to Myra and back again. "Good, then, it's settled," she said, pushing the chair away from the table and standing up. "When breakfast is over, everybody go get dressed, take showers, whatever it is you need to do, and we can plan on leaving around ten!" She picked up her coffee mug and made her way back to the kitchen, whistling a tune that sounded an awful lot like victory.

By 10:27, they were finally making their way out the front door. It was a bit more of a struggle than she had bargained for getting six of them out of the house, but she had managed. Emilia rode shotgun, staring straight ahead, her palms folded demurely in her lap. The few feeble attempts Myra had made at starting a conversation were met with silence and blank stares. Rather than continue to beat her head against a wall, she turned the music up in the Land Rover, glancing back in the rearview as she drove, giggling at Marco and Carina bopping their heads to the beat. Sammy and Ella were tucked in tight next to them sharing the middle seat belt, a situation she hadn't considered up to this point. She wondered how the thorough investigation the state had put her through had neglected to inform her she would need to trade in the Land

Rover for a minivan.

By the time they pulled up to South Towne Mall, the noise level in the car's interior had reached an all-time high. She instantly understood now why parents invested in those little headrest monitors so the kids could watch movies in the back seat. Her head was pounding.

They poured from the car as if in a comedy skit and headed toward the food court entrance. They decided to shop in order of age, so Marco got to go first. His interest declined quickly as Myra and her daughters perused racks of shirts and pants and finally decided on four outfits that could be mixed and matched. Myra let him pick a few toys from the back part of the store, and his enthusiasm poured back in. He settled on a little stuffed dog that he kept calling *Mullido*, a train kit, some Matchbox cars, three books, and a Spiderman beanbag chair.

Carina was elated when she was told it was her turn. She, unlike her brother, was thrilled at the prospect of acquiring new clothes. She raced through the girls' side of the store, plucking dresses, skirts, tees, and headbands from the shelves and racks. Myra could only laugh.

"Whoa, whoa," she said, placing her hand gently on Carina's head, as though to ground her to her place. "Not so fast, honey. We don't need to rush, okay? Let's take our time and decide together." Carina dropped her head.

"I'm so sorry Ms. ... My- ...er, Myra. I was just—"

"Don't apologize, Carina," Myra cut her off. "Let's just go through together, okay?" Carina looked up at her and nodded, and Myra could see tears welling up in her eyes. She put her arm around Carina's shoulder and gave it a little squeeze. "Come on, where to?" And she let Carina lead her through the maze of displays.

Sammy and Ella found themselves left standing next to Emilia and Marco, though Marco was fully engrossed in his new stuffed puppy. Ella shifted from one foot to the other, not sure exactly what to say.

"So," she offered, "where do you like to shop?" Emilia tossed her a sideways glance and shrugged her shoulders.

"I usually have better things to do than shop," she countered. Her negative response only further fueled Ella's desire to make friends.

"Yeah, I don't get to the mall much either. Mom used to make fun of me because she said I was obsessed with clothing, but I've kind of grown out of it," she said, flipping her hair over her shoulder. "I mean, I guess she's right. There are only so many clothes you can wear at one time, right?" She glanced up at Emilia, smiling, searching for any sign of camaraderie.

"Well, I guess your mother knows best," Emilia replied icily, her gaze fixed on the toy that Marco held in his hands. Sammy, put off by the whole conversation, rolled her eyes and marched off to find her mother.

"Yeah, I guess," Ella answered, at a loss for any more words that could possibly turn the course of the conversation.

CHAPTER **23**

By the time they walked out of the store, Myra, Sammy, and Ella were laden down with bags, and Myra's Amex was smoking. They headed back to the food court to refuel before moving on to shopping for Emilia. Carina and Marco couldn't stop talking and showing each other all of their new items, though Myra kept reminding them that it was time to eat and they could go through their bags when they got home. Marco smiled widely at her. "I'm sorry, Ms. Myra, but *me amo* Mullido," he said, squeezing the little stuffed puppy that sat by his side. Emilia, eating in silence with her head lowered to her food, suddenly threw her fork down onto her plate and snatched the little black-and-white furball from beside him.

"Mullido is gone," she scolded him. "Stop calling him that. This is just a toy, Marco." She took the stuffed dog and crammed it into one of the bags on the table, and turned her attention back to her plate. Marco's eyes began to brim with tears, and his lower lip protruded dangerously. Emilia, as though realizing she had overreacted, almost instantly turned back to face him, her tone softening.

"I'm sorry, Marco. I didn't mean to hurt you." But it was too late. Tears were streaming down Marco's face and little whimpers were coming from his throat. Sammy, already protective over her new foster brother, gave Emilia a stare that could freeze oceans and pulled the toy back out of the bag, shoving it into his little hand.

"Here, Marco," she said. "You call him whatever you want. He's yours." Emilia's face was turning an ever-deepening shade of red. She stood up abruptly from the table.

"I have to use the restroom." Her voice squeaked, and she took off in the direction of the facilities. Myra stood up to follow, but Ella placed a hand gently on her forearm, pulling her back down to her seat.

"Let me go, Mom. Maybe I can talk to her." Myra nodded consent and Ella went off in the same direction. Sammy was fuming, and Myra shot her a look, warning her not to speak ill of their sister in front of Marco and Carina. Sammy's mouth dropped open and her eyes widened.

"Seriously, Mom? Are you kidding?"

"Don't, Sammy," Myra cautioned.

"Fine!" Sammy exploded, turning to Carina. "But I just want to know, why does she care so much about what he calls his stuffed animal? What's it to her? Why is she being so mean?" Carina, soothing her young brother, looked back at her.

"Mullido was our dog when Mama and Papa were alive. This dog looks a lot like him. Marco picked it because it reminded him of her. Mullido means fluffy in Spanish. She was the cutest little thing, and she was really Emilia's dog more than anybody's. Emilia did everything for her: walked her, fed her, played with her. When we moved into foster care, they took Mullido away, and Emilia was so sad." Myra's hand had flown to her mouth at some point during Carina's speech. The giant lump re-formed in her throat, and she felt as though she might cry too. "I think she just misses him a lot, that's all," Carina said. Sammy's anger had abated, and her brows knitted together with concern.

"Oh. I'm sorry. I didn't realize," Sammy said.

"It's okay," offered Carina, wise beyond her young years. "You couldn't have known." The four continued eating in uncomfortable silence as they waited for the two older girls to return.

It took about fifteen more minutes for Ella and Emilia to finally make their way back to the table. They sat down across from each other silently, and Myra shot Ella an inquiring look, wondering if everything was okay. Ella nodded discreetly and changed the topic.

"So, I think we should head downstairs after lunch. There's an awesome store I think you'll really like, Emilia." Emilia gave a faint smile, clearly grateful for the distraction from what had just occurred.

"Okay, I'd like to see it," she consented. Myra didn't know what Ella had said to her, but it was clear that an alliance of sorts was beginning to form between them, and it offered her a sense of hope.

When they walked into the clothing store to shop for Emilia, neither she nor Myra could forget that this was the same place where Emilia had made a show of pocketing a pair of earrings the previous year. Myra could sense Emilia's discomfort as they entered, glancing nervously back and forth and plunging her hands deep into the pockets of her jeans. Ella didn't seem to notice.

"Emilia, this would look amazing on you!" she exclaimed, whisking a beautiful jade green sweater from one of the racks and holding it up to her. "That color is gorgeous with your eyes!" she gushed. Emilia blushed a little, clearly not accustomed to all the attention being placed on her. Myra had to agree. It was a stunning color on her.

"Thanks," Emilia mumbled, tucking her hair behind her ear.

"You'll try it on, right?" Ella asked. Emilia nodded sheepishly as Ella thrust the hanger into her hand and continued rapidly moving through the store, lit up at the potential of befriending her new sister through one of her favorite subjects: clothes. After just twenty minutes, Emilia's arms were piled high with items to try on and Ella was corralling her toward the dressing rooms. As Emilia exited and entered the dressing room in different outfits, Myra couldn't help but watch the reaction that she was having to her own reflection, gently fingering each material that touched her skin, and spinning ever so slightly so the dresses she tried on would catch the air and lift around her. Again, Myra saw that childlike quality that seemed so far away from her most of the time. She even caught her and Ella sharing some satisfied smiles. It was undeniable that she was a beautiful girl anyway, but when she smiled, her whole face lit up like the twinkling stars that had filled the sky on the night her world had been shattered. Myra couldn't look at the stars anymore without thinking about the accident, but watching Emilia smile reminded her that every memory held the potential to be re-created with time.

The six of them dragged their weary bodies back to the car, weighed down with bags and bags of merchandise. Marco was barely awake, Carina not far behind him, as they piled back into the Land Rover for the ride home. Within minutes, little Marco's head had dropped to one side, his mouth agape, a thin line of drool rolling down his chin, and Myra felt her heart warm at the perfection of it.

As they pulled up the long drive leading up to her house, Myra did a double take. Parked at the top was Greg's BMW. What the hell was he doing here?

"Is that Dad?" Sammy asked, having noticed the car at the same time.

"It would appear to be," Myra answered with an aggravated sigh. "You guys head straight inside, okay?" she asked. "I don't want to wake Marco up if we can help it. Emilia, could you bring him up to bed for a nap?" Everybody nodded in agreement as she pulled up in front of the opening garage door. She inched inside and shut off the engine. Greg was already opening his own car door. Myra shuffled outside, heading him off at the pass before he could yell out to either of his daughters.

"What in the world are you doing here, Greg?" Myra's hands were planted impatiently on her hips, and her head was cocked to one side. She hadn't intended to get an attitude, but she was way too tired to put up with him right now. The look on his face registered feigned shock.

"Am I not allowed to drop by and meet the new tenants?" he asked sarcastically. Myra peered over her shoulder to make sure the kids were inside. She didn't want them hearing Greg call them tenants.

"Come on, Greg, seriously, why are you here right now? We've had a long day, and Marco is sleeping, and all the girls are tired. Just go home, okay?" His arms crossed defiantly over his chest, reminding her of the childish antics Sammy exhibited when things weren't going her way.

"Me get serious? I find it interesting that you're so shocked I would have an interest in meeting the people now living in the same house as my daughters."

"I'm not suggesting that you shouldn't have an interest," she countered. "I'm merely trying to express that it's been a long twenty-four hours, and that everybody is tired and adjusting. I just don't know if now is the best time." Greg's face started to flush.

"I have every right to be introduced, and you know it. I should have met them before this even took place, if you want to know what I think. Fact is, Myra, I'm not leaving until I do, so you may as well just let me in now so we don't have to start a big scene." Myra could feel her anger mounting, but exploding on him would do no good. Technically, he was right; who was she to tell him that he couldn't meet them? She only wished he had called so she could be more prepared. Her reserve draining, she threw up her hands in exasperation.

"Fine, Greg, I'm not going to fight with you. In the future, though, please don't show up here unannounced. You know I'm perfectly willing to let you meet the kids, but they just got here yesterday and there is a huge adjustment going on. I'm just asking you to respect that, if not for me, then for your daughters." Greg made a little huffing noise as he pushed past her to the garage, waiting impatiently by the car for her to open the door and officially invite him inside. What a pompous asshole, she thought.

It was disconcerting to see his shoes kicked off by the garage entry door and to watch him roaming around the kitchen as if he still owned the place. She felt herself flinch as he opened a cabinet, grabbed a cup, and walked to the fridge to fill it with water. He felt her staring as he lifted the cup to his mouth and took a long, slow gulp.

"You don't mind, do you?" he mocked. She just stood there, feeling there was no point in responding. "Well, where should we do our introductions?" he asked.

"We can go into the living room, but do me a favor and lose the shitty attitude, okay? Don't you dare go making any of them feel uncomfortable, Greg. I mean it. I have no problem asking you to leave if I feel it's in everybody's best interest to do so." He narrowed his eyes at her.

"Right, Myra. Noted," he chuckled. "Scout's honor, I'll be on my best behavior."

Greg waited on the couch while Myra ran upstairs and gathered the girls. He would just have to wait to meet Marco until the next time. Sammy and Ella came down the steps first, bounding into the living room and throwing themselves into Greg's arms.

"Hi, Dad!" Ella said. "I'm glad you stopped by. We had so much fun today!" Greg smiled down at her and Myra had to give it to him: Despite the many undesirable traits she had seen in him lately, he adored those girls more than anything. Emilia and Carina lingered on the bottom steps as Greg and the kids finished their exchange. As they began to quiet down, Greg stood up and turned toward the Garcia children, waving them over with his right hand. They approached shyly, clearly uncomfortable at being put on the spot like this. Myra could feel the set of her jaw as she watched the whole scene. However, she was proud to see that Greg redeemed himself, at least in front of the girls. He extended his hand as they approached.

"Hi, there. I'm Sammy and Ella's dad, but you probably already figured that!" He laughed unnaturally loudly at himself. "You can call me Greg. You must be Emilia," he said, shaking her hand. "And you," he said, crouching down to be at eye level, "must be Carina. Everybody seems to be pretty excited to have you here," he said, gesturing off toward his daughters and Myra. "I'm happy to have you here, too. Are you settling in okay?" The two girls glanced back and forth from each other to Myra and back at Greg a few times before Carina spoke.

"Yes. Ms. Myra bought us some new clothes and toys today!" She smiled. "And my side of the room is painted purple."

"Purple, huh?" he asked. "Is that your favorite color?" Carina nodded excitedly. "Well, that's awesome! I can't wait to see it, but I know your brother is sleeping right now, right?" She nodded again, this time clearly disappointed and eager to show off her room. "Another time, okay? How about you, Emilia? Are you adjusting all right?" She nodded somberly. "I heard you inherited my office! Hopefully, it's a lot cleaner now that you're in there. It was a big old mess when I used to hang out in it." He offered her his biggest smile, but it was clear she was not convinced of his authenticity. "Can I see it?"

Myra could feel her hesitate and felt angry all over again with Greg. How dare he waltz in here and make them feel obligated to share anything with them? Before Emilia could answer, she interjected.

"Maybe another time. We just got back from shopping, and she hasn't been able to get anything out of her bags yet. I'm sure she'd like to feel more settled before she shows you, right, Emilia?" Emilia nodded graciously. "Okay, well, you've met everybody but Marco, so I guess we will see you next weekend when you come to get the girls, yeah?" Greg shot her a sideways glance, overtly annoyed at being shuffled from the house.

"All right. It was nice to meet you and good to see my two little ladies," he said, nodding at the Garcia girls and hugging his daughters. "I'm just going to talk to your mom for a minute in the kitchen, and then I'll be out of here. See you girls next weekend!" He motioned for Myra to join him in the kitchen as the girls shuffled off in different directions. When it was clear they were alone, she could feel the tension rise between them.

"What the hell was that, Myra?" he fumed. "I was just asking them a few questions and trying to get to know them. I don't need you undermining me by answering for them. If they're going to live in this house, they need to be able to carry on a conversation with me, don't you think?" Myra's lips were pursed in irritation.

"I do agree with that, Greg. However, I think you are forgetting that they haven't even been here for a day. They aren't even comfortable talking to me and the girls yet, and I just don't want them feeling obligated to you at all. I already told you I thought it was ballsy of you to even show up unannounced in the first place." Greg let a big breath of air out through his teeth like a hissing sound.

"Ballsy?" He exclaimed. "Myra, this whole thing is ballsy. I don't think I need to express again to you what a stupid idea I think the entire mess is." Myra's spine straightened.

"Lower your voice, Greg." But he only continued to get louder and more passionate in his outburst.

"Let's just hope you've got this one right, Myra. We all know what good decisions you're capable of making. I know you had to do something drastic to subdue your remorse, but this is still blowing my fucking mind. I can tell you with conviction that I will stop by here anytime I goddamn well please to check on the well-being of my daughters with these ... these ... fucking ragamuffins you've decided to house." Myra heard footsteps shuffle across the floor outside of the kitchen, followed by the light slamming of a door. She panicked as she wondered which one of the children had heard his terrible rant. She had the strong inclination to slap him hard across the face but remembered just in time that he was a lawyer and would have no problem taking her to court and getting a ruling that she was abusive and unfit to foster the children any longer. Her cheeks burning, she hissed at him through gritted teeth.

"Get out of my house, NOW!" She was on him before he could speak, shuffling him by the lower back toward the side door and forcefully ejecting him through it. He was so taken aback that he didn't even resist. She picked up his shoes one after another and hurled them all the way out of the garage door and into the driveway, pinging the BMW's hood with the second. He stormed out of the garage, still grumbling about something, but she didn't hear a word as the heavy garage door rumbled closed behind him.

It took Myra several minutes to compose herself enough to go in search of the eavesdropper. Her gut already knew it had to have been Emilia, as she had seen the three others going up the stairs as she and Greg had walked into the kitchen, but her head was begging her gut to be wrong. They had made progress today—however small—and it terrified her to think that it had been for nothing. She racked her brain to come up with the words she would say to Emilia that might explain away Greg's irrational behavior, but she knew that nothing she said could erase his tone as he ejected the cruel phrase, labeling them "ragamuffins." She took some deep breaths to slow the pounding of her heart before walking out of the kitchen toward Emilia's room. The shopping bags from the day's excursion had been thrown outside of the French doors, spilling some of the contents onto the tile. Myra shook her head sadly, knowing now for certain. She knocked softly on the door.

"Emilia?" She asked quietly.

"Go away. Please, just go away," Emilia sniffled.

"Emilia, please, just let me talk to you, okay?" She felt terrible, desperate to make it right.

"No. Please just leave me alone. And take your things back. I don't need them, and I don't want them!" she sputtered Myra slumped down toward the ground in defeat, her arms hanging limply toward the floor, tucking the spilled items back into the bags.

"He didn't mean it, Emilia. He's mad at me, not you." Silence. She began to speak again, but it seemed so useless. She would just have to give it time and hope that Emilia could move past yet another one of her mistakes. This time, however, she wasn't going to take the blame for Greg.

CHAPTER 24

The week that followed felt torturous for Myra. Every suggestion or comment she made was met with a snide remark or filthy look from Emilia. The shopping bags still sat outside of the French doors, stuffed to the brims with the items they had purchased on their trip to the mall. Sammy had dared comment on them one morning at breakfast.

"Why haven't you taken the tags off your new clothes, Emilia?" she asked casually. "You should wear that green sweater to school this week. It looked so pretty on you." Emilia's eyes filled with daggers.

"No, thank you, Sammy. I much prefer to go to school looking like the ragamuffin that I clearly am." Sammy, having not been privy to the conversation between Myra and her father, was clearly confused.

"Um ... okay ... I guess." She mumbled something under her breath, finished her breakfast, and excused herself from the table. Emilia and the other children followed suit and Myra was left standing alone in the dining room, picking up bowls and cups, shaking her head, and wondering if this arrangement was ever going to get back on course.

The following Saturday morning Greg was at the front door to pick up Sammy and Ella. Myra didn't bother to invite him in, but once the door was closed behind them, the realization that she was alone with the Garcia children for two full days hit her like a freight train.

"Well," she mumbled to herself, "time to make lemonade out of some very sour lemons. All I can do is focus my attention on the little ones and hope the weekend goes off without a hitch." She became aware of someone standing behind her and turned around, surprised to see Emilia shadowing her, arms crossed over her chest in her usual manner. "Oh, hi, Emilia, you startled me."

"No point in trying to squeeze this sour lemon. I promise you that you won't find anything sweet inside. By now, I think we both realize that we aren't going to get along, so let's stop pretending, okay? You can focus whatever attention you want on my brother and sister. In fact, they need it very much, but I don't. I needed you to keep my family together, and you've done that. Beyond that, there is nothing I need from you, especially your attention, so let's just keep that clear." Myra threw her hands up in the air, exhausted from playing this back-and-forth game with her.

"Emilia, I don't know what you want me to do. I really thought we made some headway last week until my ex-husband came over. I know what he said was hurtful, but you can't keep making me and the girls pay for it. I didn't say it, and I don't believe it. What can I do to show you that?"

"You haven't paid for anything you've done, Ms. Jenkins. I have. Me and my family. Maybe if you could stop feeling bad for yourself for five minutes, you would see that!" Emilia fumed. It was too much for Myra. She felt herself getting angry all over again at the situation: at Greg, at her perceived role in the whole thing, at the fact that she had never righted the inaccuracies in the story. All of it came bubbling over.

"You have *no* idea what I have gone through, Emilia. None, whatsoever. I have gone above and beyond to try to make what happened as right as I can possibly make it, but I'm human. I can't magically bring your parents back. I can't erase the past, and I can't feel like a prisoner in my own home because you hate me." Her hand flew to her curls, the nervous habit she hadn't succumbed to in months suddenly reappearing with a vengeance. She rolled her eyes up to the ceiling, exasperated. "Maybe this was a bad idea. Maybe Greg was right when he told me that you wouldn't forgive me and this could never work." She looked Emilia in the eye. "I don't know what else to do or how I can try any harder than to keep doing what I'm doing. I ask you to remember that it was you who showed up on my doorstep with this idea, not the other way around. You have me surrounded, Emilia. I throw my hands up! I don't know what you want from me." She could feel the tears coming and willed them to stay put behind her eyes. She wouldn't give her the satisfaction. Just then, Marco and Carina caught her eye, their little faces peeking out through the railing at the top of the steps. Emilia followed her gaze and a worried expression fell across her face.

"Marco, Carina, come down here. It's okay. Ms. Myra and I were only talking. We didn't mean to startle you." Myra let her handle it, happy for once—as immature as it might be—to see somebody else having to do the explaining. Marco had started to cry, running off into his bedroom, and Carina stood up, looking down on the two of them.

"He's afraid you're going to make us go back, Ms. Myra," she said, worry casting a shadow over her face. Her gaze turned to Emilia. "And he says it's your fault, Emilia." She shook her head sadly. "Why can't you just be nice?" She turned in the direction of her bedroom to go comfort her brother.

Emilia and Myra stood facing each other, discomfort creeping in to replace the anger. Emilia's face was flushed with ... with what? Myra couldn't tell for sure, but she thought maybe embarrassment. Oddly, Myra's complexion had gone a different route, the color draining from her face as she realized the impact of their argument. She had meant what she said. Maybe this *was* wrong. She certainly couldn't become a victim of circumstance, nor would she allow her daughters to feel that way. But then, how would she ever recover if she had to break her promise to poor little Marco and Carina? What would happen to them? She knew right away that she needed to call a meeting with Amanda.

***

It had been an interesting weekend, to say the least, Emilia and Myra tiptoeing around each other in a graceless dance. Monday afternoon couldn't come fast enough. Once the older girls arrived home from school and could watch over the younger children, she rushed out the door and headed to the family center building. Amanda greeted Myra with an enthusiastic embrace, and Myra felt her resolve crumble instantly. When they pulled away, Amanda's expression changed, noting the sadness on Myra's face.

"Uh-oh. Come on, let's get into my office where we can have some privacy." Myra nodded consent and followed her down the hallway into the office. She plopped down into the familiar chair, dropping her purse onto the floor beside her. "Now," started Amanda, "why so glum? Trouble on the home front, I'm assuming?" Myra dropped her forehead into her hands, nodding in defeat.

"So much trouble!" she replied, lifting her chin to rest in her palm. "I don't know what to do, Amanda. She freaking hates me! It's like everything I do, everything I say, she fights me on it." Amanda chuckled in response.

"Well, that's teenagers for you." Myra shook her head.

"No, it's not that. It's bigger than that. She just has so much anger harbored toward me. Why did I ever think this was going to be a good idea? I feel like an idiot and a failure." She couldn't help it now. She let the tears come rushing down her cheeks. She felt Amanda reach across the desk for her hands.

"Myra, listen to me for a moment. You knew that this wasn't going to be easy. You said so yourself on several occasions throughout the application process. You have been interviewed, researched, psychologized, background-checked, investigated, you name it, and you know what? Everybody came to the same conclusion, that you were *more* than capable of doing this, that you could more than provide them with a loving, nurturing, and safe environment, and that you were either superhuman or batshit crazy to take it on." Myra stopped crying long enough to let out a chuckle, and Amanda matched it with her own. "Lucky for you, they settled on superhuman, and so here you are, taking on a small army of children, and it's not going to be easy. To go right for the cliché, if it were easy, everybody would do it. You are not everybody, Myra. You are a strong, capable, extremely brave woman who clearly does not give up very easily. You *can* do this ... you just have to continue to believe in yourself and give it all you've got. It's only been a week. She'll come around." Myra sniffled and wiped her nose with a tissue.

"You promise?" Amanda squeezed her hands.

"I believe it. Now you have to," she encouraged. They chatted back and forth for a while longer, Amanda listening patiently as Myra filled her in on the goings-on of the past week. Amanda offered her advice and even agreed, off the record, that Greg was a real asshole, which made Myra feel oddly better for some reason. By the time she walked back down the front steps of the building to her car, she felt clearheaded, calm, and confident in her decision once again. She was ready for whatever round two would bring.

Myra walked into the house to the smell of something delicious. The kitchen was empty, but a large pot sat atop the stove, clearly the source of the enticing aroma. She hung her purse in its place and walked over, lifting the lid to reveal a white broth with chicken and vegetables. Curious, she walked through the kitchen and into the living room, noticing that the bags of clothing had been removed from outside of Emilia's doors. One door hung open, and she peeked in, but nobody was there. She heard whispers coming from the top of the steps and slowly crept up one stair at a time. She reached the top of the staircase and peeked around the corner to see Marco and Carina hunched together outside of the closet.

"Hi guys, what's going on?" They both whipped around, clearly startled, and Carina pressed her finger to her lips.

"Shhh. We're playing hide-and-go-seek. We're listening to see if we can hear Emilia." She giggled.

"I did see her come in here!" Marco chimed in. "She thinks we don't know!" He let out a loud laugh and Carina whacked him on the arm.

"Shh. She's going to hear you, and then she'll run away!" Myra leaned against the wall to watch them, entirely amused by the whole scene. It was rare that she got to see all three of them interact playfully together. Marco and Carina crept closer and closer to the front of the closet, snickering and whispering, until finally—

"Yaaaaaaaaaaaaaaaaa!" Emilia howled, jumping out from inside the closet. Marco and Carina both squealed with happiness and ran from the room, almost knocking Myra over on the way out. Emilia smiled and walked from the room herself.

"They love to play this game. Mama used to play it with them all the time." She shrugged. Myra cleared her throat.

"Well, they definitely seem to be having fun. Thank you for holding the fort down for me while I was gone. Where are Ella and Sammy, and ... um ... are you cooking?" she asked, motioning down the stairs toward the kitchen. Emilia's eyes widened.

"Oh, yes, I'm sorry about that. I didn't think you would mind," she said, stumbling over her words. "Marco said he missed Mama's cooking, and this is one of the few recipes I remember off the top of my head. I thought maybe, if it was okay, we could eat it for dinner tonight." Myra smiled gently.

"I think that would be a lovely idea. Do you mind if I ask what it is you are making?" Emilia nodded.

"It's called chicken pozole ... it's like a stew. Mama used to make it every Christmas. This is the same recipe her Mama used to make for her, and her Mama before that. I hope you will like it." Carina and Marco reappeared, Sammy and Ella in tow, all of them out of breath from laughing.

"It's so yummy, Ms. Myra." Marco exclaimed.

The stew was even more delicious than it smelled, and Myra listened happily as Marco and Carina chatted on about all the other traditional Mexican foods their mother had been so fond of preparing. Emilia just sat and listened, clearly proud of how well both of her siblings remembered their parents. They had been so young when they passed, and Myra was sure that Emilia had gone to great lengths to keep their memory alive and fresh in both of them.

CHAPTER 25

Myra sat in the dining room one morning, poring over her un-
checked mail. It was hard to believe, but a month had already
passed with the Garcia children living under the same roof.
She had vacillated all month long over whether or not this had
been the best decision. Just when she felt things were beginning to get better, she and Emilia would inevitably have an
encounter, and she would find herself questioning it all over
again. She was mentally drained, and her determination to
win over Emilia was fading fast. Sammy and Ella seemed
equally passionless at furthering their efforts, having been met
with resistance too many times. The tension between her family and Emilia was palpable, and she wondered how much
longer she would be able to keep up this illusion. The life she
had hoped to breathe back into the house was withering
quickly, its song fading back into the shadows of unease and
discomfort.

These thoughts kept creeping in, distracting her from the
letters and bills before her. She threw down an envelope in

frustration and dropped her head down into her hands, letting out an agitated growl. Her mind sifted through the memories of the past few weeks. It seemed as though every insult Emilia had hurled at her was cycling on repeat, wearing her down.

"Please remember that I am their big sister, soon to be their legal guardian, Ms. Myra," she had said when Myra had suggested perhaps Marco was going to bed too late. Similarly, when Carina had expressed an interest in taking ballet lessons at school and Myra had encouraged it, Emilia had stated, "Let's not get her involved in something that she might not be able to continue once we've left here. I'm not sure I should be committing to anything until I know what our situation will be." Her last confrontation with Emilia had been just that morning, over something as minuscule as how much cereal she had poured into Marco's bowl. Emilia had insisted that it was too much for her little brother and that Myra was putting unfair expectations on him, and that she would never expect him to eat that much. If that wasn't reaching, she didn't know what was. Not to mention that Marco had been happily chomping, blissfully unaware of the entire exchange. It was exhausting trying to redirect all of these petty arguments and keep her cool in the process. Emilia would take any and every opportunity she could to remind Myra that this was a temporary situation and that her part in the "favor" would eventually be over. It angered Myra in so many ways, not only because she was constantly being undermined in front of the little ones, or because naturally Carina and Marco thought their sister knew best, or even because she truly wanted them both to have opportunities that she could afford to give them. It was more than that. It was because every single time Emilia threw these little jabs, it felt as though she were issuing a warning for Myra to not get too close.

And it was working. Every time Marco or Carina did something, or said something, or smiled and laughed in a way that made her heart melt, it was accompanied by a pang of fear and sadness, knowing that they would be taken away as soon as Emilia had the opportunity to do so. Every time charming, funny little Marco danced his way across the living room, causing them all to fall into a fit of giggles, she would catch herself and tuck the love that she felt for him away, desperately afraid of feeling loss again. Every time sweet, caring Carina ran up behind her and squeezed her in a giant embrace, she felt the hesitation creep in, all the while knowing she wanted to scoop the little girl up into her arms and twirl her around the house. She just couldn't let herself fall in love with these little souls who would surely be whisked away from her.

Ella and Sammy were not so guarded. They were over the moon in love with the two children, and who could blame them? Myra felt a heaviness settle over her chest every time she thought about what the separation was going to do to her poor daughters. Somehow, Myra had convinced herself that the six of them would become a loving family, and the mistake in this was becoming gravely apparent. What would the girls say? What would Greg say (though she hated to admit she cared)? She had been so enchanted with her idealistic vision of the future that she had neglected to include this very important detail of the agreement she and Emilia had initially discussed. She had been so swept up in the fostering process that she had almost forgotten it herself, but Emilia had made it clear that she would not allow it to be forgotten.

Now, as she sat here recounting even more mistakes she would have to make right, she felt old and weary and broken. Before they knew it, summer would come and go, to be replaced by a new school year and then, just as the joy and promise of the holiday season would be approaching, Emilia would turn eighteen at the end of November and their world would turn upside down all over again. Emilia would move out and go to great lengths to have her siblings as much as possible, to keep them from Myra and the girls, and to undo all the structure that Myra had been working to give them. Essentially, they had eight months together— just enough time to form bonds. She felt nausea creeping up on her.

***

Myra was up in her room when she heard the front door slam open, and the sound of Sammy, Ella, and Emilia arguing permeated the silence of the house.

"You're a total jerk!" Sammy screamed.

"Sammy, stop!" Ella attempted

"I didn't do anything to you, Sammy!" countered Emilia. Myra, glad that the little ones were still at school and not around to witness this, came peeling down the stairs two at a time.

"Whoa, whoa, whoa, ladies! What is the problem?" Sammy's face was red and puffy from crying, a shiny stream of mucus running from her left nostril.

"*She* is the problem!" she screamed, pointing her finger accusingly at Emilia. "She's a jerk and a bully!" Myra pulled Sammy to her and smoothed her hand over the top of her head.

"Okay, take a couple of breaths and we can talk about it. Just breathe for a minute and get yourself together." She looked at Ella.

"What happened?" Ella threw her hands up in aggravation.

"I mean, she's right, Mom. Sorry, Emilia," she offered, "but that was totally not cool." Myra raised her eyebrows, waiting for an explanation from anybody at all. "Sammy was getting picked on in the hallway by a couple of older kids at the end of school. They were calling her names and circling around her, just being really nasty. I came around the corner to head out

166

to our bus line and saw the end of it. I walked over and got them to leave her alone." Ella looked pityingly at her sister.

"So what does that have to do with you, Emilia?" Myra asked. Emilia did her typical shrug in response, and Myra felt Sammy pull away from her.

"Yeah, Emilia, why don't you tell her how you just sat there leaning up against your locker, watching the whole thing? Why don't you tell her about the big, happy smile you had on your face while they told me I was the daughter of a murderer and that you were going to kill us all in our sleep as sweet revenge?" Myra tried to calm her, but Sammy pushed her away and took another step toward Emilia. "You know what? We were so excited to have you come and live with us. Ella and I talked about it every day, about how much fun it would be to have an older sister. We wondered what you would be like and we talked about all the cool stuff we could do together." A sob escaped her throat, and she hiccupped it back. "But you know what? You're just a jerk. You're a mean, angry jerk with a bad attitude and the personality of a … a … a shoe!" She whipped her backpack off and flung it across the space between them, hitting Emilia hard in the right shoulder. "Maybe you should just go back where you came from!" With that, she stormed up the stairs, into her bedroom, and slammed the door behind her. Myra took a deep breath before turning back to face the oldest girls.

"Ella, thank you for telling me the story and for helping your sister out. Emilia, we will talk shortly."

"I didn't do any- —" Emilia began defensively.

"Enough!" Myra put her hand up. "I don't want to hear it. Right now, I have some damage control to do and I will be down shortly." She left the two girls standing at the bottom of the stairs to marinate in her anger and went up to calm down Sammy.

Forty-six minutes, one box of tissues, and countless curse

words later, Myra emerged from Sammy's room, leaving her exhausted daughter to rest on her bed. Poor Sammy, who had come so far in the past few months, once again cast into the fires that had been ignited all around her by the actions of one night. Ella emerged from her room when she heard Sammy's door click shut.

"Mom?" she asked. Myra turned to face her. "I'm really sorry that I didn't get there sooner. I was back in class talking to my teacher about a project I have due, and—"

"Shh." Myra cut her off. "It's not your fault. Go finish your homework, honey. I have to pick up the kids. I'll be back in a bit, okay? Ella nodded. Myra padded down the stairs and rapped three times on Emilia's door.

"Yes?" Came the response.

"Get your shoes on, please. I'd like you to come with me to pick up your brother and sister. I'll meet you in the car." Without waiting for an answer, she walked through the kitchen and out the garage door and turned on the Land Rover to wait.

Emilia opened the door and slipped into the passenger seat quietly, her face and posture void of any sign of emotion. She clipped her seat belt without a word and stared ahead through the windshield. Myra backed the car out of the garage and slowly down the long drive and out onto the road. The silence in the car was deafening, yet neither made any effort to speak. Finally, feeling clear in thought and emotion, Myra punctured the silence. Her voice was flat.

"There were a lot of people who thought I was crazy when I told them I was going to try to foster the three of you." She gave a small sniff. "Hell, I thought I was crazy half the time, but you know what? I decided to do it anyway. I didn't decide to do it because of guilt or shame. I didn't decide to do it because I pitied you, or even necessarily because of the sad thought of the three of you being separated. I didn't do it because I'm a particularly nice person, or because I felt I owed it to you, although I'm sure that all of these factors played a small part. Do you know why I did it, Emilia?" Silence. "I did it because of my girls. I did it because when I brought the idea up to them after you came to visit me, not only did they agree without hesitation, they did it with so much excitement and enthusiasm that it blew my mind. Not once did they consider it might be hard adjusting to having three new personalities in the house or that they might have to share the time they spend with me. Not once did they voice concern over how it would inevitably change our schedules with five sets of after-school activities and interests. Not once did they worry about sharing TV time or computer time or about losing the guest bedroom so that when their grandma comes into town, they will likely have to share a room. Not once.

"I was the one who worried about these things, and they worked diligently to talk me out of every fear or hesitation that I came up with, coming up with creative solutions to all of it. They dove right in, clearing out space, painting, decorating, food shopping! I was so impressed with how big their hearts were and how amazingly open they were to the idea of sharing their entire life with three strangers that I realized I was the one being crazy, not them, because people should lift each other up and help each other out. That, Emilia, is why I went through this entire process, and you know what? I'm glad that I did because it's taught me a lot about myself.

"First and foremost, it's taught me what amazing young women I have somehow raised even through all of my faults, and it's also taught me how very much they mean to me. So, that being said, I'd like to address what happened at school today." She paused, giving Emilia a chance to respond, but was met with nothing.

"Time and time again, since you moved in, I have tried to talk to you, to convince you that I'm doing my best and trying my hardest, to no avail, and I understand that. I get why you

169

are angry with me and why you don't trust me and why you dislike me, and I have accepted that. My girls, however, are a different story, as innocent, unassuming, and deeply wounded by this accident as you are . Their family was broken through this too, just in a different manner. You can no more understand what they are going through than they can understand what you are going through because none of you has walked a day in the others' shoes. They adored you before they even met you, Emilia. You can hurt me and try to derail me as much as you'd like, but don't you dare do it to my girls. They have been your biggest fans and your biggest supporters throughout this process, whether you know it or not. I'm not suggesting that you all have to be best friends, but you know just as well as I do that Sammy did nothing to cause the pain that you have gone through, and for you to find joy in watching her suffer doesn't serve anybody.

"Like it or not, Emilia, we all agreed to this, and November is a long way off. Until then, you are stuck living with me, and, even afterward, your brother and sister will remain in my care for three years before you can legally adopt them. It would be appreciated if you would at least try to put forth an effort with the girls until that point. I don't want to talk about this anymore after we get out of this car. I've spoken with Sammy and I know she is hurt, but she really does still want to be your friend. I can't promise what her reaction will be tonight when you see her back at the house, but I have her word that she will talk to you calmly and kindly if you two choose to discuss it, and I'd like that same promise from you. I don't want any more animosity in this house. It's been going on for a month now and I won't have it any longer. There are six of us living there and each of us deserves to be considered. We're about to pull up to the school and Carina and Marco will be waiting outside, so if you have anything to say, let's do it now, okay?" There were a few moments of silence, and Myra glanced over at Emilia's profile, noticing a single tear rolling down her cheek, which she quickly wiped away.

"I understand, Myra. I'm sorry that I hurt her. I don't know what I was thinking. It wasn't fair. You have my promise that I will be more thoughtful of their feelings."

"Thank you. It means a lot," Myra acknowledged as they turned into the school lot.

CHAPTER 26

Once all the kids were settled into bed, Myra poured herself a glass of wine and sat down at the dining room table, focusing on the steady tick of the clock. She replayed her conversation with Emilia over and over again, searching her response for any sign of sarcasm, happy when she was unable to find one. For the umpteenth time, she found herself hoping that perhaps they had rounded the corner. Although her faith in this was plagued with uncertainty, she couldn't help but wonder if she hadn't finally gotten her point across that she was not a terrible person—or at the very least that her children were completely innocent. She felt herself craving guidance from somebody who might understand her plight and reached for her phone. She wanted to talk to her mother, the only person who knew the truth and might therefore be able to relate to the anger she was experiencing. Initially, she had chastised Myra for not speaking up about Greg's involvement, but Myra had been quick to remind her how many times she had been there to protect her own husband in Myra's youth. Her father, a diehard workaholic, was constantly in search of excuses, and Myra's mother was always more than happy to provide them.

"Daddy couldn't make your recital because he just closed a huge deal at work, and they are throwing a party for him! Isn't that wonderful?" her mother would exclaim joyfully, clasping her hands together as though Myra should be as excited as she was at the new opportunity. Eventually, as Myra grew, she began to notice how her mother's eyes glazed over with a light dusting of tears or the corners of her mouth turned down ever so slightly each time she had to deliver these blows to her daughter, but it never stopped her from doing it. Myra was taught that family was family, and family members protected one another—good or bad, right or wrong—even if it was at your own expense.

Given that type of upbringing, Myra didn't feel her mother had any say in the situation, and clearly, her mother agreed, as it was never brought up between them again.

But tonight was different. She needed to speak frankly with somebody without consequence. She found her mother on speed dial and hit the call button.

"Hello?" Myra felt herself instantly dissolving into the sound of her mother's familiar voice.

"Hi, Mom."

"Hey there, little lady. How are my favorite girls?" Myra sighed, trying not to burst into tears before she even got out a full sentence. "You sound stressed out. Want to talk about it?"

"Ugh ... yes ... and no ... but yes! I'm going to lose my mind if I don't. Mom, this is so much harder than I bargained for. Not just on me, but the girls, too. Something really crappy happened at school today and poor Sammy —shit, Mom. I just feel awful." She heard her mother take a deep breath on the other end of the line.

"Myra, you know I love you, right?" Oh geez, where was this going? "I told you this might not work out the way you or the girls thought it would. Can we admit that it was a little over-romanticized?" Myra rolled her eyes. This was *not* what she needed right now.

"Mom, yeah, I get that, okay? I'm not calling to be berated though ... I really just need you to listen. The fact is, I did it, and now I'm in it, so looking back on my potentially poor decisions isn't going to do anything other than make me feel more like shit than I already do. Can you do that? Can you please just listen and let me vent?" Her mother gave a little chuckle.

"I suppose I can probably do that for you, Pea." Ever since Myra could remember her mother had had this pet name for her. While it usually bothered her, tonight it eased her tension.

"Thank you, Mom."

She proceeded to fill her mother in on all the details of the past month. Although she had spoken to her several times since the arrival of the Garcia children, she had been sure each time to keep it light and positive, refusing to let on that there might be any problems. By the time she had finished speaking about the events earlier that afternoon, her voice had broken and she was in full-on tears. She let herself cry as she awaited her mother's response on the other line. "Well," she choked, "say something! Tell me I'm an idiot and I'm fucking my daughters up. Tell me I made another huge mistake! Go ahead! Honestly, Mom, at this point it doesn't matter, right?" Her shoulders heaved with all the anger, sadness, and anxiety she had felt over the past year and a half.

"Myra, I'm not going to tell you that you're an idiot because you're not. You have done what you can to make the best out of a very difficult series of events, and I commend you for that. What I am going to suggest to you is that maybe it's time to tell the truth." Myra, just finishing her second glass of wine at this point, let out a puff of air and topped off her glass.

"Oh, yeah, that would go over well!" She laughed. "I'm

sure that would be very believable."

"Myra, truly! If she just knew the whole story—"

"C'mon, Mom ... if she knew the whole story she would tell me I was full of shit, just like everybody else would. What person in their right mind takes the blame for something of this magnitude, only to change her story almost eighteen months later? It's bullshit! You see it on the news all the time, people accused of crimes getting off free and then working even harder to prove their innocence to evade the social stigma. I won't be that, Mom, I can't be that. Nobody ever believes that guy!" She sobbed. "I made my bed and I'm going to have to lie in it." The weight of it battered her like a ton of bricks. "I created this scenario one way or another, Mom. I may not be guilty of the crime the way it was reported, but I'm certainly guilty of taking the blame." Her body collapsed into a string of tears and it suddenly felt hard to breathe.

"Myra," her mother attempted, "breathe, baby. Blame or no blame, the fact remains that it wasn't you. I know I made the mistake of covering for your father all those years, but don't make the same mistakes as me. Be better than that, because you deserve it, and the girls deserve it. All of those kids deserve to know the truth, and you deserve to tell it." Myra wanted to believe her, but by the same token, she knew it was too late for all of that. The anger and frustration boiled over, only further fueled by the wine.

"You're right, Mom, that's what I'll do. I'll just sit them all down at breakfast tomorrow and let them know." She laughed sarcastically. "I can see it now. 'Girls, Garcias, I have an admission to make. I know it seems unlikely, but in all honesty, it was your father who caused the accident that led to the Garcia parents' deaths, and I only took the blame to protect our family. I had no idea the impact my lie would actually have. By the way, we're having lasagna for dinner. Anybody opposed?'" She giggled unnaturally, becoming acutely aware that she sounded half mad.

"Myra, have you been drinking? I think you should go to bed." That was literally the last thing she needed to hear as she threw back the remainder of her third glass of wine.

"Wouldn't you be? Have you been listening at all? Aw, forget it, Mom. I've got to go. I love you. Good night!" She pressed the red button on her phone and chucked it across the dining room table. "Fucking perfect!" she slurred.

***

Myra woke abruptly and peered around her in confusion. It took her only a moment to realize she had fallen asleep on the couch, drowsy from the wine. A blanket had been placed over her, and she felt slightly embarrassed, noting the empty wine glass on the coffee table next to her. She imagined one of the girls must have gotten up for water in the middle of the night and tried to wake her. She glanced at her Cartier: 3:36 a.m. She'd better get upstairs.

THE SONG OF
FLOWERS

CHAPTER 27

The following morning, nobody made mention of her passing out on the couch, so, naturally, she didn't bring it up either. It didn't go unnoticed that Emilia, though still quiet and detached, was unusually helpful, clearing the breakfast dishes from the table and loading up the dishwasher. Myra was pleased with the shift, sure now that their conversation had had some sort of impact, however fleeting it might be. At one point, Myra watched Emilia open her mouth to critique the way Myra was braiding Carina's hair. She paused, however, seemed to think better of it, and walked from the room.

Myra felt for the very first time since Emilia's arrival that she had some semblance of the upper hand, but she certainly wasn't convinced of it. She had gotten her hopes up so many times only to watch them deflate before her eyes, that she made an internal pact to move through the next few days erring on the side of caution with any civil gestures Emilia tossed her way. Her actions over the next weeks would speak more loudly than any niceties from her mouth.

By the weekend, things were still going smoothly, and Myra felt herself relaxing ever so slightly. On Saturday morning she came into the kitchen to see Emilia standing at the dining room slider, looking out over the backyard toward the lake.

"Good morning, Emilia." She jumped, startled by Myra's voice.

"Oh, good morning."

"I'm sorry. I didn't mean to startle you! What are you looking at?" A self-conscious smile passed over Emilia's face.

"Oh, I was just watching Sammy play." Myra, taken aback, looked at her watch: 9:10 on a Saturday and Sammy was not only up but outside?

"Sammy's out there? Playing what? She's never up this early on a weekend."

"I came in to get some water a while ago and saw her out there kicking around her soccer ball. She is really good." Myra came up to stand next to her. She sipped her coffee as they watched out the slider together. Sammy had her lucky soccer ball bouncing from knee to knee before letting it skillfully slip down to her foot, tapping it meticulously across the expanse of lawn, and shooting it into her makeshift goal post.

"Yeah, she's pretty incredible. I think it's what keeps her sane. She's always the happiest when she's on the field. Season starts officially in May, but now that it's getting warm, she'll be out there every single day. Do you play?" Emilia dropped her gaze.

"I did. I mean, I used to."

"Oh, yeah?" Myra asked. "That's great. Why did you stop?" Emilia took a deep breath and Myra instantly knew the answer to that question and regretted asking.

"It just wasn't as fun when there was nobody there to cheer for me, you know?" Myra took another sip.

"I can imagine that was very difficult, Emilia." There were

a few moments of awkward silence before she spoke again. "I know it wouldn't be the same, but if you were to sign up for the upcoming season, I know we would all come cheer for you." Emilia seemed instantly flustered.

"Oh, that's very nice of you, but it's been so long. I'm probably not even very good anymore." She shifted uncomfortably from one foot to the other.

"I'm sure it's like riding a bike," said Myra. "Either way, you never know unless you try. You should go out and play with her."

"I don't know," replied Emilia. "She's still pretty mad at me about school."

"Well, once again, you never know unless you try, right?" With that, Myra patted her on the back and walked off through the house to find the other kids.

She found Marco and Carina snuggling with Ella in bed watching Saturday morning cartoons and thought what a beautiful picture it would be. She told them they had another half an hour before it was time to get up and get started with the day and wandered off into her bedroom to take a hot shower.

She emerged feeling refreshed and awake, which was only furthered by the beautiful spring weather she viewed out of her bedroom window. She walked to her dresser, wrapped in her bathrobe, pausing to get a closer look at the lake. It was a sight that had always brought her joy since the day that she and Greg bought the house. She thought back to the day.

They had been looking for months, determined to find the perfect house to start their family in, but time was running short. They pulled up the long drive to a house far larger than anything Myra had been anticipating.

"Greg, this is way too much house for us!" she protested, but already she could see that he was in love and they hadn't even opened the front door. He got out of the car and walked around to the passenger side, opening her door and extracting her eight-and-a-half-month pregnant self through the opening.

"No way, baby! This is exactly what we need. It says here it's 3,500 square feet, four beds, three and a half baths, with an office, vaulted ceilings in the main living space, a gourmet kitchen, and lake views!" he exclaimed excitedly, referencing the sheet their Realtor had provided. She giggled at his enthusiasm.

"What are we going to do with 3,500 square feet? We're coming from a 900-square-foot apartment!" she laughed. "What are we going to fill all that space with, and who do you think is going to clean all of it?" He smiled and planted a big kiss on her cheek.

"We'll hire a cleaning lady, beautiful wife! You know why? Because that is one of the many benefits of being married to one of the best damned lawyers in Wisconsin. I promised you when we married that I was going to give you the life you deserved, and I'm making good on it, right?" She rolled her eyes playfully and took him by the hand.

"Come on, big shot, let's go inside." Upon entering, Myra had instantly felt overwhelmed. It felt cavernous and empty compared with their dinky apartment, and the thought of being alone in all this space with a brand-new baby terrified her. Greg, however, was visibly captivated as they wandered through the house room by room. It was everything the paper had promised, but something felt missing to Myra until they made their way upstairs. They checked out the three guest bedrooms, the Jack-and-Jill bath, and the disconnected full bath before entering the master suite. It was another huge, empty room with an equally huge, empty bathroom and huge, empty closet attached; but what caught her eye was the giant bay window at the far end of the room. She wandered over and touched the glass, instantly infatuated with the amazing lake view and knowing immediately that this was the view she wanted to wake up to every morning.

They signed the papers two weeks later, just days before Ella was born. Greg worked around the clock with the Realtor and her contractor, getting it painted and ready for move-in while Myra stayed back at the apartment with the newborn. They hired a decorator, a luxury Myra had never even considered until Greg suggested it, and, within a month, Myra was carrying her baby over the threshold of their beautiful new home. She cried when she walked in and saw that Greg had paid the contractor to blow out almost the entire length of the back wall, as well as a section in the dining room, and had it replaced with beautiful sliding glass doors so that she could have her amazing view from the entire downstairs. She had never felt so special, and she recalled that this was the first time she truly heard the joyous song of the house.

She was startled back to reality by the sound of the soccer ball nailing the side of the house. She looked down at the backyard and saw that Emilia and Sammy were taking turns seeing who could boot it the hardest. Sammy looked surprised as she high-fived Emilia, and Myra couldn't help but keep watching. They moved on to a game of scrimmage, with "goals" set up at either end of the lawn, and took turns trying to score on the other. Emilia was fast as lightning and clearly competent at working with the ball. Her feet moved so quickly that the ball became a blur between her feet, allowing her to score on Sammy every time she approached. Sammy just kept laughing and shaking her head, clearly impressed at Emilia's skill. Myra smiled to herself, glad to see that maybe the girls had found a way to relate to each other that didn't feel forced. They had struggled the most of all the children, and it felt promising to see them working it out in a way that obviously came so naturally to both of them.

The next week passed seamlessly. Every day after school

and homework, Myra would see Emilia and Sammy out back with the soccer ball. Some days she would notice one teaching the other some new skill, and she could almost see both of them visibly improving before her eyes. She had never seen Emilia talk so much or seem so animated. It was just like watching Sammy; she was so in her element.

Oftentimes, Ella and the two younger kids would go out and join for a while and the backyard would echo with their laughter and squealing. Myra would sit on the back patio sipping a cup of tea, watching them race back and forth across the yard, delighted with the whole scene. In these moments, the possibility of them all becoming a family would creep back up on her, but now she was quick to catch it and let it fall back into the shadows of her mind. She still wasn't quite ready to let her hope come back to life.

When Saturday morning rolled around, Greg called to say he was running a little bit late to get the girls. They left their bags ready by the front door, and, as was becoming their habit, headed out into the backyard with the Garcia children. The soccer ball was unearthed from the back shed and the laughter and play began. Myra rose from her observation chair only when she heard the doorbell ring. She opened the door, waving Greg in nonchalantly as she walked back toward the kitchen. He stood there for a moment, looking a little confused. They hadn't had many civil moments since the day he had unexpectedly shown up at the house, and he was surprised at her willingness to invite him in. He closed the door behind him and cleared his throat.

"Where are the girls?" he asked, glancing down to see their backpacks resting against the wall.

"Out back," Myra called from the kitchen. "I'll let them know you're here." He wandered in behind her, taking stock of the pictures covering both sides of the refrigerator.

"Nice artwork." He laughed, running a hand through his

silver hair. It appeared that he may have at some point realized that he had acted like an ass the last time he stood in this kitchen, as he seemed determined not to make the same mistake today. "Been a while since we had pictures of rainbows and stick figures up there, huh?" Myra nodded sentimentally, only mildly aware of his use of the word "we."

"Mm-hmm. It sure has. Marco and Carina like to color a lot. Usually, Ella sits and does it with them. I like it. It makes the fridge look so cheery." She could feel Greg watching her, and for the first time in a long time, it didn't make her feel uncomfortable. Let him watch her, judge her ... he was going to do what he wanted to do and view her in whatever light he chose to, so it seemed pointless to care too much. She was sick of trying to prove herself to everybody. She finished washing out her tea mug and set it upside down on a towel to dry. Greg wandered into the dining room toward the slider, and Myra followed him, noticing the slight cock of his head as he surveyed the scene on the lawn. She reached in front of him for the handle on the slider and he stepped back.

"Wow, they look like they're having a lot of fun together, huh?" he noted. Myra nodded as she slid the door open.

"Don't jinx it this time, okay?" she prodded. "It hasn't been an easy road to get to this point, and I'm starting to get used to it." She stepped onto the patio. "Girls, your father is here!"

"Aww, c'mon!" yelled Sammy. "Can't we have five more minutes?" Her face scrunched up in a pout, which made both Greg and Myra chuckle. She was the master of dirty looks.

"No, Sammy. You were supposed to leave forty-five minutes ago. I'm sure your dad has plans and..."

"No," Greg interrupted, "we don't have any plans. They can have a few more minutes if they want."

"Yes!" Sammy and Ella exclaimed in unison as the game resumed. Myra eyeballed Greg curiously, wondering whether or not she should trust this kinder side of him and where the hell it had come from.

"What?" he asked, feigning shock. "I'm not an asshole *all* the time, Myra. Listen, I owe you an..."

"Nope," she responded. "No, you don't. Don't even say it unless you mean it, Greg. You haven't given me an apology in upwards of three years, so there's no point in starting now unless it's 100 percent genuine. I mean it." She could feel her jaw stiffen, not even remotely ready to believe his sincerity given his recent actions.

"No, really," he responded, peering down at his feet. "I was a real jerk last time I was here. I know there's no excuse for it, but I was feeling really left out of the whole thing, and it just pissed me off. Still, I shouldn't have said what I said. Don't get me wrong," he rationalized. "I'm still not saying that I agree with all of this, but I could have thought it out a bit better." And there it was, a lawyer's apology, laden with just enough authenticity to make it believable to anybody who didn't know better, but still with enough wiggle room that he didn't *actually* have to admit real fault.

"Okay," Myra allowed with a slight roll of her eyes and a chuckle. "Half-assed apology accepted. Thanks for that. Probably should get going, Greg. I have to head to the grocery store, a pretty extensive task these days with six of us to feed. I'd like to be back by early afternoon so Marco can take some quiet time," she said, checking her watch. "He's not quite six, and he still gets pretty cranky if we go all day long with no downtime. You remember those days? Come on girls, five minutes are up!" she yelled out into the yard. The game broke up, and all five kids came marching up the steps, sweaty and winded. While Emilia sneered as she passed by Greg, Marco introduced himself to him with his big, characteristic grin spread across his adorable face. He extended his hand like the little mayor that he would inevitably become one day, and waited for Greg to return the gesture. Greg giggled, crouched down, and reached for his outstretched palm.

"Hola, Mr. Greg. My name is Marco. I'm five, but I'm going to be six in June. It's nice to meet you!"

"Well, aren't you a little man, then!" replied Greg. "It's very nice to meet you as well, sir," he said, shaking Marco's little hand enthusiastically before standing back up. "I think I should hire him to be the liaison between me and my clients. What do you think?" he laughed to Myra. She shook her head and laughed back, steering Marco back into the house.

CHAPTER 28

The house was calm and quiet as Marco and Carina played with Legos upstairs in their room. Emilia was lying on her bed, scribbling furiously in a notebook, her door actually left ajar for a change, when Myra walked into the living room and plopped down onto the couch with her book. She opened to the dog-eared page and settled into the cushions, promptly picking back up on the plot line where she had left off the night before. Typically, suspense wasn't her genre of choice when it came to leisurely reads, but this one had been recommended by her mother, and she had to admit she had been on the edge of her seat since the first page. She was flipping through the pages rapidly, thoroughly engrossed, when she heard Emilia clear her throat. She jumped a little, placing the book down on her chest. Emilia stood at the end of the couch, her long black hair cascading down over her shoulders. She was staring down at a scrap of paper in her hand, rolling it into a little ball with her thumb and pointer finger. Myra sat up further on the couch and swung her legs off to the side, patting the seat beside her.

"Hey, what's up? Everything okay?" Myra couldn't help but notice the apprehension on Emilia's face. "Come, sit down."

"No, that's okay," she replied emphatically. "I'll stand. I just ... I just had something that I wanted to tell you." Myra nodded slowly, her curiosity piqued.

"Okay, what's that?" She couldn't help but wonder if she was wandering into another trap. Things had been going so well, it almost seemed inevitable that the bottom should drop out now. She thought back to the comment she made to Greg about jinxing the situation.

"I didn't do it, you know," Emilia said quickly as she glanced up at Myra, the ball in between her fingers getting smaller and smaller. Myra tilted her head, not sure of what she was referring to. She continued, "I didn't take the earrings that day at the mall, and I just ... I guess I just wanted you to know that, so ... now you know." She shrugged. Myra, taken aback by the admission, picked the book up from her lap and placed it face down on the coffee table.

"Oh" was all she could manage. "Well, I don't really know how to respond to that." She let out a nervous little giggle. "Please, come sit down." She patted the cushion beside her again. Emilia reluctantly made her way to sit down, and Myra adjusted her seat so that she was facing her. "Well, I have to tell you, I do appreciate you telling me that."

"I'm not a thief, Myra. I don't know why I did it." She sighed heavily and then finished her thought slowly, carefully choosing each word. "I have felt so out of control since my parents died, and I just ... I guess I just wanted to feel powerful, and for some reason seeing you there and making you believe that I would do something like that, it just made me feel like I was stronger than you. I believed that if I could challenge you like that to your face, then maybe all of this couldn't hurt me anymore. Maybe I could be bigger than everything I was going through, you know?" Myra nodded her head understandingly.

"That's pretty insightful stuff, Emilia, and you know what? I do know what it feels like to be powerless, and I understand why you did what you did."

"You do?" Emilia asked hopefully, meeting Myra's gaze. Myra couldn't help but notice how innocent she looked, just a wounded little girl trapped in the body of an almost adult. She imagined that this same look must have come across her own face several times throughout the course of the past two years. It was amazing how grief could reshape you like that.

"I do. More than you know," she replied sadly, reaching over to place her hand on top of Emilia's. Emilia instinctively pulled away, but then allowed her hand to settle back where it had been, pinky finger grazing Myra's own.

"That's not all, Myra."

"Oh?" Myra breathed. "Okay, go on." She watched as Emilia struggled to hold back her tears, eyes darting back and forth. She was clearly nervous, and Myra couldn't imagine what she had to say. She could feel her palms starting to get clammy again, still waiting for the ball to drop. Emilia gulped hard, and the words that followed were forceful enough that Myra felt as if Emilia had reached into her chest cavity and stilled the very beating of her heart.

"I know you didn't do it. I know you didn't kill my parents," she choked. Myra's eyes grew wide, never having heard these words spoken by anybody but her mother. A million emotions raced through her body in an instant: relief that somebody else knew the truth, irrational hope that perhaps she would be vindicated, and the most debilitating fear that she had ever felt, knowing that this one girl held a truth that could further destroy her family. But, more prominent than any of the others was a feeling of shock and disbelief so potent that she could practically feel it in every cell of her body. She needed to clarify the words that she had just heard.

"I'm ... I'm sorry. What did you just say?" she managed.

"I know, Myra." Emilia lamented. "I know that you didn't do it, and I'm so sorry. I was horrible to you, and I just ... I'm so sorry." Myra shook her head in confusion.

"No, that's not ... how could you ... where ...." Her thoughts wouldn't form a complete sentence; so many questions were running through her mind at the same time. She felt herself becoming lightheaded, the room swirling around her, and then suddenly she got it. She raced back in her head to the conversation she had been having with her mother a week and a half ago. How stupid she had been to assume that all the kids were asleep! How many nights did she lie in bed with the lights out, her mind racing all over the place? Did she think she was the only one? Even so, she thought she had been so quiet. Suddenly, that third glass of wine seemed like not such a good idea. "The phone —my mother— you were eavesdropping?" she asked, staring blankly at Emilia.

"No," Emilia shook her head. "I was asleep and I woke up to go to the bathroom. I came out of my door and I heard you crying. Initially, I was so angry hearing you feel bad for yourself, and I almost came around the corner, but we had just had the argument on the way to the school earlier that day, and I just thought it was best if I laid low for a while because I was afraid you would ask us to leave. Then, well, yes, then I eavesdropped, but that's not the point. The point is that I heard it all and I know it wasn't you and I'm just ... I'm just so sorry, Myra. Please don't be upset." Myra just sat there like a stone, unsure of what to do, finally settling on the only thing she deemed important.

"You can't tell my girls, Emilia." Emilia looked confused.

"But, why? Don't you want them to know? Everybody should know! It's not fair!" Myra was furiously shaking her head back and forth now.

"No, no, no. It has to be what it is, Emilia. If I were to

change my story now— don't you see? It would just start the whole process over again for them, and I can't do that. They'd have to live through every taunt, every nightmare all over again, and, on top of that, they'd never believe another word I said. It would only confuse things at this point. I should have told the truth from the beginning, but I was scared and shocked and I didn't, and every day that went on that I didn't speak up, I dug myself further and further in, until it was too late."

"I don't get it!" Emilia spewed. "You would rather let the whole town —no, the whole state —hate you than let their father pay for what he did?" She was the one shaking her head now, and Myra could feel herself losing control of the situation. She had to make her understand.

"Emilia, think about how you feel about Marco and Carina for just a second, okay?" She took a few deep breaths and willed Emilia to do the same. "I want you to walk through this with me for a moment. What do they mean to you?" Emilia's eyes welled with tears.

"They mean everything to me. They are my world. They are all I have left." Myra nodded emphatically.

"Yes, exactly! I feel the same way about Ella and Sammy. Do you understand that? Good. I never bothered to correct the story because of them, and it's taken me a long time to pinpoint it. Initially, like I said, I was just confused and shocked. However, at some point, I became really afraid. I had no alcohol in my system, Emilia, despite whatever the papers led the public to believe. Greg, on the other hand, was completely intoxicated!"

"Then why did you let him drive?" Emilia squealed, slamming her hands down on her thighs.

"No, no, no, it's not like that, Emilia. Please, let me finish!" She begged, frantically smoothing the skin on the back of Emilia's hands. "I drove the car that night. That part is true." She went on to explain the details of the gruesome scenario, and by the end of the story both of them were lost in sobs. It took a few moments for either to recover enough to speak.

"I just still don't understand why you didn't tell the police," Emilia sniffled.

"I couldn't, Emilia. If Greg had been put on trial, the charges would have been far greater. The alcohol is one thing, but the fact that he is a man alone put him at greater risk. Don't forget he is an amazing defense attorney and I've watched him perfect his craft for years. I know a lot about all these little nuances, and a woman has a far greater chance of getting off. If he had been convicted and gone to jail, we stood to lose everything. As it is, his law practice took a small hit, but if it had been him on trial, his practice would have been annihilated. Where would that have left the girls and me? I have no career or fancy skill set. I'm a housewife, Emilia. And who would I have hired to defend him and with what money if all of his assets were frozen? He's the best lawyer I know, and I knew if anybody could defend me, then he was the man for the job. All of these thoughts kept popping up over and over again, and it just seemed the most logical route for our family. Then, by the time I had the clear head to think better of it, it was already too late and I was heading off to trial. It would have drawn out the whole process and tortured my girls all over again. Do you understand that?" Myra stared into her eyes pleadingly, so desperate for the truth to never come out. "Please tell me you understand that." Emilia nodded her head.

"I do understand it, Myra, because that same fear for Carina and Marco is the only thing that got me to knock on your door that day. It would have ruined them if we had been separated after everything they had been through." Myra closed her eyes and squeezed Emilia's hands in her own.

"So maybe you and I aren't so different after all," she said, and Emilia let out a tired sigh.

"Maybe not," she agreed. Myra opened her eyes and reached gently for Emilia's chin.

"Look me in the eye." Emilia did. "This is our little secret, no matter what, okay? Promise me." Emilia stared right back at her, seeming suddenly protective of this mother that she had never wanted.

"I promise you. Our little secret." Myra pulled her into the tightest embrace that she could muster and was relieved to feel Emilia hug her back.

"Thank you," she whispered in her ear, and Emilia responded by squeezing her even closer.

Marco came peeling down the stairs just as they were collecting themselves. "What's for dinner tonight? My belly is hungry!" he yelled, lifting his shirt and wiggling his belly as he danced across the floor into the living room. He stopped short when he saw their faces. "Aw, are you okay?" he asked, concerned. Myra and Emilia both smiled at him.

"Better than ever," Myra responded. "Now get over here and let me see that belly!" she teased, jumping up off of the couch and chasing him into the kitchen as he squealed with laughter.

CHAPTER **29**

Soccer season was upon them before they knew it. Emilia and Sammy had been eagerly awaiting tryouts and busily practicing together every day. On a Tuesday afternoon, as Myra sat at the dining room table, paying bills, a loud commotion and the bang of the front door slamming into the wall made her jump right out of her seat. She turned the corner to see Emilia and Sammy both laughing and playfully pushing one another, clamoring to get to Myra first.

"I'm telling her!" squealed Sammy.

"No way, get out of the way, I get to tell her!" Emilia giggled back. Ella stood in the doorway, grinning from ear to ear.

"If you two don't hurry it up, I'm going to blow it for both of you!" Myra was approaching the front door now, curiosity piqued and a big smile on her own face.

"Tell me what?" she asked. Sammy turned to Emilia.

"Count of three?" Emilia nodded. "One, two, three! I'm on the varsity team!" Sammy screamed, Emilia echoing it with her. Myra's jaw dropped.

"What? The varsity team!? But you're only in seventh grade! How is that possible?" She laughed. Sammy was beaming.

"*She* is the reason it is possible!" she exclaimed, pointing her finger at Emilia. "The coaches said they have only ever done it one time before, but that they've never seen a person my age with the skill set that I have. I swear it's all the new stuff Emilia has taught me. I can't believe it, Mom!" Myra couldn't remember the last time she had seen Sammy this spirited. "I'm going to be the youngest girl on varsity soccer. Even some of the girls in junior varsity are older than me. This is like a dream!" Myra scooped her up in a huge hug.

"I am *so* proud of you! You've worked really hard for this, and you deserve it." She noticed Emilia staring down at Sammy, a proud look on her own face. "How about you, Emilia? How did you do?" Emilia's face split into a wide grin.

"I also made varsity, which means that I and little squirt here are going to be playing together!" Sammy broke into a little dance and they all laughed.

"Well, this is very exciting stuff, ladies. I think this calls for a celebration. Let's go out to eat tonight, yeah?" All three girls nodded in unison, and a night of festivity was planned. That same afternoon, the family learned that Carina had landed a leading role in her ballet recital. Emilia had conceded to allowing her to start shortly after her talk with Myra, and Carina had fiercely embraced the art of dancing.

"She moves like our mother," Emilia was fond of saying as Carina practiced her pliés and pirouettes, twirling around the living room. That night at dinner, she made the comment again, which sparked a question from Ella.

"You talk about her dancing a lot. It must have been beautiful."

Emilia's shoulders sagged a little bit and a soft smile came across her face.

"It truly was, *she* was. My father and her, they used to dance in the kitchen every single night while dinner was cooking."

"And they'd kiss!" Marco added, visibly disgusted by this fact. Myra laughed.

"Yes," Emilia giggled, "that too. They were very happy with each other." Myra's mind flashed back to the empty turquoise glove, fingers still interlaced tightly with the hand of Mr. Garcia. "They used to tell us stories about Mexico, about all the amazing adventures they had there." She cleared her throat, clearly sniffing back the emotion that was making its way to the surface. "They met on a coffee plantation in Cuetzalan where they were both working. Papa used to pack picnics and surprise her by taking her to explore, and he used to say that was how he made her fall in love with him. She wasn't originally from there and didn't know the area well, so he would take her to the mountains or off to visit the waterfalls, the caves, and the botanical gardens. She used to tell us that he was so full of surprises that she never knew what each date would bring. In turn, she taught him how to dance. He used to joke that he didn't actually know how to dance, that he would just stand on the tops of her feet while she moved." Carina and Marco giggled.

"That's why Mama's feet are so flat!" they all said in unison. Myra and the girls had all stopped eating, riveted to hear so much information being offered about their life before the accident and the history of their family.

"After I was born," Emilia continued, "Mama had to stay home with me. Her parents had passed away, and Papa's mama was very sick and couldn't help take care of me. Papa wasn't making enough at the coffee plantation to take care of us both, and so they decided to come to America and make a new life. He found work through an immigrant program, and

197

that's how we ended up here. He went on to become a citizen, and he became pretty successful. After Marco and Carina were born, Mama opened her dance studio." She smiled gently, clearly lost in her own thoughts. "They were so proud of what they had accomplished, as they should have been. They taught themselves English, got their citizenship, opened their own businesses. They were very strong people." A silence came over the table as everybody digested all that they had learned. Myra finally broke the silence.

"Well, then I suppose we know where you get it from, yes?" Emilia looked up and smiled.

"I suppose we do, don't we?" she said.

"Thank you for sharing all of that, Emilia. It's nice to be able to learn more about your parents." Dinner was finished as the regular banter ensued, and by the time they left the restaurant to head back home, everybody was full, happy, smiling, and feeling more connected than they ever had before.

***

Before Myra knew it, she was on the phone organizing the twelve-week check-in with the state. Amanda and her team would come back and verify that everything was still up to code and that all the children's needs were being met as agreed upon. Myra was practically singing when she heard Amanda's chirpy voice on the other end of the line.

"It is *so* nice to hear your voice! How have you been?" Myra asked. Amanda responded with her characteristic chuckle.

"Well, aren't you perky today, Myra? A lot better than the last time we spoke, I see. How are things going in the Jenkins-Garcia household these days?"

"Well, amazing, actually! It's been a pretty incredible experience, in all honesty." Myra could picture Amanda's face, brows knitting together with confusion as she leaned further back in her desk chair.

"Really? Well, that's pretty incredible, isn't it? I'm happy to hear it, although I don't mind telling you that I'm a little curious about where this change of heart came in. You're getting on all right with Emilia?"

Myra laughed.

"We are getting along famously, Amanda. She is such an incredible help with her siblings, and, oh, she and Sammy have been helping each other brush up on their soccer skills. I've never seen Sammy this good, and she was already good! She made the varsity team ... in seventh grade! If she keeps up like this, she's almost guaranteed a scholarship to college!" Myra could hear Amanda tapping her pencil against her desk, still likely a little confused, even though genuinely happy that things were on the upswing.

"And how about Ella? How is she adjusting?" she asked.

"Also well! She and Marco and Carina are practically inseparable. The little ones follow her everywhere she goes, and she's sure to include them even when her friends are over. They look up to her so much, and I think she likes the admiration." Myra laughed. "Honestly, Amanda, I'm so glad I stuck with it. It's been a great experience getting to know them all."

"I'm wondering, Myra, where you think the shift happened between you and Emilia. Pardon my confusion, but the last time we spoke, she was being so difficult. You were about ready to call it quits, if I remember correctly."

"Oh yes, I remember," agreed Myra. "We had a long, eye-opening conversation shortly after our meeting. She and Sammy had had an altercation at school and ... "

"An altercation of what sort?" Amanda interjected, suddenly all business. Any altercations were to be reported to the state.

"No, not that type of altercation. Just an argument, really.

You know how siblings can be. Anyway, it turned out to be a blessing in disguise, and, like I said, it's blossomed into a very good friendship. However, it was big enough that it needed to be addressed, and so I did, and, well, we haven't had any problems to speak of since." Amanda again let a little chuckle escape her lips.

"Well, well, well. I am very happy to hear this, Myra. And what about Greg? Has he finally come around to the idea?" she inquired.

To be honest, Myra hadn't given much thought to Greg lately, but as she recounted the time from his first interaction with the children until now, she realized that he really had begun to step up his game. He had been helping more and more with carpooling the girls to and from their various activities, and he sometimes came to the door for pickup and drop-off. Occasionally, he might even hang out for a while, talking to Carina and Marco, who swarmed him the moment he entered. Now that she thought about it, she had even noticed him kicking a ball back and forth with them as they sat on the sidelines of Emilia and Sammy's soccer game one day. For a while there he had neglected to come to the games at all, but now his presence was more and more frequent.

"You know, Amanda, that's going pretty well too. I can barely believe I'm saying it, but he's been really engaged lately, even a little supportive if you can wrap your head around it." She laughed.

"More good news! Well, I can't wait to come by and see everybody. How does next week sound?" Myra skimmed over her calendar, joyfully littered these days with sports practices, school plays, dentist appointments, and parent-teacher conferences, among other activities. They settled for the following Monday, with Amanda and her crew planning to arrive while the kids were still in school and stay to briefly interview them after they had come home.

When Monday rolled around, Myra felt herself agitated and antsy, racing from room to room, re-stacking magazines, and fluffing pillows, although she knew this wouldn't be half as intense as the first home visit. She couldn't quite place her anxiety, but she thought perhaps it had something to do with the fact that she hadn't been fully honest with Amanda. She could still sense Amanda's bewilderment when they had hung up the week before, and it made her nervous that she would have more questions to answer on the subject of her and Emilia's prospering relationship. Myra was a bad liar to begin with—although, given the whole car accident story, that might not be so obvious. Amanda was one of those people who, though unassuming, seemed to know exactly what was going on in your head, maybe even better than you knew yourself. Myra couldn't fathom having to tell her a lie to her face, sure her guilt would be plastered all over her own.

As it turned out, she seemed to have worried for nothing. Amanda, Bob, and Annette moved through the house at record speed, stopping to comment on how beautiful Emilia's room had come to look. Bob ticked off all of his little boxes one by one, having apparently no reasons to scribble or hide the clipboard from her view today. Upon completing their rounds, they sat down at the dining room table with tea and talked casually about the beautiful weather, the success of the girls' soccer season, and how all the children were doing with school and after-school activities.

It wasn't long after that the first round of kids arrived home from school. The three girls were cheerily yapping away as they came into the house, discarded their backpacks by the front door, and made their way into the kitchen. A round of greetings ensued, followed by each child breaking off with one of the social workers for a brief interview. Myra was left alone in the kitchen with her thoughts as they dispersed throughout the house. Emilia, as though sensing her anxiety, turned to look over her shoulder as she followed Amanda out of the dining room and winked at Myra. She couldn't help but smile.

Amanda settled into the couch, half-facing Emilia.

"Well, it really seems as though you and Ms. Jenkins have turned a corner, huh?" Emilia nodded in agreement. "I have to tell you how happy I am to hear it, but I would be lying if I didn't admit that I'm a little bit curious as to how this came about." It was clear that Amanda had a sneaking suspicion that she wasn't being told the whole truth. Emilia shrugged.

"Well, I had an argument with Sammy a while back, and Myra and I talked about it. I guess I realized I wasn't being very nice to them, to the girls. I mean, none of this is any more their fault than it is mine, right?" Amanda nodded, one eyebrow raised as she listened.

"Do you mind if I ask what the argument was about?"

"Well, some kids at school were making fun of her in the hallways, saying that her mother was a murderer. I ... I kind of just stood there and let it happen. I might have even liked that it was happening. It was really mean of me, but at the time I was just so angry at all of them. When we came home that day, Sammy told on me. Myra and I had a long talk about it, and I guess she just helped me realize that we are kind of all in this together, you know? Sammy and Ella are as much victims here as me."

"Yes," Amanda agreed, "that's true. How do you think this has affected your relationship with Myra, then? I understand it with the girls, but I'm still a little confused as to how you two came to such a nice arrangement." Amanda knew she was prying, but it was her job to make sure that everybody involved in the situation was in a healthy environment, and she couldn't take any risks. Who knew if perhaps there had been threats or bribery that had taken place between the two of them? Emilia cleared her throat, realizing what Amanda was getting at, and put on her most convincing smile.

"Honestly, Ms. Cooper, when I saw how passionate she was about her children and how upset it made her that I had hurt Sammy, it made me realize that she is a lot more like me than I thought. I've had to make some tough decisions to protect Marco and Carina, and I guess she has had to as well, you know?" She shrugged again, hoping that she sounded convincing, not sure how else she could make Amanda understand without disclosing the truth. She wanted to scream "She didn't even do it!" at the top of her lungs and finally let the truth be heard, but she had made a promise and she didn't take it lightly. Amanda still looked confused, but apparently, Emilia had said enough to appease her for now, which was quite a relief. This line of questioning could go on in circles forever.

"Well, whatever it is, I'm happy to see you both happy and getting along. Now, how about school? I hear you are playing soccer again. The season started up just a while back, right? Varsity for both of you, I hear!" Emilia nodded, glad for the change in subject. She could talk about soccer all day.

By the time Myra came home from picking up Marco and Carina, the older children's interviews were over and everybody seemed genuinely satisfied and impressed with the way the family was settling in together. The interviews with the younger siblings were short and sweet, and, shortly thereafter, the whole family was gathered at the front door escorting the three social workers out into the drive. Amanda stopped and turned back to Myra before she left.

"Now, Myra, I'm not sure how you did it or what really took place between you and Emilia, but I have a funny feeling I'm not hearing the whole story." Myra felt her stomach flip a little, but Amanda broke into a huge smile. "Whatever happened, I truly am genuinely pleased to see you getting along so famously. Sometimes these things are of a sensitive nature, and perhaps the human connection doesn't always come with textbook answers. I'm perfectly willing to let this be on a need-to-know basis, and, currently, I don't think my knowing the whole truth is necessary. I just hope that you keep on this path together. I can't wait to see you in six months." She reached over and gave Myra a squeeze. "You truly are a remarkable woman, Myra. I admire all that you've done here." And with that, they were gone.

THE SONG OF FRUIT

CHAPTER 30

Summer came upon the family fast. Myra had been so busy attending soccer games and ballet rehearsals, driving Ella to and from her various clubs, and trying to keep Marco entertained, that it felt as though the school year had flown. June was here, and with it came a whirlwind of activity. Marco's sixth birthday was coming up, as well as Carina's recital. Sammy and Emilia had been asked to join a summer all-star soccer team, and Ella would be starting her internship with an underprivileged youth organization in Madison as a part of its mentor program. Myra was so proud to see how the relationship with Marco and Carina had inspired her to work with children, although they were reluctant to share her.

Myra had spent the week before Marco's party racing all over town. She and the older girls had stayed up late decorating, and, by Sunday morning, it looked as though a party bomb had exploded throughout the lower level of the house. Every surface was littered with confetti, streamers hung from the ceilings and doorways, and superhero balloons floated lazily to and fro, only kept in place by little weights attached to their strings. A picnic table had been purchased and erected in the backyard, and it was equally well-adorned and set for all the partygoers. In the far corner of the yard, Ella had set up a table full of goodie bags and a variety of party games, which she had agreed to be in charge of; Emilia had wrapped all of Marco's presents; and Sammy had stacked all the presents on their own table, leaving plenty of room for the gifts from his friends. Marco came down the stairs slowly, rubbing sleep from his eyes and pushing his hair back off his forehead, so that it stuck up at an amusing angle. He got only about halfway down the steps when he seemed to notice his surroundings, and the look that came across his face filled them all with joy and laughter.

"Surprise!" they all yelled together. He took the rest of the stairs two at a time, his mouth wide open in surprise, a happy smile dancing behind his eyes.

"Is this for me?" he exclaimed. Myra giggled and tousled his hair.

"You're the only birthday boy I see!" He ran toward a cluster of balloons and started slapping them out of the air excitedly. "Careful, buddy. You don't want to pop them before your party!" He turned around with a dramatic sigh, clapping his palm onto his chest.

"*Como mola*! I am *so* excited for today! When are they coming? When is my party?" He was hopping back and forth from one foot to the other, hand still clasped over his heart as though the anticipation might be too much for him to handle.

"Calm down," Myra laughed, "you can't have cake before breakfast! Everybody will be here in a few hours." Before she could even finish the sentence, Marco was off, racing toward the back sliders, having noticed the backyard complete with the stack of presents.

"Are those all for me?" he asked incredulously. Emilia walked up behind him and placed her arm adoringly around his shoulder.

"*Si, hermano*. Today is going to be a fun day for you! We have lots of fun games planned." Marco turned around and wrapped his arms around his sister's waist.

The doorbell began ringing just before noon, and the partygoers poured in. Myra hadn't had this much company in what seemed like ages, and she looked on apprehensively as mothers, fathers, and children entered her home. It was clear that some were more familiar with her situation than others, and those busybodies she found freely roaming "accidentally" into rooms where doors had been closed, or disapprovingly watching every movement she and her five children were making. Quite honestly, she had become so accustomed to being judged that it shouldn't have bothered her much, but being scrutinized in her own home was more unsettling than she had prepared for.

When Greg walked through the door carrying gifts, the whispers and glares of the other mothers were not lost on her. He whizzed past Myra with a little nod of his head, the stack of presents carefully balanced on his open palm.

"Could you grab the slider for me?" She laughed a little and followed him through to the dining room slider, pulling the handle so that he could navigate with the leaning pile out onto the porch and down the steps. A swarm of children followed him, tipped off that the fun must be on the other side of the door if that's where the presents were headed.

Within minutes the party was in full swing. It felt as if there were kids —and parents—everywhere. Myra tucked herself behind the table of presents, halfheartedly rearranging them to look busy. She watched Greg flitting from parent to parent, his most winning smile plastered onto his face, charm oozing from every pore. She noticed the other mothers, both married and single, letting their gaze linger a little longer than appropriate as he wandered off toward the next willing admirer. She couldn't help but find the humor in it. As much as

Greg could rub her the wrong way, she had to admit that he was a pretty good schmoozer. People ate it up. She had once too, though it felt like a long, long time ago now.

She was surprised, too, that it seemed Greg had become somewhat of her ally in the past month or two, especially since he had noticed so many positive changes in the attitudes of his daughters. She recalled how the past few weeks in particular he had lingered longer than usual after dropping the girls off, asking Myra a myriad questions about the progress of the living situation. He had even gone so far at one drop-off to compliment Myra on whatever she was doing that "seemed to have Sammy so much more engaged." She took the compliment with a grain of salt, but, admittedly, it felt nice to be acknowledged after all the harsh things he had said to her in the past regarding the situation.

He had been cordial with Emilia and Carina as well, offering for them to join Sammy and Ella for weekends at his house (never quite understanding Emilia's refusal to acknowledge his existence, let alone accept the invitation), but it was Marco, in particular, who had stolen a little chunk of his heart. He had always wanted a boy, and it was funny to watch him dote on Marco. As if he could read Myra's thoughts, she watched him break away from the pack of parents and make his way out into the yard in search of his little buddy. He came up behind the birthday boy and scooped him up from under his arms. Marco squealed and giggled as Greg spun him around in circles before placing his very dizzy self back onto the ground.

"Happy birthday, little man!" he bellowed.

"Hi, Mr. Greg!" Marco responded, throwing his arms around Greg's neck. Out of the corner of her eye, Myra noticed Emilia. She was stone still, anger flaring her nostrils, her gaze trained on the scene taking place between the two of them. Myra hurried over to Greg and Marco to defuse the situation.

"Marco, you've got so many friends here. Why don't you

go and play?" she said, shooing him off toward the other children. Greg turned to face her, his face reflecting his wounded pride.

"Geez, Myra. Can't I say hello to the little guy on his birthday?" Myra tucked a curl behind her ear.

"Oh, Greg, I didn't mean anything by it ... just let him play, okay?" Greg looked aggravated, but shrugged his shoulders up by his ears and headed back toward the adults. She looked back to find Emilia, but she was no longer behind the table. She turned again just in time to catch sight of her back foot moving into the house, the slider door slamming closed behind her. She sighed and went back to rearranging presents.

When the door closed behind the last guest, Myra hesitated before turning around to survey the damage. She was exhausted and mentally vowed to never do another birthday party at the house again. The kids were equally exhausted, and she'd sent them all up to Ella's room to put on a movie and unwind. Balloons lay popped and scattered across the floor, the confetti was everywhere, and dirty footprints marked up the living room rug. The kitchen counter was piled high with empty pizza boxes, used paper plates and cups, and the giant cake box. The backyard was littered with pieces of the piñata, scattered party favors, and the remnants of party games. It was going to be a nightmare to clean up. Greg had lingered to help her send off the last guest, and she found him now in the kitchen pressing down the pizza boxes to bring out to the recycle bins in the garage— one benefit of his knowing the layout of the house.

"Thanks, Greg, but you don't have to do that." He shook his head.

"Myra, I know I can be an ass, but even I'm not going to leave you to clean up this entire mess by yourself. Let me stick around and help you." She was too tired to argue.

"Whatever floats your boat, Greg. I'm going to get started

out in the yard, I guess."

"I'll go out with you. Just help me get these boxes out to the garage." She was reluctant to admit it, but it was nice to have the help. They moved through the house at a breakneck pace, and she couldn't believe how fast they got everything back into order. What would have taken her the rest of the day managed to only take just over an hour. She leaned against the wall in the foyer, watching as he sat on the bottom step of the staircase lacing up his shoes.

"Thank you again for your help. I really appreciate it. You didn't have to do it." He rose to stand and took a step closer to her.

"It was my pleasure. We make a pretty good team, don't we?" He took another step closer and reached out, taking her hands into his own. "We always were better together." Myra felt beads of sweat beginning to form at her temples. She pulled her hands back toward herself and shifted uncomfortably on her feet.

"I think you've had too much cake, Greg." She moved to walk away, but he had taken another step closer and had her cornered against the wall.

"Come on, Myra, you don't ever miss me? You don't ever think of the way we used to be? I've been thinking a lot and I think we could have that back." She felt her face beginning to flush. She had no idea where the hell this was coming from, but she was in no way prepared to deal with it, especially after the day they had just had. She pushed him back gently.

"Jesus, Greg, are you feverish? Give me some space," she replied in a high whisper. "I don't know where this is coming from, but I think it's time for you to leave." She glanced up the staircase toward the banister.

"Come on, Myra, you know me better than anybody in the world, and I know you. We could make this work. I want to help you with the kids, all of them. We could all be a family again. Like I said, I've been thinking about it a lot lately, and it just makes sense. If those kids can accept you, why wouldn't they be able to accept me, right?" He reached up to brush a curl from her forehead and she just stood there, lost in her own thoughts.

Was he serious? Could it maybe work between them? Had she truly never even considered it? But, wait a second, who the hell was she kidding? This was the man that had called her insane, who had ridiculed her in front of her daughters, who had crucified her for the mere thought of adopting these children, and now he had a sudden change of heart? Not to mention that Emilia would never accept Greg, and Myra would never get her to keep her secret if she even considered this. A million thoughts filtered through her head. A rustling noise at the top of the step snapped her back to reality, and she looked up in time to see Sammy's face disappear behind the bathroom door. Fuck, what was happening right now?

"Greg, you need to leave right now," she said, forcefully shoving him away from her toward the door.

"Myra, come on, at least talk to me about it." Her hand reached for the door handle and she pulled the door open, her other hand still on the small of Greg's back, ushering him out of the house.

"There's nothing to talk about, Greg. You need to go." He pressed his hand into the door jamb, blocking the door with his knee.

"At least tell me you'll think about a date, hey? For old time's sake." Her jaw fell open in utter disbelief that he was pursuing this so strongly.

"No, Greg, I won't think about it. The answer is no." He threw his hands up and released his knee from the door, sending her lurching forward before she caught her balance.

"Fine, if that's the way you want it, Myra. I can't believe you." He started to walk away as she stood peering through the opening in the door, but halfway down the drive he turned back to face her. "I just have one question: Do you think you're ever going to find anything better than me? Honestly, Myra, think about it. How many dates have you been asked on since we split? Nobody wants to try to get to know you anymore. They think they know all they need to about you because they read it in the goddamn paper. I hope you're okay with being alone." Just like that, his profession of love had turned into the rantings of a selfish, angry little boy.

"That's where you're mistaken, Greg. I'm not alone. Not even a little. And for the record, that was two questions." She closed the door gently and turned the lock, taking stock of how quickly her heart was beating and willing it to stop. She was sickened that, even for a brief moment, she had considered what he was offering. She was disgusted that a few weeks of cordial behavior from him could so easily erase the myriad little cruelties he had committed against her. Was she that simple? She breathed deeply, bringing two fingers on either hand up to her temples. No, simple wasn't the word. Hopeful. She hadn't even realized it, but somewhere deep down within her she had been allowing an ember of hope to burn for her relationship with Greg. How had she been so unaware? Her hands dropped down to her sides, and she closed her eyes, feeling her pulse begin to slow. This was no time to get weak. She had a family to raise, five children who relied on her to be strong, competent, and aware. Greg did not need to be thrown into the equation. She marched over to the fireplace, plucked the family picture in Vale from the mantel, opened the top drawer on the nearby hutch, and placed the frame face down inside. She closed the drawer with a slam.

CHAPTER 31

Dinner that night was quiet. The kids were all sunburnt and exhausted, picking at their food. The tick of the clock and the clanging of utensils against plates provided a soothing background. Sammy cleared her throat a few times, and Myra saw Ella give her an impatient look. She cleared her throat again, this time followed by a wail from Ella.

"Ouch! Stop it!"

"Girls what is going on?" asked Myra. Sammy and Ella exchanged another look, and Sammy nodded encouragingly at her sister. Ella rolled her eyes in concession.

"Oh, fine. Mom, Sammy wants *me* to ask you something, although I'm not sure why she can't just do it herself," Ella said, shooting another dirty look in Sammy's direction. "She thinks she heard something today." Myra waited, knowing full well where the discussion was headed. She nodded her head patiently. "Well, for whatever reason, she is pretty convinced that you and Daddy are getting back together. I told her it's stupid—"

"Don't call me stupid!" shouted Sammy. "I *did* hear them talking, right, Mom? Tell her." Emilia's fork had dropped from her grip and was now balancing threateningly off the edge of her plate. Her eyes were wide with an emotion Myra couldn't quite pinpoint.

"Now, girls, your father was here helping me clean up, and that's it. We are not getting back together," she replied.

"But, Mom, I heard him! He said that we could all be a family. I know what I heard," Sammy exclaimed, crossing her arms over her chest. Myra sighed.

"I know what you *think* you heard, but it's not accurate." Sammy was shaking her head adamantly.

"Mom, I'm not deaf."

Emilia stood up from the table abruptly.

"Emilia, where are you going?" Myra asked.

"If you will all excuse me, I'm not feeling so well. I'm going to go to bed." Sammy slammed a hand down on the table.

"Emilia, what is your problem? Why do you hate my dad so much? You're the only one who isn't happy about this, and I want to know why. I see the dirty looks you give him all the time." Sammy stared at Emilia, waiting for a response, and Myra interjected.

"Sammy, stop it, and there is nothing to gloat about because we are *not* getting back together." But nobody was listening to her, because all eyes were focused on Emilia, whose face had turned maroon.

"I do hate your father, for what he's done to my family." Myra's eyes widened and Sammy jumped up from the table, toe to toe now with Emilia.

"Of course you do, Emilia, always looking for somebody else to blame. First it was my mother, now my dad. Maybe one of these days you could try being grateful for a change. And you," she turned toward Myra pointing. "I know what I heard, and I heard him tell you that we could be a family again!" Her eyes filled with tears.

"I think everybody is tired, it's been a long day," Myra replied, desperate to defuse the situation before Emilia could divulge her secret. "Let's talk about this in the morning and- "

"I don't want to talk about it! Not with any of you!" Sammy screamed, storming out of the room. Myra shot Emilia a pleading look, and she too turned and stormed from the room. The rest of them sat there for a few moments, Myra's anger toward Greg bubbling up within her as she now realized she had two new fires to put out before bedtime, again, no thanks to him. As if on cue, Marco burst into tears. Myra's shoulders slumped.

"What's the matter, honey?" she implored weakly.

"I just don't like seeing everybody so mad," sniffled Marco. "I'm sad because today was my birthday, and that means that Emilia's birthday is coming up next." Myra knitted her brows together in confusion.

"Birthdays are supposed to be fun, Marco. Why would that make you sad?" His lower lip puckered out and a new deluge of tears came on.

"B-b-because when Emilia's birthday comes she's going to be eighteen, and she's going to leave us. Then, she'll take us away from you and then none of us will be a family anymore and so I just want us all to be happy." He threw his face down into his hands and burst into a fit of sobs. Carina, too, started softly crying on the other side of the table. Myra met the gaze of Ella who threw her a gentle smile.

"Well," Ella remarked, "this isn't turning out so well, is it?" Myra laughed. Ella was good at finding the humor in difficult situations. "Why don't you let me get Marco and Carina to bed, and you can go deal with Sammy, okay, Mom?"

"Thanks, Ella. You're a great kid, you know that? You're a great sister too." She stood up from the table and made her way around, kissing each child on the head and giving each a little squeeze before heading off to deal with Sammy and Emilia.

217

Emilia refused to talk, and Myra wasn't going to press the issue tonight. She headed up to Sammy's room, where she found her with her head buried in her pillows, sobbing. It took a good half hour to explain to Sammy what had actually happened, and another ten minutes or so to calm her down enough to get her to sleep. It never ceased to amaze Myra how emotional her youngest daughter was, though she always put on such a brave face.

By the time she left Sammy's room, the house was quiet. She made her way into her own room and readied herself for bed. As she slipped under the covers, she couldn't help but wonder if she shouldn't have hired Greg to dress up as a clown at Marco's party. He probably could have made just as much of a mess of things and provoked just as many tears. She laughed to herself as she drifted off to sleep, the image of him with a bright red nose and a curly orange wig fresh in her mind.

CHAPTER **32**

After breakfast the following morning, Myra found Emilia in her room, humming an unfamiliar tune while she put her folded laundry neatly into her drawers. Myra leaned against the door jamb, listening, waiting for Emilia to notice her there. When she did, she abruptly stopped her song.

"May I talk to you for a moment?" Myra inquired. Emilia responded with her characteristic shrug.

"I guess so. What about?" Myra moved into the room, gently closing the French doors behind her.

"I think you probably have a pretty good idea what about," Myra coaxed. She had made a promise to herself this morning to go at the situation gently, understanding Emilia's fear and hesitation at the dinner table the night before and filled with appreciation that Emilia had not spilled the beans to the other children. Emilia sighed heavily.

"Yes, I'm pretty sure I do, too. I'm sorry if I caused a scene at dinner last night. It's just that—"

"Please," Myra said, holding up her hand in protest. "I

didn't come in here for an apology. In fact, I came in here to thank you for using your discretion with what you let out. Also, to make sure that you are okay and to offer you an explanation if you would like it." Emilia walked over and sat down on her bed.

"I don't need an explanation so much as ... well, I just want to know if it's true. Is their dad really going to come and live here again?" Myra laughed softly and shook her head.

"Not if he offered me all the money in the world, Emilia." Relief washed over Emilia's face and Myra went and sat beside her. "Greg is a smooth talker, Emilia. He likes to think that he can have whatever he wants and with a lot of people he can, but I've known him a long, long time. I made a promise to you and to your brother and sister, and Greg was not a part of that promise. Sammy was understandably confused by what she heard take place between us, as I imagine anybody would be if it had to do with their parents' marriage. Sammy is young, and even Ella. Well, they don't know the truth as you and I know it, and so it's harder for them to understand. Just, please, continue to keep that knowledge between us and I will handle the rest, okay?" Emilia nodded. "Good. Now, there are a few other things I'd like to discuss with you as well, that are of far greater importance than Greg." Emilia furrowed her brow in confusion and Myra smiled. "How about a lunch date today, just you and me? We can go anywhere you want." Emilia squinted at Myra curiously, a shy smile starting at the edge of her mouth.

"Okay, what's it about?"

Myra shook her head.

"Not telling, not until we have some time to really sit and discuss. I'll see if Ella minds babysitting and we'll head out around noon. Think about where you'd like to go," she said, as she rose from the bed and made her way back to the door.

Ella readily agreed to watch the younger kids, although

that didn't stop her from asking twenty questions about what it was Myra had to discuss with Emilia and why the rest of them weren't invited to lunch.

"Don't be so nosy!" Myra joked back with her. She was much more reluctant to tell Sammy where she was going, as Sammy was visibly still miffed by her exchange with Emilia the night before. She was surprised, however, when her admission was met with nothing more than a disinterested thumbs-up, after which her earbud was promptly popped back into her ear and the nodding of her head resumed to match the beat of the music she was listening to.

Myra tossed a handful of restaurant suggestions to Emilia, but they settled on a tiny authentic Mexican place across town that Myra had never heard of.

"Papa used to take us here for our birthdays each year!" Emilia offered, as they sat down at their table. "The food here is the closest I have ever had in taste to the way Mama cooked. It reminds me of home." Myra perused the menu, which was mostly in Spanish, and finally pushed it away from her.

"You pick. I trust your judgment." She cleared her throat. "Speaking of home, that's kind of what I wanted to talk to you about." She shifted in her seat, eager to get right to it, but unaware until this moment how nervous she was to have this conversation with Emilia. She supposed she was afraid of the answers she might get when she began asking questions. Emilia looked up from her menu, perplexed.

"What about it?"

"Well," Myra began, "Marco was a little upset last night after you left the table." She watched as Emilia's brows knitted with concern.

"Is he homesick? Poor little hermano."

"No, no, not home like that," Myra interjected. "This home, our home. Marco seems to be worried about September when you turn eighteen. He is very concerned about you leaving."

She felt her voice quaver under the weight of that thought. "I ... well, I know that was the original plan, but I thought that maybe if you wanted to ... well, you are more than welcome to stay." There was a silence between them for a moment. "I mean, I'd like it—we— would like it if you stayed, Emilia."

The waitress appeared just at that moment, introducing herself with a cheery smile and breaking the sobriety of the conversation. Emilia looked eager for the distraction and started in immediately ordering a beverage for herself and also a few different dishes for Myra and her to share. The waitress looked momentarily flustered as she dug through her apron for paper and pen, while Emilia pointed intently to different menu items as she spoke. The waitress documented it all and sped away to collect their drinks, leaving the two of them to again broach the sensitive subject.

"I appreciate your offer, Myra. It makes me sad that Marco is hurting, but I know I can provide them with a happy life. They are my family and I have to take care of them, you know? If I move out and get a job and an apartment, I can start making some money so that I can legally adopt them when I turn twenty-one. It just seems like the right thing to do to raise them on my own. Mama and Papa would have wanted that, I think." Her fingers fidgeted with a cloth napkin on the table, and her eyes darted here and there, not wanting to meet with Myra's.

Myra sighed slowly, realizing that she had been holding her breath. Although she didn't know exactly what she had been expecting, it had not been this response. While Marco had been assuming that Emilia would still leave, Myra realized she had been assuming that, now that things had been good between them, Emilia wouldn't want to leave. She hadn't even really given it much thought until Marco had brought it up the night before, and she had realized that morning, lying awake in bed, that she needed to find some answers for the benefit of all the children and herself.

She took a few moments to formulate her response before speaking. The waitress placed their drinks on the table and was gone.

"Emilia, what will you do? Where will you work? How will you make enough to pay for an apartment? How will you afford healthcare and food? You will need a car, as well, to get back and forth, and what about school? Even if you manage to find a job that can pay for these things, how will you do that and finish high school at the same time?" Emilia straightened in her chair, eager to prove to Myra that she had already considered these things.

"Well, naturally, I will have to leave high school and get my GED. I know that already. As far as the money goes, don't forget I have the money left over from my parents' home and from their businesses. It's not much, but it will last me a while if I am smart with it. I know I can make it work." Although Myra admired her tenacity, her heart was breaking watching this young woman force herself into unnecessary adulthood. A pang of guilt she hadn't felt in some time seized her, forcing another deep sigh from her throat.

"So you have some money, but what about when that runs out?"

"Money isn't everything, Myra," Emilia snapped defensively. Myra saw for a brief moment the frightened child that sometimes haunted Emilia's expression, and her heart opened more.

"That is a very true statement, I admit, but children are expensive to raise, and what about your education? You are so smart, honey. You got all As and one B last year. That's not to be taken lightly, particularly with all that you've been going through. You could go to college and educate yourself for a career." Emilia huffed.

"If I don't have enough money to support myself and

eventually raise my sister and brother, where would I get the money to go to college?" she retorted sarcastically. "I mean, just because I've worked hard and gotten good grades doesn't mean I have to go to college. I know of lots of smart people who never went to college and made a life for themselves. Look at my parents, they did it!" Emilia was getting more and more passionate as she spoke, and Myra was almost sure she saw tears beginning to well up in the corners of her eyes. Her anger gave way to frustration and sadness as she continued. "I mean, who doesn't want to go to college? Of course, I'd love to go to college. I have wanted to be a veterinarian since I can remember, but plans changed, you know? Life happens and you have to go with the flow. Isn't that what all the experts say?

"So I am, Myra. I'm just going with the flow, and my sister and brother mean more to me than any degree, and certainly more than any other little creatures that might one day need my help. When they are grown I can go back to school and pursue my own dreams. Family comes first."

A little smile crept across Myra's face.

"You're right, Emilia. Family does come first." Emilia dabbed at her eyes with the corner of the napkin and reset her jaw.

"Yes, always." she agreed, though her disappointment was evident.

"And that is why I am insisting that you stay with me and finish school and go to college." Emilia again looked perplexed and Myra continued. "Family comes first, and you are our family. It wouldn't be right if I let you throw your future away to take on a responsibility that doesn't have to be yours right now. They are still your brother and sister, and that will never change, and should you decide one day later down the line to adopt them, I will readily agree to it and sign whatever paper-work is necessary, but for now, put yourself first while you can." She reached across the table for Emilia's hand, which was still working the napkin into a tight knot. "Please, Emilia. Don't take this opportunity away from yourself. I will take wonderful care of Marco and Carina, as if they were my own family because they are ... you all are. Follow your dreams so that they don't escape you. I had dreams when I was your age, and I met Greg and fell in love and started a family, and I never pursued any of them. Don't get me wrong, I'm happy with the decisions I've made, but I have those moments when I wonder how my life might have been different if I had finished college, waited to get married and have children. Live life with no regrets, right? I think I've heard some so-called experts use that line, as well!" Before Emilia could respond, their server was back at the table, hands full of plates, which she placed, one by one, across the table.

"Anything else I can get you?" she asked brightly.

"No, thank you. I think we have everything we need!" Myra answered, giving Emilia's hand a little squeeze. The server nodded and left. "What do you think, Emilia? Will you stay?" Myra watched her expression, noting how tired the conversation had made her, again hardening her features into that of a woman well beyond her years. Emilia placed her thumb and forefinger wearily to the space between her brows.

"I just don't know, Myra. Before Mama and Papa died, they would tell us that we needed to be good to each other, that we were all each other had, and that if anything ever happened to them, we should stick together and be everything for one another."

"And you took that to mean that you were never to ask for any help? Do you think they would expect you to be both mother and father on your own, particularly if there were other options available to you?" Myra asked, genuinely trying to understand Emilia's mindset. Emilia's face crumpled, no longer able to carry the burden of this feeling by herself. She nodded her head, blinking back tears.

"Yes, I'm afraid they would be ashamed of me if I didn't raise them with our traditions and morals and values," she choked. "I just want to do right by Mama and Papa and by Marco and Carina." Myra moved to Emilia's side of the booth and tucked her arm around her shoulders, thankful that they had chosen a seat in a remote corner of the dining area. They sat like this for a while, Emilia quietly crying and Myra gently rubbing her back and offering her napkin after napkin to clean her face. The waitress approached at one point to ask about their meal and kindly kept walking when she saw them. Finally, when it felt as though Emilia had cried out all the guilt and fear and shame she had been carrying around with her, and the pile of napkins on the table was inches deep, she lifted her head again, her breath hitching in her throat, and she sat there, defeated and exhausted.

"That's a lot of stuff to have been carrying around with you," Myra said quietly. "Do you feel any better?" Emilia nodded. "Well, it's a good thing," she said, "because it appears as though they are officially out of napkins." Emilia laughed, louder than she meant to, and Myra gave her another squeeze and giggled herself. "I will make you a promise right here and right now. Any morals, traditions, or values that you want your brother and sister raised with, I promise you all you have to do is tell me what they are, and I will make sure that it happens. No matter what it entails. So, that being said, do you think you might like to look at some colleges this summer?" Emilia was still dabbing at her eyes and nose, trying to slow her breathing. She nodded her head again, and then slumped over, apparently defeated yet again by another bullying thought.

"What is it?" Myra asked.

"It's just the money!" Emilia hiccupped. "I have some, but I still don't have enough money from my parents to pay for it all, and— " Myra placed her hands on either side of Emilia's face and cupped her chin.

"Emilia, do you remember the first day that I met you?" Emilia nodded, again blinking back tears. "Do you remember what I gave you that day?" Emilia thought back for a moment before recognition dawned on her face.

"But ... I ripped those up!"

Myra laughed.

"Well, fortunately for you, the papers I gave you that day were of no more value than this napkin," she said, dangling one of Emilia's makeshift tissues from her thumb and pointer finger. "They were just statements. The original documents for the trust funds were given to your caseworker and are safely tucked away in your files." Emilia's face was a mixture of relief, bewilderment, joy, and disbelief.

"So, does this mean that you'll at least think about it?" Myra pressed. Emilia smiled.

"I'll think about it," she agreed, although she knew full well that her mind was already made up. All the emotion had caused her to lose her appetite, but although she couldn't eat the food they had ordered, her mind began to wander ravenously through all the new possibilities that had been created for her through this one conversation. She might actually get a chance to be a college student, maybe even to live her dream of becoming a veterinarian. She could hardly believe it. In the short span of a lunch meeting, the course of her life had been, yet again, rerouted into uncharted waters.

Emilia's announcement later that week to stay at the Jenkins household and finish school was met with unanimous jubilation from all the family members. Ella immediately took an active role in helping her research schools she might be interested in applying to, while Sammy willed her to keep practicing her soccer skills each and every day, in hopes that she might be offered a scholarship.

The family spent the rest of the summer on an extended road trip of sorts, touring campuses from Michigan to Minnesota, Iowa to Illinois, and all through Wisconsin. By the time school started back up in September, Emilia had made a definitive decision to stay in Wisconsin so she would be close enough for regular visits with the family. She had narrowed down her search to four top picks, and she felt more prepared than any of her friends for whatever lay ahead. She sped through the application process, sending out one query after another in quick succession, and, by early November, all that was left to do was stay on track with her good grades and wait to hear on decisions.

CHAPTER 33

Myra's white van, having some time ago replaced the Land Rover, crept up the icy driveway at a snail's pace. The back bumper, heavy under the weight of bodies and shopping bags within, dug a wide line through the accumulating snow. "Jingle Bells" blaring from the speakers made Myra's head pound, but hearing the sounds of her five children singing along joyfully was the best medicine she could ask for. Christmas decorations spangled the lawn and the rooftop, and bright lights swayed lazily from the eaves of the house and the tops of trees. A wreath hung crookedly from the front door, an indication of the joyful chaos that lay on the other side. This year, Myra had not needed to hire help to decorate the house or convince anybody of the importance of trimming the tree together. Instead, everybody had eagerly played a part, and the result was magnificent.

The group of them spilled from the van, laden with bags filled with gifts, and stomped any residual snow from their boots before taking them off and walking into the house. The interior of the house sparkled from the rafters to the floor-boards with both homemade and store-bought decorations. Spruce garlands interspersed with twinkling lights wound around the handrail leading upstairs and framed the wall of sliders at the back of the house. Colorful drawings of Christmas trees, Santa Claus, elves, and presents adorned the front of the refrigerator, windows, door faces, and empty wall space, courtesy of Marco and Carina. Two life-size nutcrackers stood guard at the front door, and the dining room table boasted a large bowl of pinecones sprinkled with glitter and spruce-scented candles. Tabletops and shelf space had been rearranged to make room for decoration after decoration, and Myra couldn't remember if she had ever seen the house shine so brightly. Every day that drew them nearer to Christmas Day, its song became louder and fuller, peppered with the delightful squealing of Marco and the awe on Carina's face as she gently shook each package that magically appeared below the tree. And the tree was a thing in and of itself. It was the tallest they had ever purchased. So tall, in fact, that she did have to request help. She did not, however, hire anybody, but instead cornered Greg one day as he dropped the girls off from their weekend visit and slyly coerced him to go with them to get the thing. Since Marco's birthday, he had tried diligently to convince Myra that they should try again, and each time she rejected him, knowing that it was only a matter of time before he would again make the suggestion. She tried not to entertain it, but for the sake of their Christmas tree, she didn't think it was such a bad thing to use his newfound interest to her advantage.

Myra started a pile of bags in the living room, instructing each of the children to remove anything she wasn't supposed to see and label who the gifts were for before gathering them together so that she could wrap them once everybody was in bed. Myra was astonished at what an undertaking wrapping for such a large family could be, but the lines at the mall for gift-wrapping stretched out into the common area, and so she decided that it would be better to do it herself. The pile seemed to grow and grow, as one bag after another landed on top of the pile. Once everybody had eaten and been sent off to bed, she pulled out the box filled with wrapping paper, scissors, tape, and labels and diligently got to work, one item at a time.

About halfway through her third present and fully lost in thought, she became aware of Emilia standing near the couch, holding something in her hand.

"Hi, sweetie," Myra said, glancing around quickly to make sure nothing was left hanging out of any of the bags.

"Hi," Emilia said with a smile. "I just wanted to give you these. They're for Marco and Carina, but I had to put pictures in them first," she said, handing Myra two beautiful hand-painted glass frames. Myra turned them around so that she was looking at the pictures upright. The frames had been split into two horizontally, the top half a picture of the Garcia children with their parents and their little black-and-white dog, and below a picture of all of them with Myra and the girls, taken during one of the road trips the previous summer. Myra teared up as she looked at them, gazing up at Emilia. "Our family," Emilia explained. "Or families, I should say. I want them to always know that they have both, and I thought this might be a nice way for them to remember where they came from, as well as where they are going." She paused for a moment, letting Myra take in what she had said. "When you think about it, maybe it's not so different. There were six of us to begin with, and there are six of us now, only nobody has fur this time around," she joked. "Either way, we are all still together, even if with Mama and Papa it's just in spirit." Myra, touched by the gesture, brought a hand to her heart.

"They're beautiful, Emilia. I think Marco and Carina are going to love them. I don't even know what else to say. I couldn't think of a nicer gift that you could give them." Emilia shrugged, embarrassed.

"Well, do you need some help wrapping?" Myra shook her head.

"No, no, you go to bed. Have a good sleep. I'll make sure these get wrapped carefully for you and tucked in the back of the tree so they don't get broken." Emilia began to walk away as Myra's gaze fell back down to the picture. She ran her fingers across the surface of the glass. "Emilia?" she asked.

"Yes?" she responded, twirling around, her hand resting on the edge of the door.

"What was your dog's name again? I forgot." Emilia smiled softly at the memory.

"Mullido. Sweet, silly Mullido." She grinned.

"That's right. What does it mean again? Furry?" she asked. Emilia smiled in amusement.

"Fluffy, but nice try. Good night, Myra," she said and left Myra sitting there laughing at herself.

"Right, Fluffy," she muttered to herself. She sat staring at the picture even as Emilia closed her door and turned out her bedroom light. She imagined what life must have been like in their home before this home. She sat mesmerized by the chubby cheeks of Marco's baby face, the characteristic mischief in Carina's sweet eyes, and the easygoing smile on Emilia's face as she crouched down next to her siblings, Mullido on her lap licking at her chin. There was so much she would never know of their past, so much she had missed, so many gaps she couldn't fill, but still, she felt in many ways as though they were all meant to find one another. She hoped with all hope that they knew how much they meant to her, how their presence in her life and the lives of her daughters had lifted them from bleakness and added color and music back into their existence. In many ways, they had all saved one another from being broken apart.

***

In Myra's dream, she held Emilia's frames in her hand once again. Before her eyes, the pictures began to bleed and morph into one another, until Mr. and Mrs. Garcia and the little black-and-white puppy were standing side by side with Myra and the children. Then she became the mirror image of her photographed self, standing among the others, watching as they all came to life around her. The dog stood frantically wagging his tail while Emilia fawned over him, and Sammy, Ella, Carina, and Marco gathered around her, competing for his attention, licks, and kisses. Mr. and Mrs. Garcia watched on admirably, holding tightly to each other's hands. Myra felt out of place for a moment, not sure how she fit into this picture she had become a part of, but her separation was replaced with relief when the Garcias turned toward her, extending their arms in a gesture of inclusion.

"Come, Myra," Mr. Garcia beckoned, a compassionate smile spreading across his countenance. "Come stand with us." She felt herself floating effortlessly toward their outstretched arms until she was pulled into a warm embrace by the two of them. "Look at how they play together." He gestured toward the group. "The dog and the children, they are from two different worlds, and yet when they play, they play as a pack. It is humbling to see how they transcend the boundaries we blindly put upon them." Myra nodded agreement, her gaze wandering to Mrs. Garcia, standing stoically by her husband.

"Myra, it is similar to what you and the children have created, isn't it?" Mrs. Garcia said. "From two walks of life, these children have been brought together by tragedy, yet they have formed a bond that is strong and everlasting. You did this, and we thank you." She gave Myra's hand a little squeeze. Myra began to understand as she watched the children rolling

233

1

around with the dog, expressions of carelessness and joy covering each of their faces. She watched as Emilia swatted the dog's playful jaws away from Sammy's hand and Sammy's nod of thanks back at her. She watched as Ella lifted Carina and twirled her around in circles, and how Carina playfully rolled into Marco when she was placed back down, knocking him gently to the ground. They had become a pack. They loved one another. They were a family. When she looked back to the Garcia parents, they had vanished, and here she was, left alone to admire this brood she had helped to create, even if out of her mistakes. She felt a blissful peace and happiness sweep over her body, and when she awoke the next morning in her bed, she let herself lie and revel in the feeling for a while.

CHAPTER **34**

Myra was hesitant to admit that she would need to ask for Greg's help, yet again, but Christmas was only days away and there was one surprise she knew she wouldn't be able to pull off without his assistance. The children were already on their holiday break, so finding a moment when she could call him without interruption proved a tricky endeavor. Finally, late one night, when she was sure that everybody was asleep (she had gotten better about checking rather than assuming), she pulled out her phone, snuck out onto the back patio, and reluctantly dialed Greg's number.

"Hello?" He answered, his voice emoting a mixture of puzzlement and curiosity. "Myra?"

"Hey, I'm glad you answered. I'm sorry it's so late."

"No, no, no … " he interrupted, and his voice dropped down to a husky murmur. "I've been waiting for you to call. I'm glad you did." Myra rolled her eyes, never ceasing to be amazed by the incredible size of his ego. It was clear to her that he assumed her reasons for calling had to do with reconciliation, and she let out an inadvertent laugh.

"Why have you been waiting for my call, Greg? Did the whiskey tip you off that I might need a favor?"

"Huh?" he asked, genuinely confused. She laughed again.

"Never mind. I have a favor to ask you." There was a moment or two of silence on the other end of the line, as it finally became clear to Greg that she had reasons outside of lust for dialing him.

"Oh, uh, a favor? What kind of favor?" he asked, still far too much hope in his voice.

"Not that kind," Myra replied. "It's about the kids."

"Oh," he responded disappointedly. "I thought ... never mind. What's up?" She had a brief moment in which she truly felt bad for him. She imagined him sitting in his fancy, too-large house, all by himself, a half-empty glass of whiskey resting by his hand. She knew what a gnawing, raw feeling it was to be lonely, especially around the holidays, and she wouldn't wish it on anybody, but she reminded herself that, realistically, Greg had chosen this for himself. She brought herself back to the real reason she was calling.

"I have a surprise that I'm going to need your help with. I'm not going to lie, it's asking a lot, but I don't really know who else to ask, so, do you think you could help me?" She heard him emit a little snicker.

"Oh, geez, Myra. Well, it certainly sounds interesting, as most things seem to be with you these days." She could almost see him shaking his head, swirling his glass of whiskey around in gentle circles. She clearly never ceased to amaze him these days. "Let's hear it. I think I could be game." Myra felt an excited tingle run through her body.

"Okay, great, perfect!" And she began to talk a mile a minute, disclosing all the details of her secret plan, peeking over her shoulder every so often to make sure there were no children eavesdropping on her conversation, even though she stood outside, wrapped up like an Eskimo to keep out the cold. Twenty minutes later, she was met with silence on the other end of the line. "Hey, are you still there? Greg?" She asked, and she realized he was giggling. "Are you laughing?" She giggled back.

"My, my, my ... you know. There was a day when I called you crazy and thought better of it afterward, but this time, I think you've really gone and lost it," he teased. She grinned like a Cheshire cat, knowing him well enough to sense that this meant he was on board.

"Stop it!" she laughed. "So, you'll do it?" She bit her lip as she waited for his response.

"Of course I will, you crazy woman! When do you want to meet?" By the time they hung up the phone, the plans were laid.

***

Myra awoke to the sound of delighted shrieking outside her door. She smiled to herself, threw back her covers, and reached for her robe. She yanked open her door to see Marco and Carina peering wide-eyed through the slats in the banister at the pile of gifts under the giant well-lit tree, and the over-stuffed stockings hanging side by side on the fireplace.

"Did Santa come?" she asked eagerly, and both children nodded their heads simultaneously. "Well, we'd better wake up the girls, then!" she suggested. With that, the two jumped up and raced into first Sammy's and then Ella's room, rousing them with their excessive animation. Each at their own pace, the girls strolled into the hallway with sleepy eyes and messy hair, but even at their ages, the magic of the holiday was not lost on them. One look at the scene below them seemed to wake them right up, and the commotion stirred Emilia from her room off the living room as well, evoking the same reaction. The children clamored to the bottom of the steps, heeding Myra's warning to wait there until she reached them. As soon as her foot hit the bottom step, the four of them raced into the living room, but Emilia hung back, mouth agape. Myra came upon her as Sammy's voice rose from the fireplace.

"Mom, can we get the stockings?" Myra laughed, also lost in the magic of the moment.

"Of course you can." She turned to Emilia. "How about you? Do you want to see what Santa put in your stocking?" she teased, well aware that Emilia, Sammy, and Ella knew that Santa was no more than a myth.

"Ho, ho, ho! Merry Christmas!" Emilia joked back and walked toward her stocking, still astonished. Myra had to admit, it was quite a sight. She had never before had a tree this size, let alone gifts for six people wrapped and underneath it. It looked like something out of a catalog. She watched on with amusement and wonder as the children tore into their stockings, creating little stockpiles of their goods around them.

As was the custom in the Jenkins household, Myra made coffee before they began opening gifts, and the youngest, now Marco, got to put on the Santa hat and make piles of presents for each person. Carina helped him read the labels so that he got them in the correct piles, and by the time Myra came back in with her coffee, she was pleased to see that the spot underneath the tree was almost bare, save the gifts they had for people outside the immediate family. The children were all buzzing with enthusiasm and anticipation.

"Can we start yet?" asked Sammy.

"Yes, can we?" chimed in Marco and Carina. Myra giggled.

"I think since there are so many of us, maybe we should go in order from youngest to oldest. What do you think?" Marco started right in on a little victory dance and everybody began to laugh. Marco began tearing into his first gift with vigor, sending bows and bits of paper flying through the air.

He squealed with excitement when he saw the remote-control car inside, and he didn't stop admiring it as Carina started in on her first gift. They made their rounds like this until piles of clothing, toys, accessories, and decorations lay mounded up around each of them. It was Emilia's turn, and she hovered over the three boxes left in front of her before picking up the smallest and turning it over in her palm.

"To Emilia. Love, Myra," she read as she began to untie the bow slowly and carefully, much to the aggravation of the others. She removed the tape piece by piece so as not to rip the paper until a small, white box was all that remained. She glanced up at Myra and smiled curiously as she removed the lid and a little white square of cotton material. She gasped at the tear-shaped dangle earrings encrusted with shiny, clear stones. "Oh, wow, Myra, they are beautiful!" She held them up to the light of the sliders, watching them sparkle and dance.

"I thought you would like them," Myra smiled. "They reminded me of that pair we saw in the store last Christmas," she said, without thinking. "The stone in the middle there is a diamond, the others are white topaz. Now that you are eighteen, and officially an adult, I figured it was time for you to have a little sparkle," she jested.

"Wait," Sammy interjected, "last Christmas? They moved in after Christmas, Mom," she said in confusion. Myra caught Emilia's eye and didn't skip a beat.

"That's right, it must have been when we went shopping after you moved in. I'm getting old, Sammy. Bear with me," she joked. "Besides, it feels as though you have all been with us forever, doesn't it, girls?" Sammy and Ella both nodded in agreement. Myra was glad to have averted any further questioning, but it was clear by Emilia's face that she knew exactly which day Myra was referring to. A little smile passed between them.

"I adore them, Myra. Thank you so much! I'll take such

good care of them, I promise. They're amazing!" The other girls crowded around her and each took turns holding them up to her ears and marveling at how brilliantly they shone. Marco, having completely lost interest in this, took the opportunity to tear into his remaining presents, which made Myra chuckle.

When, finally, they had finished unwrapping the mountain of gifts, the living room lay littered with tape, bows, and torn remnants of paper. Myra got a giant trash bag and began cleaning up as the children busied themselves with their new items. She checked the face of her Cartier as she picked up the last of the trash and tied off the top of the bag. They appeared to be right on schedule. She cleared her throat to get everybody's attention.

"I almost forgot," she stated, though she had done nothing of the sort. "I think there is one more gift." All the children perked up at this, except Emilia, who shook her head.

"No, Myra. This is already too much. Please—" but Myra held her hand up in objection.

"No, no, none of that," she insisted. "Do you think you could all have a seat on the couch for me?" she asked, pushing piles of presents out of the way to make room for all of them. They scrambled to their seats, curious and perplexed, looking at one another for an explanation. Just like that, a knock came on the door. "Well, would you look at that? Something to be said for perfect timing." The five children wiggled excitedly, now even more confused, as Myra headed toward the front door. She opened it just a crack and peered out, whispering something to the person on the other side. She peeked back over her shoulder with a grin on her face. "No peeking!" she yelled, but all the children were already craning their necks in anticipation. "Ready? On the count of three: ONE, TWO ... THREE!" she yelled and flung the door open to reveal Greg standing there holding something inside of his coat. He stepped in and crouched to the ground, opening the front of the jacket and placing its contents on the floor. A puppy sat there blinking sleepily for a moment, before taking in its surroundings and wagging its fluffy tail.

"Mullido!" Marco cried, and indeed it was true, the puppy they had found resembled the lost dog of the Garcia family to a *T*. The little puppy tore off toward the couch, wagging ferociously as it was scooped up into the air by Ella and placed on the couch with them.

"Oh, Mom, he's so cute!" she squealed. "Where did you get him?" Myra and Greg stood there watching, grinning from ear to ear at what they had pulled off.

"I couldn't have done it without your dad," she admitted. "It's not easy keeping secrets from five nosy kiddos!" she laughed. "I did some research online and when I found him, Dad met me there. Well, clearly, he is adorable, and I thought he would be a perfect fit, so Dad took him home and he's been there for the past couple of days waiting to surprise you." The children were beside themselves, particularly Emilia, who hadn't said a word or taken her eyes from the small pup once.

"What's his name?" Sammy asked, and Myra shrugged.

"Well, I thought you guys could come up with a name together." Ella and Sammy smiled at each other, completely on the same page.

"I think we should name him Mullido," said Sammy, and Ella nodded in agreement. Marco clapped his hands together in excitement and Carina gave him a little squeeze. But Emilia looked sad and shook her head softly.

"No, Mullido is gone, and no other dog will ever be Mullido," she said quietly, shifting in her seat. But then, a thought came to her, and she smiled. "Besides, you guys don't even say it right," she teased, and all the others laughed because, of course, she was right. "Why don't we just call him Fluffy?" she offered, and everybody seemed content with that.

"That's perfect!" agreed Sammy. "Fluffy it is!" she said, scooping the dog up into her arms as he deliriously licked at her face. Myra walked to the couch and crouched down in front of it as the puppy moved from one of them to the other. Greg stood awkwardly by the front door for a moment, watching before clearing his throat.

"Well, I guess I'll be on my way, then. Merry Christmas, you guys! Girls, I'll be here to pick you up in a couple of days, okay?" he said, blowing a kiss in their direction. Myra felt herself soften, but it was only when she saw the same emotion come over Emilia's face that she spoke.

"Nonsense, Greg. Take your coat off and stay a while, would you? Girls, go grab the gifts you got for Dad, huh?" Greg smiled sheepishly from the doorway.

"Are you sure? I mean, I know you guys probably have plans. I don't want to impose." But Marco was already upon him, pulling at his jacket.

"Come on, Mr. Greg! We have a big breakfast ready, and there will be lots of extra food for you." Greg smiled and ruffled the hair on Marco's head, letting his jacket slip off of his shoulders.

"Well, we don't want too many leftovers, I suppose." He kicked off his shoes carelessly and headed into the living room to join the festivities. The girls jumped up to hug him and then raced to the tree to grab his presents, leaving Emilia and Carina alone on the big couch. Emilia picked up the puppy and placed him in her lap as she scooted over to make room for Greg. It was perhaps the first time she had ever acknowledged his presence, and he was visibly surprised.

"Oh, well, thank you," he muttered, lowering himself onto the cushions. Emilia nodded and looked back at the puppy who was already exhausted and curling himself into a neat little ball on her lap.

"Thank you," she said to Greg quietly, still not quite ready or willing to make direct eye contact with him. "He is amazing." Greg looked at her thoughtfully as she fawned over the animal.

"You're very welcome, Emilia, although Myra did all the hard work. I just had to snuggle with a puppy for a couple of days," he conceded. She smiled, still looking down.

"I suppose that wasn't very tough to do with this guy," she replied, gently scratching the top of Fluffy's head. Ella and Sammy returned to the couch with presents for Greg, and Emilia was glad for the distraction.

By breakfast, Fluffy was snoring happily on the dog bed that Greg had retrieved from his car, and the children were content and tired from the busy morning. Myra turned on Christmas carols on the radio in the living room as everybody settled around the dining room table. She laughed out loud when she heard Elvis singing his version of "White Christmas," and no sooner had she begun, then Greg's booming voice joined in.

THE SONG OF SUSTENANCE

CHAPTER **35**

The next year passed at an alarming speed, and Myra found herself constantly reminded to cherish the moments that were left having all five children under one roof. Emilia had been accepted by each of the four schools she had applied to, but the partial soccer scholarship she had been offered by the University of Wisconsin had been enough to sway her decision. The other perk was that the campus was relatively close to home so that, though Emilia had opted to live on campus, she could come home any time she wanted.

The school year gave way to summer and then, as suddenly as it had begun, it inched toward fall and Emilia was packing up her things to begin her first year at college. The week leading up to the big day was filled with excursions to Target for dorm accessories, stops by the campus bookstore for all the textbooks she would need, and clothes shopping at Emilia's favorite places.

In retrospect, Myra had perhaps gone a little over the top, but she didn't have a single regret. Emilia and Myra had grown closer and closer since the night the truth had come out between them, and now it felt like a truly authentic mother-daughter relationship. Emilia pushed her boundaries now and again, and Myra pressed back; Emilia asked for advice and Myra did her best to steer her in the right direction; they agreed, they disagreed, and argued; but through it all, a fierce bond was created between them and there was no doubt that they loved each other. It was similar with the children. Of course, they all had moments when they fought over silly things and egged one another on for no other reason than aggravation, but through all the ups and downs, they were always there for one another.

Ella and Emilia had become particularly close as they navigated the world of college applications together. Although this fact often made Sammy a bit jealous, she and Emilia had continued to build upon their love of soccer. Also, as Sammy grew in age, so did she develop patience with the younger siblings, which proved extremely helpful to Myra and seemed to appease Marco and Carina now that Ella was no longer at their beck and call.

Greg, too, had become a staple in the household, much to Myra's surprise. At Christmas, it seemed as though he had finally been able to see all that Myra had been working toward with the children. He quickly realized that there was no chance of a romantic relationship between him and Myra again, and he stubbornly accepted this fact and fell into the surprising role of Myra's biggest supporter. He never missed a game, recital, or event for any of them, and he consistently backed up any punishments, consequences, and decisions that Myra made concerning them. He frequently came to dinner on the weekends, and even he and Emilia seemed to have come to a silent understanding. Harmony had once again returned in full to Myra's home, and it was sweet music to her ears.

If anybody had told her a few years ago that life could ever

THE SONGS OF MY FAMILY

be like this, she never would have believed it , but, of course, it hadn't come without a price. She had begun to play with the idea of going back to work part time at the school, but every application had been met with enthusiastic promises that were never fulfilled. Her social life, too, continued in its hum-drum manner, but she was so busy with the activities of the kids that it failed to bother her much these days. She resigned herself to the fact that the day would come when people would stop associating her with the mistakes of her past and that only when that day came might she again establish friendships outside the few she had. But, for now, she was content with the laughter, chaos, and energy brought on by a house full of children.

The night before Emilia's big day, Myra made her favorite Mexican dish, sweet chiles stuffed with chorizo and cheese. She had scoured the internet looking for the perfect recipe un-til she found one that hailed from the region where the Garcias had lived. Fluffy danced around her feet as she carried the plates two at a time into the dining room and placed them down. Emilia eyeballed the dish excitedly, taking her place at the head of the table.

"Myra, you have certainly outdone yourself. This smells amazing! How did a lady from Madison, Wisconsin, figure out how to make real Mexican food?" she teased. They all took their seats, and each of them seemed equally impressed.

"Geez, Mom, I hope you don't expect us to eat any more of your casseroles after this!" Sammy joked. Myra made a face at her and everybody laughed.

"Well, I hope it tastes as good as it smells. Before we eat, though, I'd like to make a toast." Marco jumped at the oppor-tunity to take center stage, reached for his fork, and dinged it against the side of his glass three times. "Thank you for that, Marco," Myra laughed. "I'd like to make a toast to Emilia. Best of luck tomorrow as you take the first step of your new journey into adulthood. I wish you success and happiness, although you will be truly missed around here. Just promise us you won't get so caught up in college life that you forget to come home and visit, okay?" She smiled. Emilia nodded her head. "Good! Well, in that case, cheers to Emilia!"

"Cheers!" the rest of them echoed, clinking their glasses of milk across the table. Myra looked on happily as they all dug into their plates of food, but she couldn't help but feel an emptiness in her stomach, even as she ate. Not for the first time, she found herself wondering how life would be different without Emilia's constant presence. It was amazing to her how this girl, who had initially challenged her so much, had become such an important fixture in her day-to-day life. What a journey they had been on together— all six of them. It was almost unbelievable, and yet she couldn't imagine her life any other way. She sat admiring Marco and Carina and then turned her focus on her own two beautiful daughters, so thankful that they had been brave enough to push her to make a decision she surely never would have made on her own. As the moon rose, casting a silvery glow over the backyard, Myra's heart swelled with an emotion that she could only associate with tranquility and contentment.

***

Greg's rapping on the door was drowned out by the hustle and bustle inside, so that when his head appeared in the foyer, Myra jumped backward from her position at the coat closet.

"Jesus! You scared the crap out of me!" she exclaimed, playfully smacking at his arm. He chuckled a little and pushed the rest of the way through the door.

"Wow, why all the chaos in here?" Myra shook her head.

"I know. It's been like this all morning. Everybody is excited to get up to the college and help Emilia move in. Between that and Emilia and Ella feverishly packing up all of her last-minute items, I feel like I haven't had a moment to breathe!" Greg kicked off his shoes and put a hand on her shoulder.

"Why don't you go take Fluffy for a walk and I'll hang out here with the kids. Take a break." He checked his watch. "What time are we supposed to get her there?" She was thankful that he had come to help with carrying the bigger items.

"We were planning on arriving at eleven." He nodded.

"Well, good, that means we have plenty of time. I'll take the little kids to the backyard to play some soccer, so Emilia can finish getting herself situated in peace and quiet. You go." She nodded her head, gracious for a moment of relief. She lifted Fluffy's leash from its hook beside the door, at which the little dog came racing from some unknown corner of the house and began running little circles about her feet.

"Come on, Fluffy. Sit still for a minute," she laughed, attempting several times and failing to clip the leash onto her moving target. Finally, pressing her hand firmly onto the dog's backside to hold him in place, she was able to attach the leash and head out the door. She heard Greg's booming voice as she closed it behind her.

"Who wants to play soccer?" This was followed by the high-pitched squealing of Marco and the sound of footsteps storming down the staircase. The early morning sun was already beating down on the pavement and Myra was thankful for the slight breeze coming off the lake. She walked down the steep driveway and crossed the road to the sidewalk on the opposite side. She let Fluffy set the pace, stopping here and there to sniff, mark his territory, and continue on his way. Her mind, grateful for a little quiet, began to wander without her intention, and she found herself revisiting the first day that she and Emilia had laid eyes on each other. It was funny in some ways to reflect on that, because nowhere now did she see the steely eyes or stony jaw of the girl she had met that day. She remembered Emilia's unforgiving words as she chastised Myra and the way she had torn up the paperwork that Myra had handed her. Who knew that her anger would be transmuted into the kindness and love that Myra now saw in her?

She thought back to the day Emilia had confronted her about knowing the truth. She had been so adamant that Myra exonerate herself from the blame, so hungry for others to know what had really happened, and yet she had swallowed up the truth with grace and stoicism. She didn't have to do that, and Myra knew it. She reached into the back pocket of her shorts, making sure that the letter was still safely there and hoping that it expressed all the things Myra wanted to say to her. She planned on tucking it into Emilia's suitcase when she had a moment.

When she walked back into the house, Emilia's things lay neatly stacked by the front door, reminiscent of the day she had moved in, and Myra stared at them nostalgically as she bent to unhook the leash from Fluffy's collar. She hung the leash back on its hook and went in search of everybody. From the living room, she saw Greg, Carina, Marco, Ella, and Sammy in the backyard engaged in a halfhearted soccer scrimmage. She turned back toward Emilia's room and peeked through the crack between the two French doors. Emilia was lying on her bed, staring up at the ceiling.

"Hey there. You almost ready?" she called.

Emilia sat up and scooted back on the bed.

"Yeah," she said neutrally, but Myra was not convinced.

"May I?" she asked, gesturing toward the empty space at the foot of Emilia's bed, and Emilia nodded. "Do you want to talk about it?" Emilia shrugged slightly and then nodded.

"Yeah. I'm just a little sad, I guess. This just feels so final, you know?"

"Yeah, I know, but it's not final, Emilia. If you're not

enjoying campus life, your room is always here for you. You can come home anytime you want, including every weekend, if that's what you want."

"You mean you aren't going to turn it back into an office?" Emilia joked, cracking a smile. Myra mirrored her expression.

"What the hell do I need an office for, anyway?" she countered. "Even if I had any paperwork, it's not like anybody around here would let me get any of it done." They laughed, and Myra put her arm around Emilia's shoulder. "Try to be excited, okay? This is a big day for you. Everybody feels a little scared on their first day of college, but look at all the other scary things you have done in the past couple of years. This is a piece of cake."

"You have a good point there," Emilia agreed. "There was nothing scarier than coming to live with you —no offense!" She smiled.

"And look how that turned out," Myra said. "I think we did all right together, yeah?" Tears welled up in Emilia's eyes as she nodded her head and leaned into Myra's shoulder.

"Yeah, it worked out pretty amazing," she agreed. "Myra? I don't know if I've ever really told you how thankful I am for what you did for us. I mean —"

"Shh," Myra hushed her. "You don't need to tell me. I know, and I'm equally thankful for what you've done for me and the girls," she said, stroking Emilia's long black hair.

"Still," continued Emilia, turning to face her. "I really want you to know how much it means to me. I want you to know how much *you* mean to me and Sammy and Ella. I really love you all so much," she said, starting to cry. Myra wrapped her in a huge hug, feeling her own tears coming on. She reached behind her to grab the box of tissues off Emilia's nightstand and placed it in between them. Emilia grabbed for one as she sat back up, dabbing it at the corners of her eyes and her nose. "I even kind of like Greg!" she said, rolling her eyes sarcastically and letting out a little snort of a laugh. Myra chuckled and handed her another tissue.

"Yeah, he can be charming, but don't worry, he's still not getting his office back." They exchanged another hug just as they heard the dining room slider open up and the panting of the soccer players spill back indoors. Greg showed up at the door a moment later, flushed and near breathless.

"So, these kids have officially kicked my butt," he admitted with a laugh. "Are you girls ready to go?" And then, noticing the tears, he added, "Oh, is everything okay?" His brow furrowed in concern, and Emilia and Myra both laughed.

"Yes, just a little girl talk," said Myra, and together they walked out to join the rest of the family.

CHAPTER 36

They pulled onto the campus just after eleven-fifteen, a new record for them staying close to their time frame. Most of the dorm dwellers had shown up with a mother or father in tow, perhaps a brother or sister, but when Emilia and her entourage spilled from the cars and into the dormitory carrying her belongings, they drew gazes from every direction. Myra was worried that all the attention might embarrass Emilia on her first day, but Emilia stood tall and proud, corralling her siblings through the foyer, up an elevator, and down a winding hallway of the Sellery Residence Hall until they found Emilia's room.

"Well, this is it," she said, glancing back down at the slip of paper in her hand to be sure. The whole crew poured into the room, which, though more spacious than many Myra had seen, was not ready for the Garcia/Jenkins crew. Myra was glad that Emilia's roommate was not yet there, and judging by the look of relief that washed over her face, it was pretty clear that this thought had entered Emilia's head as well. Greg took

Sammy and Ella to help him get the remaining bags, and Marco and Carina amused themselves by climbing the ladders of the loft beds to see who could reach the top first.

"I guess you should probably pick your bed, huh?" Myra suggested.

"Yeah, I guess so. I think I like this one near the window," she said, walking over to the far bed. The beds were raised up high and had desk spaces built underneath. "That way I can see outside when I'm sitting at my desk to do my homework."

"Maybe you can see our house from here!" Marco exclaimed, having suddenly lost interest in the ladder and racing toward the window.

"I don't know, buddy. We're up pretty high, but I don't think we're that high," Emilia laughed.

"Well, maybe you can just pretend then," offered Marco, and she smiled and nodded.

"That I can definitely do." Myra and Emilia busied themselves opening the tops of bags and boxes to see what was inside so that they could begin organizing. Greg and the girls came back up with the final load and stood in the doorway after dropping it off.

"What can I do?" he asked, his eyes darting from Marco to Carina as they raced around the room. Myra shrugged busily.

"I don't know. We just have to work to get her unpacked," she said. "Emilia, do you know where the showers are? We have to make sure we find that out before I leave; don't let me forget. And you should get to meet your neighbors too." Greg watched on admiringly at how diligently Myra handled the situation, treating Emilia just as she would have her own daughters.

"You know, Myra, now that all the stuff is carried up, I think it makes more sense for me to take the kids back to the house so you can get some stuff done with Emilia." Myra stopped what she was doing and shot him a grateful look.

"Really? You'd do that?" He chuckled and crossed his arms over his chest.

"Well, they can't possibly get me much more exhausted than they already have. I think I can handle it. Toss me your keys and I'll leave mine here for you," he said, gesturing toward a hook by the door. "I won't be able to fit everybody in mine." Myra dug through her purse and tossed them across the room.

"You're a lifesaver, Greg. Thank you!" she said, turning back to the boxes. Greg began shuffling the kids back out the door, eliciting protests.

"Come on, even I can't stay?" groaned Ella. "I'm going to be doing this next! Shouldn't I at least know what I'm in for?"

"When it's your turn you can stay, Ella, but today it's about Emilia and they have a lot of work to get done," Greg said. "Come on."

Myra and Emilia giggled as they listened to the sounds of the entourage get fainter and fainter, and finally disappear altogether. They set straight to work, unpacking, organizing, and decorating. About halfway through, Emilia's roommate made her way into the room, followed by two adults and two younger children. Myra was again thankful that Greg had gotten their crew out of there.

"Hi, I'm Emilia. You must be Grace?" Emilia asked enthusiastically, offering her hand. "I meant to write you this summer and introduce myself, but I got really busy. I have four siblings and our house gets a little chaotic." Grace smiled and took Emilia's hand.

"I totally get it," she said, gesturing to the two young children behind her. "Annie and David are pretty wild —notice I didn't write either." The two laughed. "Is this your ... mother?" Grace asked, and the hesitation in her voice was not lost on either of them. Myra's blond curls and Emilia's dark features didn't exactly make sense.

She stood to introduce herself by name, figuring she would allow Emilia to fill in the blanks if and when she wanted to, but Emilia spoke before she had a chance.

"Yes, she's my mother," Emilia agreed. "Obviously I'm adopted, but this is my mother, Myra." Myra was overcome with emotion by this introduction and struggled to contain her pride. She shot a warm smile at Grace and her family and extended her hand.

"Myra Jenkins. It's a pleasure to meet you." The rest of the introductions were made, and Myra and Emilia got back to work, a smile of acknowledgment passing between them.

As the last items were unpacked and placed in their new homes, the lot of them stood back to admire their handiwork. The once-lackluster room had been transformed, and it appeared as though the two girls had lived there for some time. It was with a bit of reluctance that Myra realized this was her cue to say goodbye and allow Emilia to get comfortable and familiar with her surroundings.

"Well," she said, fidgeting with the hem of her shirt, "I guess this is it." She took in a deep breath and let it out slowly, willing the tears not to come.

"I guess so," agreed Emilia, and then, jumping up, "Oh, I almost forgot." She reached into the bottom of her backpack and pulled out a present wrapped in purple paper with a little white bow. "This is for you. Don't open it until you get home." Myra took the package carefully, the tears coming freely now.

"You didn't have to—"

"Shh," Emilia mocked, "you don't need to tell me." They both laughed. "I wanted to, okay?" Myra conceded with a nod.

"Okay, well, thank you, then." She reached her hand into her back pocket and pulled out her letter, squished and wrinkled and written on lined notebook paper. It seemed pale in comparison, but every word had come from her heart, and so she handed it over. "I know this isn't much, but this is for you.

I was going to slip it into your bag, but now feels like the right time to give it to you. Read it when you're alone, okay?"

Emilia nodded.

"It's perfect. You've done so much already, Myra." she said, gesturing around her at the decorated dorm room. "I'm here, aren't I?" Myra shuffled her feet a little.

"Well, I'm going to let you get to it then, okay?"

"Okay. Do you want me to walk you out?" Emilia offered, but Myra shook her head.

"No, I want you to get settled. I can find my way out. If you need anything, I'm just a phone call away, you know."

"Yes, I know," Emilia agreed. "Myra, I love you a lot. Thank you for everything." Before Myra could respond, Emilia had scooped her into a giant hug.

"I love you too, Emilia," she whispered into her hair, giving her an extra squeeze. They pulled apart, and both wiped away the tears from their eyes. Myra turned toward the door with her gift and grabbed the keys dangling from the hook. "Remember, just a phone call away," she reminded.

"Just a phone call away," Emilia repeated, and Myra walked out the door.

CHAPTER 37

When the house was quiet that night, Myra poured herself a glass of wine and sat down on the couch with her gift. She turned it over a few times in her hand, feeling secretly guilty that she hadn't thought to get Emilia a gift before sticking her finger under the tape and peeling the paper away. An envelope fell onto her lap, and she let it sit there as she continued to unwrap the layers of tissue paper from her gift. The last piece fell away to reveal a heavy, gilded frame containing the most beautiful picture that Myra had ever seen. It had been taken the previous Christmas by Greg. Myra and Emilia stood side by side in the center, Ella and Sammy on either side of them, with Marco and Carina doing their best to hold Fluffy still in the foreground. They were standing in front of their giant Christmas tree, and everybody was smiling and laughing. She stood there staring at this picture for what seemed like ages until it dawned on her that she had the answer to a question she had so often pondered in the years previous. What would her family look like after all the tragedy that had befallen it?

Here she was staring at it. *Her* family. She hugged the frame into her chest before placing it on her lap and picking up the card.

Dear Myra,

I've always been raised to believe that truth is the best policy, and so even back when I blamed you for things, there was a part of me that honored your bravery in taking responsibility for your actions. When I found out the actual truth, it derailed me, because I realized that a lot of what I had believed my whole life wouldn't hold up against what I was hearing. It was hard for me to fathom that anybody would deny a truth that might prove their innocence, and so initially I became angry with you, yet again, for not letting yourself be vindicated. I've grown up a lot since then, and I just wanted to tell you that I honor your bravery even more now.

You have shown me the true meaning of love, Myra. It goes beyond the boundaries of right and wrong, or truth and lies. You were willing to take the blame for something that you didn't do to protect the two people you love most fiercely in this world, and then maintain this weight even as I asked you to do the unthinkable for me and my siblings. You put up with so much from me, knowing that at any time you could have told me what really happened and all of the problems I was giving you might have ended.

It's funny to me that the thing that tore us apart in the most horrific way ended up being what brought us back together in the most amazing, loving way imaginable. Thank you for being the glue that held both of our families together, and for bonding those families into one. Nobody has ever shown me an act of compassion so great.

Thank you for helping me to become a woman who knows how important the difference is between telling the truth as it is and telling the truth as your soul calls you to tell it. You continue to inspire me. I love you always.
Your Daughter,
Emilia

Myra reached for the box of tissues on the end table and dabbed at the corners of her eyes. She folded the card back into itself and placed it back into the envelope. She held the picture before her once again and smiled more brightly than she had remembered smiling in years. She walked to the mantel and placed the photograph right in the center, and as it settled into its place, she could have sworn she heard a faint chorus rising up into the cathedral ceilings of the house.

ABOUT **ATMOSPHERE PRESS**

Atmosphere Press is an independent, full-service publisher for excellent books in all genres and for all audiences. Learn more about what we do at atmospherepress.com.

We encourage you to check out some of Atmosphere's latest releases, which are available at Amazon.com and via order from your local bookstore:

Icarus Never Flew 'Round Here, a novel by Matt Edwards

Hope Dares to Blossom, a novel by Elisabeth Conway

COMFREY, WYOMING: Maiden Voyage, a novel by Daphne Birkmyer

The Chimera Wolf, a novel by P.A. Power

Umbilical, a novel by Jane Kay

The Two-Blood Lion, a novel by Nick Westfield

Shogun Of The Heavens: The Fall of Immortals, a novel by I.D.G. Curry

Hot Air Rising, a novel by Matthew Taylor

30 Summers, a novel by A.S. Randall

Delilah Recovered, a novel by Amelia Estelle Dellos

A Prophecy in Ash, a novel by Julie Zantopoulos

The Killer Half, a novel by JB Blake

Ocean Lessons, a novel by Karen Lethlean

The Church of Unrealized Fantasies, a novel by Marilyn Whitehorse

The Mayari Chronicles: Initium, a novel by Karen McLain

Squeeze Plays, a novel by Jeffrey Marshall

JADA: Just Another Dead Animal, a novel by James Morris

ABOUT THE AUTHOR

Jillian Arena lives in Jupiter, FL with her husband, children, and countless pets. When she's not writing stories, digging her toes in the sand, or hanging out with her family, she spends her time running her holistic coaching practice and empowering amazing humans of all walks of life to dream big and take life by the horns. Her experiences doing deep inner work with others has shaped her heart-centered writing style and all of the characters she has developed.

For wholesale book orders, or to learn more about Jillian's other offerings, visit www.intuitivebalancecoaching.com

Made in the USA
Columbia, SC
21 November 2022

ISLE OF
SIN

S. FIRECOX

Isle of Sin

Editing by: A.S. Grayson

Cover Design: Raven Designs

Cover Photography: CJC Photography

Models: Eric Guilmette & Lauren

ISBN: 978-1-68530-113-2

Published by: Ninja Newt Publishing, LLC

Imprint: Sin Cave Publishing

Print Edition

ISLE OF

SIN

ISLE OF SIN

There are three rules on Sinners Isle.
Submit.
Obey.
Consent.

Adalyn Rose didn't consent.
And the one who brought her here paid the ultimate price.
Now she's mine to care for. Mine to train. Mine to protect.

A sweet little heiress with a heart of gold.
And a body built for sin.

She'll kneel for me because she wants to.
Then we'll explore her limits.

Assuming her past doesn't come for us first.
Because her world of wealth and sin is filled with dark
secrets.
Including one that may just cost me my life.

Turns out my isle was meant to be a training ground.
For *her*.
I ruined the game by claiming her as mine.
This affair of seduction and intrigue just turned into a battle of survival.

But they made one crucial mistake.
They brought this fight to *my* island.

Welcome to Sinners Isle.
Where dark fantasies come alive.
Allow me to be your guide...

ABOUT THE SINFUL 8

Isle of Sin is part of The Sinful 8 Collection, which is a series of standalone novels featuring the eight children of Mr. Sinner, a wealthy businessman who enjoyed indulging in the darker pleasures of life. Upon his death, he left a significant inheritance behind for his children, as well as a collection of eight dungeons that he'd purchased throughout the world.

All with the sole purpose of passing on one location to each child.

He only had one stipulation: *Each location is designed to cater to the various kinks of the BDSM community and cannot be used for anything else. However, my children can run the location as he or she chooses.*

The eight Sinner siblings divided the locations accordingly, agreeing as a unit to fulfill their father's wishes.

This novel features Asher Sinner, Mr. Nicholas Sinner's seventh child. Asher took over *Sinners Isle,* located on a private island in Fiji. His location specializes in wealth, secrets, and decadent pleasures.

And his story entangles him in a whole different world of pleasure and pain.

One none of the other Sinner children know about.

The world of Sin Cave and the Elite.

INTRODUCTION

Sin Cave is a global organization owned by four influential families, each of whom takes responsibility for a single arm of the business.

Sin Cave Fantasies—A members-only club that meticulously designs sexual fantasies to their clients' specific requirements. You won't find evidence of their locations online, but they're there—in every major city in the world. Membership is strictly by invitation only.

Elite Brides—Future wives of the world's elite, these women are provided with the best education money can buy, including a warfare-style program on elegance and societal expectations. In later years, they receive extensive education on the sinful deeds husbands enjoy behind closed doors.

Elite Maidens—Trafficked virgins who are put through a series of tests by a member of the Sin Cave Elite, including their tolerance to pain and sexual deviancy. If they meet the stringent expectations, they join the "Elite," a club with enormous privileges, where they are matched with a small selection of men whom they serve. Those who fail the tests are sold into brothels, where they will remain for the rest of their lives.

Ecstasy—A high-end chain of nightclubs catering to the rich and famous. Those deemed worthy are invited to become members of Sin Cave Fantasies or, in rare cases, to the Elite.

Welcome to Sin Cave.
You are about to enter the Elite Bride Training Program.
Where every path is carved and cultivated to suit the future husband's needs.
Each journey is woven with darkness and depravity.

Consent is not an option.
You either bow.
Or you endure a fate worse than death.

This world is not kind.
It's cruel.
It's corrupt.
And it's deadly.

But Adalyn is about to find her light...
Assuming she survives.

A Note From Sin

This novel contains scenes of
non-consent, sexual violence,
torture, blood play, and suicidal
thoughts. These scenes involve
the antagonists of the world, not
the hero. Because Asher Sinner
believes in consent and safe play.
And with those notions in mind,
he helps our heroine thrive. For
this story is about healing,
growth, and learning to
overcome a horrific past.

S. Firecox

PROLOGUE: ADALYN

STAY SILENT.

Submit.

Survive.

That mantra radiated through my mind as I bit my lip to keep from screaming. Everything hurt. Everything stung. Everything *vibrated*.

The male behind me grunted, his release throbbing between us as he finally found his happily-ever-after. I hated him. I hated them all.

But I despised Nate most of all.

My *trainer*.

The fucking devil incarnate.

He smiled at me now as though he knew exactly what I was thinking. How badly I wanted to kill him. How much I loathed every fucking thing he made me do.

This was his idea of a celebration.

The end of my college education.

The beginning of my real future.

He saw this as an introduction to what my future husband would require of me—*sharing*.

My so-called freedom had come to an end. Tomorrow, we would leave for Nate's version of a graduation ceremony.

In Fiji.

Most people would be ecstatic by the prospect of going somewhere so exotic as a "graduation gift." But I knew better. I knew exactly what would happen there.

Wealthy sadists from around the world were being invited to partake in open season on my body.

It served as the culmination of all my mandated training.

Nate considered it a bachelorette party of a sort since I was scheduled to be married in a month. My husband-to-be might even come join in on the fun. However, I doubted he would bother. The whole purpose was to train me so I knew exactly what to do on our wedding night.

To spend time with me beforehand would prove futile.

This was the world of the rich and powerful.

A world I had been born into without any say as to my future or whom I would end up with.

They'd called me an *Elite Bride* from the day of my birth. Fruitful arrangements had been made, and my training had begun.

There were no alternatives.

Nowhere to run.

Nowhere to hide.

Not when it came to this society of dominance and prestige.

To escape would result in a fate worse than death.

My father expected me to show up at that altar, trained and prepared to be a proper high-society wife. Nate was the one assigned to ensure that happened.

And he was *very* skilled at his job.

Except for one minor detail—he hadn't broken me yet.

It was a secret I harbored deep within, a secret he almost brought out to the surface tonight.

But I dropped my gaze with a forced grimace, submitting once more.

Stay silent. Submit. Survive.

I knew how to play this game. I'd mastered every angle.

And in Fiji, I would finally make my move.

CHAPTER ONE
ASHER

Is she there yet?

The text sprawled across my phone, disrupting my morning routine of reading current news reports from around the globe.

Yeah, I typed back. *Just going through a final security check at the gate.*

Bet she loves that was Tru's reply.

I expected your message to be another rant from her, I admitted, my lips twitching at the sides. *She's already sent three.*

Sounds like our baby sister. His words deepen my amusement. Darby hates when we rag on her for being the baby of the family. *Give her a hug for me,* Tru adds.

I'd invite you to join and give her one yourself, but I don't really want you on my island, I replied, smirking as I imagined my older brother's resulting expression from reading my message.

Worried I may run that isle of yours better than you, hmm? he taunted.

Worried you might try to turn it into a voyeuristic playground, I retorted.

Isn't that what it is already?

I snorted. *Only for those who want it.* Which wasn't many, considering the clientele I serviced at Sinners Isle.

All seven of my siblings had inherited a club after our father's death. I'd taken the one out in the middle of the Pacific Ocean. Mostly because I preferred isolation and had a knack for keeping secrets. The elite of the world frequented my club because they enjoyed the anonymity my isle offered them.

Which was also why Darby had chosen to come here for her belated honeymoon with Yon and their now one-year-old son.

I'd made nanny arrangements for them for the week to ensure they had some private time, too.

Private time that I didn't intend to be involved with whatsoever.

It was hard enough knowing my younger sister was into kink, just like the rest of us. I didn't need to know what type or how far that kink went.

Which probably made me a hypocrite because I didn't care at all about Truman's preferences. Which was how I knew about his penchant for voyeurism and exhibitionism.

Most of my other siblings were pretty open about their likes and dislikes, too.

I supposed that came with the territory of owning a string of dungeons and sensual clubs around the globe.

My phone dinged again, this time with a message about another incoming arrival—Nathan Spencer and his guest, Adalyn Rose.

I didn't typically greet my guests personally at the airport, but as I was already here to collect my sister, I opted to also make myself available for Mr. Spencer. His seven-year-old membership to Sinners Isle had placed him on a priority list, yet we'd never had the pleasure of meeting.

Mostly because Mr. Spencer had only visited twice during that period of time. Both times had occurred during one of my many trips to New York City to see Tru.

So this would be our first proper introduction.

I shot another text off to my brother with a promise to call him later, then slipped my phone into my pocket and stood.

There were only a few lingering employees at the private lounge inside the airport, all of them mine.

Because I owned this entire island.

It was arranged with water bungalows and huts along the shores, offering the privacy my clients craved.

With a variety of play areas set up throughout the island.

An erotic paradise that many celebrities and wealthy patrons fancied for their own lurid affairs. Discretion was the name of the game. And sex was our primary currency.

Our resort catered to every need and kink, and we took our security very seriously.

Hence the men outside scrutinizing the jet my sister had just flown in on.

You're going to be an old man by the time I get off this jet, Gramps, she told me in a new message now. *All gray and decrepit.*

Already halfway there, Kid, I sent back to her, chuckling at the nicknames we'd given each other years ago. I was the second youngest in our family of eight, with her being the baby.

She was almost twenty-eight now.

And I was only a few months shy of turning thirty.

Making us less than two years apart.

Yet *I* was the old man.

I shook my head, chuckling to myself. I supposed that made our oldest brother, Damiano, positively ancient in comparison.

"Yep, totally gray," my sister said as she burst through the loading door ahead of my personnel. They would be annoyed, but they wouldn't dare comment. The Sinner children were infamous and very much in charge.

And Darby was no different, even as the youngest.

"Can you see me from all the way over there?" she asked, squinting at me. "I hear old age impacts vision and all that."

"Maybe you should call Eli or Damiano and ask them about it," I suggested, starting toward her. "They're almost forty, right?"

"And you're almost thirty," she replied, visibly shuddering. "When did you and Tru get so old?"

I laughed and wrapped my arms around her in a hug while meeting the dark gaze of her husband over her head. "I have no idea how you put up with her full-time, Yon."

He chuckled in response, his hands busy guiding the stroller before him. "I'll have help soon once the little man starts growing up."

Darby rolled her big brown eyes as she released me. "Cute." The word seemed to be directed at both of us. At least until she added, "Let's see if you get laid later."

"Oh, I definitely will be," Yon replied, a hint of his dominance underlying those words as he glanced down at the collar around Darby's neck.

Her cheeks turned pink, her long eyelashes fanning downward as she gave him a demure look.

A look I really did not want or need to see on my sister's face right now.

I cleared my throat. "I know you're eager to start the honeymoon, but how about we wait until you reach your bungalow, yeah?"

Their son, Graham, chose that moment to coo, almost as though to say he agreed. Darby immediately turned toward him, fussing in a way our mom used to do over us as kids.

At least over me, Darby, and Tru.

We all shared the same biological mother and father, while our siblings had other mothers. Two, to be exact.

But it didn't stop us from being close.

And while our father had been married three times, he hadn't exactly been a bad dad or husband. He'd just liked variety and struggled with the concept of monogamy.

A trait some of us shared with him.

Others, like my sister, not so much.

However, we all enjoyed various levels of the lifestyle. Probably because of our father's influence and the clubs he'd gifted us upon his death.

"Mister Sinner?" David's voice came from behind me, causing me to turn toward him. "Your guests are deplaning."

I nodded. "Can you escort my sister and her family to the car? I'll join after I finish the introduction."

David dipped his chin. "Of course, sir."

Darby raised a brow at me. "Guests?"

My lips twitched. "Guests who prefer their anonymity, Kid. Follow David and I'll be right out."

She scoffed at that. "I'm part owner."

"An owner of the London location who is on her honeymoon and not working," I clarified for her. "Just let

9

me handle this one thing, and I promise I'll give you a proper tour after."

Yon pressed his palm to her lower back, his opposite hand still on the stroller. "It'll take us a few minutes to get everything situated anyway."

Darby considered him for a moment and shrugged. "I'm on vacation."

"You're on vacation," he echoed, giving me a knowing look as Darby's focus shifted to little Graham again.

Thank you, I mouthed.

He dipped his chin slightly, then escorted my sister away from the airport lounge and through the exit with David leading the way.

I ran my fingers through my hair and fixed my tie, then blew out a long breath and waited for Mr. Spencer to arrive.

Unlike my sister, he didn't barge through the loading doors, instead allowing my security to enter first. He stepped through the threshold with a stern expression, his demeanor all dominant male as he moved.

This was the kind of guy used to being the alpha in the room.

I'd allow it.

Even if it wasn't accurate at all.

This island was mine, making me king of Sinners Isle. However, I could pretend to bow if it put my clients at ease. That ease made them easier to read.

And I prided myself on being able to understand the intentions of others.

It was what made me a good Dominant—the ability to understand body language and discern the less-than-obvious cues.

Cues like Mr. Spencer's astute gaze and the sharp look

he gave my security as he realized there were more of them in this room.

They were here to protect me, and Mr. Spencer knew it, too.

His focus turned to me as he openly debated my trustworthiness and evaluated my worth.

I didn't let the scrutiny bother me. I merely stood in the center of the room and waited for him to approach.

Because this wasn't a typical hotel operation. I had a general manager who oversaw the accommodations, while I maintained the entire operation.

That distinction provided me with a very different role in this relationship.

Because in my world, the customer was not always right.

I decided who maintained membership here and who did not.

Thus giving me an air of superiority in this situation.

However, I affected a casual front, allowing Mr. Spencer to feel like he owned the room. That lie caused his lips to curl a little, his overconfidence leaving a hint of distaste in my mouth.

A distaste that worsened as a female with dark hair stepped into view behind him.

She kept her eyes on the ground, exuding the picture of perfect submission.

Which would have been fine if we were in the club or in an open play area, not in the middle of an airport lobby. That posture alone told me a lot about Mr. Spencer's dynamic with Adalyn Rose—Master and slave.

Except she didn't wear a collar around her neck.

Nor did she appear to have any other markings on her that denoted her as *owned*.

Her heels clicked lightly against the tiles, her legs long and athletic like a dancer, moving gracefully with every step.

A gorgeous woman.

With a body built for sin.

Yet those lowered eyes grated at my instincts. Something felt wrong with her submission, almost as though it was forced rather than readily given.

A strange inkling, one that had me looking at Mr. Spencer again.

He'd caught my perusal—something that seemed to amuse him more than anger him.

He must be into sharing, I thought, recalling some of his requests for his visit. A private bungalow—a standard requirement. But with an open entertaining area.

Because he intended to have friends stop by to visit his sub.

How do you feel about that, little one? I wondered, glancing at her again. *Do you like to be shared?*

Her dark irises lifted as though she'd heard me, her cheeks darkening to a pretty ruby shade as she found me openly evaluating her.

A hint of defiance crossed her features, causing her nostrils to flare.

And then she was staring at the floor again.

Just as Mr. Spencer glanced back at her.

Almost like she'd known to expect his look.

An odd dynamic, I decided, making a mental note to keep an eye on Mr. Spencer and his activities.

There were very few rules at Sinners Isle, as I preferred to allow my patrons to set their own limits. But consent sat at the top of the list in terms of items I would not negotiate on.

Safewords were paramount. While the word "no" could often be heard from various areas of my island, it was always moaned in a way that actually meant "more." And that was absolutely tolerated, if not *expected,* here.

But consent still mattered.

"Mr. Sinner," Mr. Spencer said, holding out a hand. "It's a pleasure to finally meet you."

"My father was Mr. Sinner," I replied, accepting his palm. "Please call me Asher."

"Of course." He tightened his grip just a little, exerting his dominance. I didn't react, just shook his hand and released him.

"I don't often greet my guests, but I saw you were flying in today and thought it would be good to finally introduce myself," I told him, making sure he understood that this wasn't typical and that I'd given him special attention.

It served as an ego stroke.

And also a warning.

Because now that I'd seen his little sub, I would be watching him.

My senses told me something just wasn't right here, and I'd learned long ago to never ignore my instincts.

However, I hid that inclination now with a smile. "Your accommodations are ready, and your driver will take you directly to your bungalow. Then Cassandra will be by in an hour to discuss your meal preferences for the week." Each guest was given their own private chef, as well as a housekeeper, for their stay. Of course, my staff didn't reside in the bungalow with them. They had their own lavish apartments elsewhere.

And they were invited to play as the mood struck them.

An employee perk.

One I sometimes indulged in myself.

With females like Adalyn Rose, I thought, glancing at her again. *Beautiful brunette with curves in all the right places. Absolutely my type.*

Except for that hint of wrongness.

Hmm.

I refocused on Mr. Spencer. "I'll be around for the week as well. My private line is in your welcome materials. If you need anything at all, please let me know directly and I'll see to it personally."

"Thank you. I actually may need to take advantage of that offer sooner rather than later."

"Oh?" I raised a brow, genuinely intrigued. His concierge should have handled any and all preliminary requests. "Was something missed in your initial booking?"

"No, I've just had a few colleagues inform me that they are planning some spontaneous visits to the island this week. I'd like to organize a gathering, if possible."

"In a play area?" I guessed aloud while mentally making a note to check on these "colleagues" he was expecting this week. I had a list of all anticipated arrivals and their known associations. I would have to check them against Mr. Spencer's dossier.

He nodded. "Yes, and I will have a list of necessary instruments."

Adalyn flinched with the words, the movement barely perceptible but there. And it wasn't the kind of flinch that told me she was excited by the prospect of his request. "I see," I said, in reference to both her grimace and his statement. "I'll see what I can do."

And I'll absolutely be watching you, I added in my mind.

"I assume this will be a private affair for just you and your colleagues?" I guessed, still holding his gaze while observing Adalyn's reactions from the corner of my eye.